CW00384462

24 Hour Renewal Service
Phone 0845 330 4442

City Library
Communities

The last date entered is the date by which
the book must be returned. You can renew
books by phoning or visiting the library.

Nottingham
City Council

Madhuri is a multifaceted media professional, having worked in all forms of the visual medium—as a senior producer with Zoom TV; on advertisements with White Light Motion Pictures, as a director in her own production house, Grey Matter Solution; as a freelancer on documentaries with PSBT; and as assistant director of commercial Bollywood films. She has worked with stalwarts like Subhash Ghai, Karzad Gustad, and Rohan Sippy, and music director Anu Malik.

Madhuri graduated from Lady Shri Ram College, Delhi and she has a master's in Mass Communication and Films from Jamia Millia Islamia. Her thesis film *Between Dualities* won her the National Award for best documentary on women's issues. She is an avid reader, world traveller and film watcher. She gives relationship advice in a column called *Love Guru* in the *Asian Age* and *Deccan Chronicle* and writes a blog called 'Chastity Belt' for CNN-IBN.

Currently, she has finished work on a commercial film script.

Madhuri's debut novel *Losing My Virginity and Other Dumb Ideas* was a runaway bestseller. She blogs at www.madhuribanerjee.blogspot.com and tweets with the handle @Madhuribanerjee.

Visit her at her website: www.madhuribanerjee.com

MADHURI BANERJEE

Penguin
metro reads

PENGUIN METRO READS
Published by the Penguin Group
Penguin Books India Pvt. Ltd, 11 Community Centre, Panchsheel Park,
New Delhi 110 017, India
Penguin Group (USA) Inc., 375 Hudson Street, New York, New York 10014, USA
Penguin Group (Canada), 90 Eglinton Avenue East, Suite 700, Toronto,
Ontario, M4P 2Y3, Canada (a division of Pearson Penguin Canada Inc.)
Penguin Books Ltd, 80 Strand, London WC2R 0RL, England
Penguin Ireland, 25 St Stephen's Green, Dublin 2, Ireland
(a division of Penguin Books Ltd)
Penguin Group (Australia), 707 Collins Street, Melbourne, Victoria 3008, Australia
(a division of Pearson Australia Group Pty Ltd)
Penguin Group (NZ), 67 Apollo Drive, Rosedale, North Shore 0632,
New Zealand (a division of Pearson New Zealand Ltd)
Penguin Group (South Africa) (Pty) Ltd, 24 Sturdee Avenue, Rosebank,
Johannesburg 2196, South Africa

Penguin Books Ltd, Registered Offices: 80 Strand, London WC2R 0RL, England

First published in Penguin Metro Reads by Penguin Books India 2012

ISBN 9780143418375

Typeset in Bembo Roman by SÜRYA, New Delhi
Printed at Manipal Technologies Ltd, Manipal

ALWAYS LEARNING   **PEARSON**

To Papa: I miss you every day and hope you will always be proud of me. I work with your blessings.

And to Ariaana: My precious joy. Without you I would not know what to do with my life. I do this all for you.

Prologue

Wide awake. Sunlight filters in, spreading across the room, through the sheer. The smell from the bakery below wafts in—an essence of vanilla and cinnamon. It mingles with the beads of perspiration on my body. The overhead fan moves at an excruciatingly slow pace. Ray is asleep. I sit up and look at him. The stubble on his chin barely visible, but eminently desirable. Thick, gorgeous brown hair that falls over his eyes. His back bare, tanned and firm. Boxers with horses drawn on them—liketh the boxers, liketh the man. Hmmm . . .

I slide my foot against his leg, slowly. Deftly finding the contours I have gotten used to. He turns over onto his back. The corners of his lips curl into a smile as his eyes rest on me. Lazy. Teasing. I move over him and straddle his hips. He looks at me, curious. I reach up and slip the straps of my negligee off my shoulders. The red satin falls, bunching around my hips, exposing supple, white, full breasts. Firm. Erect nipples. I slide over his body, smooth, lithe, naked and run my mouth on his ear, his neck, and softly circle his nipples with my tongue. Remember last night, I whisper. He nods. That was a breeze, this is the storm. He's hard in an instant. Yearning. He pushes up and sucks on my breasts hungrily. I arch my back, wanting more. He runs his finger down my back, lightly, barely touching, then the inner thigh, tracing words on my soft skin. He moves his finger, slowly sliding it into me. Moistness. Thrust after thrust, deeper. Just ... there. Aaahh. Heaven. His uncanny ability to find the spot, while looking into my eyes. I stare right back at him, taking in his beautiful face, his blue eyes, sculpted lips, the rough stubble on his jaw. I decide to take matters into my own hands. I grab the scarf that was thrown carelessly on the chair last night and blindfold him. He wants it now. Urgently. I refuse to give in. I gently push him down and graze my fingertips down his body till I reach his shaft. Steel. Hard. I take him in my mouth. Rolling my tongue over his head. Licking. Nibbling. Tasting. Feasting. I cup his balls and rub him. He begs me to stop. Almost to the point of bursting. Screaming in pleasure. Pause.

One last taste, then I turn around, my back to him. Slowly, I lower myself onto him. The dark crevasses of my body envelop his desire. He cups my breasts as he moves to sit. And penetrates deeper. Measured movements. Gentle strokes. Rhythmic. He groans. A familiar action that makes it suddenly comfortable again. I moan softly. Faster. Harder. He removes the blindfold and, in one motion, picks me up and pins me to the bed. He looks at me, drinking in my body, trembling with desire, teasing me with his shaft. Smiling, he drives himself into me with one swift stroke. I lunge to hold him as he works up a rhythm. Our bodies move together in the synchronized harmony of rocking. We've been doing this for two years. An intense love making that is beyond our wildest imagination. Biting. Scratching. Fiercely kissing. Pure ecstasy mingled with the sheer power and force of our lust. Relentless. I tighten myself just as he releases his grip. I feel him come. Again and again. I shudder as I feel the light pass through me. A magnificent, crazy, wholesome feeling that leaves me drained and complete.

Spent, we lie back. I reach for the lighter. The Zippo flicks, and I inhale a long, deep drag.

'Coffee?' I smile with a twinkle in my eye.

I knew this relationship would last forever. How could it not? The sex was simply brilliant.

1
Heartbreaks Happen to Everyone

The best way to break up with a man is to tell him that you can't live without him. After that the chase is over.

All men primarily want to be hunters. It is women who, with their soft, manipulative ways, turn them into farmers and gatherers. But soon enough most of them rebel and wish to run wild and free again, leaving the woman to wonder what she did wrong.

Love and heartbreak are two sides of the same coin. Heartbreak happens to every human being. And one must *always* be prepared.

One week after the most glorious sex of our life, Ray cheated on me. Two wonderful years, during which I thought I was doing everything right and that Ray was the most amazing man I knew, and here I was ... heartbroken once again. I was so shocked and devastated that I couldn't speak for a whole day. And that is saying a lot since I am known to be a chatterbox and as a teacher of art history in Barcelona I spoke continuously for ninety minutes three times a week!

But I knew I had to talk to him about this situation because, to me, loyalty is extremely important. I had been in a relationship where the man had lied to his partner for me and I had lived

3

with that guilt for a year. I could not be in the same situation again. I could not let him continue to lie to both of us. It was going to be difficult, since Ray and I lived together, and neither of us could kick the other out.

I spent the whole night sitting in our pristine white kitchen wondering what to say and as the sun rose through the Gothic quarters the next morning, I decided to be honest and direct with Ray as he sauntered in, yawning and stretching. Damn! He looked good. His dark hair that fell over his eyes was his best feature. He had flicked it back and tied it into a small ponytail. His bronzed body clad only in those boxers with little monograms of the Spanish flag made him immensely desirable. But I knew that even though I still found him attractive, I had to let him go. So I began what would be one of the most painful conversations I would have that year.

'Ray,' I said, clearing my throat, 'we need to talk.'

He nodded, 'Sí,' and went to make himself a cup of coffee from the new cappuccino maker we had bought together last week for our house. Our house. How strange that sounded. I had been living with this man for two years. We had this lovely apartment with my favourite artists' replicas and framed photos of us from our trips across Europe hanging on the white walls. Sunlight filtered in through the curtains, a soft yellow material with green and pink flowers that Ray found too girly but let me have after I fell in love with the pattern at a crafts bazaar on our trip to India six months ago. I had introduced him to my parents then who thought he was a lovely 'boy'. They weren't too thrilled with the fact that I was in a live-in relationship with a Spaniard who was several years younger than me, but they saw how happy I was and gave their blessings, provided, they added, that we chose a wedding date soon.

I reached for a cigarette and lit it before I spoke again. It was a bad habit I had acquired in Europe, one I thought took away stress but really there was no such thing. 'I was at the Fiona on Monday,' I said. 'I saw you there, making out with a blond girl.

Who was she?' I asked calmly. See, I didn't think for a minute that losing my head, screaming at him and crying was going to solve anything. I had already done that, alone. I wasn't about to show him that I was an immature little child who believed that all men would be faithful forever. In fact I think I stopped believing it from that moment.

He froze. With his back towards me, he countered, 'What were you doing there? You don't even like the Fiona.'

His reaction made sense. He would hardly have taken his new girlfriend there if it was a place I frequented. But that was not the answer I'd expected. What I wanted was an apology, a plea for forgiveness, and far more importantly an explanation.

'Ka,' he started. That's what he called me. Never Kaveri. Just Ka. It was a soft purr rolling off his tongue. He shrugged, then sighed and sat down. Away from me. Far away. On the other side of the table. He probably thought I would hit him. Whenever men want to create space in a relationship they always start by creating physical space. They'll start sleeping in another room, won't touch you that often and always be away from home or wherever you are most likely to be. Watching him sit at a different corner of the table instead of beside me like he usually did, I knew that Ray had already made up his mind that this relationship was over. But I needed honesty and I needed to hear it from him.

'Well?' I insisted since a shrug wasn't an explanation.

'It's not like that,' he responded with a cliché and took a sip from his coffee. Clichés just make me angry. Honestly, I think there should be a better way to break up and if all the clichés have been used in the movies and books, we need to find a better way to tell a person why we're doing what we're doing. Honesty is of prime importance, even if it is brutal. 'What's it like then?' I asked.

I waited for him to speak. I was willing to wait there the whole day. And if we had to sit in silence, so be it. But I would not speak since I was the one who needed the explanation.

'I didn't see myself being a *family* person,' Ray said a little too harshly and looked away. 'I mean, we live together and we buy stuff for my house together, and then I meet your parents . . .'

'Your house?' I interjected. 'I thought it was *our* house?'

Ray smacked his lips and knew he had made a mistake, but he couldn't take back his words. 'Yes, but that's not what I meant.' He fumbled with his sentences, but I knew where he was going with it. 'You know the whole Indian thing is not me, Ka. I loved you for you. I don't want an Indian wedding and all that.'

'When have I ever brought up a wedding?' I enquired with rage.

'All the time. You hint at it. You speak to your mom and you tell me that she was asking if we've set the date and you joked about it with her. It's tremendous pressure on me. It's not about not being committed to you, but I don't think I want to be part of an entire family. I barely have a family of my own. My dad's in London and my brother is in Seville, both of whom I never meet. And, lately, I've started feeling that maybe I needed to explore a little more about myself. I need a breather. I've just turned twenty-eight and already you're talking about having kids and stuff.' He ran his fingers through his hair in exasperation. Ray spoke with his hands. It was one of the things we had in common. Maybe the only thing.

I could feel the earth moving. As if there were tectonic plates beneath my feet. *You have to start all over again*, a voice said in my head. I was feeling overwhelmed with this realization. My eyes grew moist.

'What's this really about Ray? We've talked about these things before. You're the one who wanted to get married and have kids. I didn't, but I began to because of you.' It was the truth. When we met, I had reconciled to the fact that I was going to be with a younger man and he might take time to mature into ideas of a family and marriage. And then love for me never became about a marriage. It was just the thought that

I would spend a life with him. But I could see he was partially right. After our trip to India I had started asking him about it and he had gone along with the idea with a nod of his head or a smile post coitus assuring me whatever I wanted was okay with him. Now I could see he never meant any of it.

He shrugged, 'Maybe I've changed. Maybe I need more from life right now than a family. Maybe the age thing is playing on my head now. There are other things too. I need to set you free, Ka. You're not living an entire life here. There are days when you're unhappy, when you complain that you want to go back to your family. And then we make mad love and you seem better for some time before you want to leave me again. This constant pulling and pushing me away is confusing. A part of you wants to be with me here forever and a part of you wants to go back to your native home. I haven't slept with anyone. Sofia and I connected. We got caught up in the moment and kissed . . . we could not stop ourselves. It happened just once but maybe it was because we have lost something as well. I still love you and want you in my life. But I need to *live* my life. I'm sorry.'

We had been together for two years. We had discussed marriage and we had discussed babies. Perhaps that's when the disintegration began. As soon as you start discussing the names of your unborn kids, your romance is over and boredom sets in. But it was not just boredom that had brought us to this point. It wasn't even the fact that Ray was younger than I was. There were some glaring differences between us that I suddenly started seeing. He loved to party till dawn and still found the energy to go to his morning collective art class that I taught. I was the one who went to sleep early so I could teach the class and earn enough money to stay in Barcelona. Which was another thing. For Ray, money was money. He didn't care how he got it and when he needed it he always found something that he could do. Waiter, bus-tour conductor, guide at one of the many museums, puppeteer at Las Ramblas every Sunday where people would throw money into a hat. I was of a different mindset. I couldn't take odd jobs to earn money as he did. I was from a family where education was the most important aspect of our lives. Education led to the right career, which in turn earned one money. We would never soil our education for the sake of money. And even if I didn't have enough money, I could never do odd jobs to get extra cash. Maybe Ray was right when he said he wasn't like me. But I didn't want to agree with him. Partly, because I didn't want to give him the satisfaction and in part because I was terrified of what to do next.

After a few minutes, when I had not responded, Ray just sighed and said, 'Can I buy you lunch?'

Lunch! Really? Was he truly that stupid? No, Ray, eating paella was not going to make me feel better about my life falling apart! Unbelievable!

I took a deep breath and looked around the apartment. It had been my home for a better part of the last two years and now I would have to leave it. I felt this overwhelming sense of loss. Maybe it was time to go back, to go home. To start afresh in Mumbai. To Bangalore to my parents. But what would I tell them? How would I start all over again? As I grappled with self-doubt, a little voice inside me whispered that I wasn't weak. I could take all this and make something of it. That there were many adventures that lay ahead in the coming year. And I needed to take this as a sign of good things to come.

2

You Can Count Your Life by the Boxes You Own

Packing up my life took a little longer than I expected. I had to give notice to the university where I was teaching and say goodbye to the few friends I had made. But the worst part was having to give away the things Ray and I had bought together; he didn't want to keep anything and I couldn't carry too much back to India. But I didn't want to part with the objects that had made our life so important.

I was apprehensive about my return. I knew things would have changed in Mumbai. I didn't know what I was going to do there. I had a job here, a home here. At least I had till I realized that things change. Ray had advised me to stay on in Barcelona in 'our' house instead of going back to India. He would move out. 'Ka, you're not going to be able to adjust to it anymore. Places are like people. They change too. They are organisms that grow. People proliferate, poverty increases, madness escalates. And while that may be okay for the people who have been living there and changing with it, it won't be okay for you. You've been away for so long that it will be very difficult for you to adjust. There will be no regular system as you have here. Don't leave because of me. Go for some time and come back when you need to. Get your fill of the country and return back home,' he had said to me before he left to stay at a friend's house while I sorted out my things.

But as I put my life into boxes I realized that it was the only option. I was in Barcelona for Ray. And if he wasn't a part of my life, my stint here was done.

I needed to go home. I missed my parents. I missed Mumbai. I missed my best friend. Aditi and I had been speaking over web chat occasionally and she 'liked' everything I put up on Facebook. And that was so not her. I could tell that something was wrong. This was a woman who was a cynic, a pessimist and a sarcastic bitch, but also sharp and brilliantly witty. That's why she was my friend. I refused to buy her fake happiness and after some careful prodding she finally sent me a mail telling me she was thinking of getting a divorce. I knew I had to step in and save the day. I was slowly beginning to find purpose in moving back.

Packing finished, I decided to go to the bank. As I walked through the neighbourhood where Ray and I had lived, I was overwhelmed by familiar sounds and sights—children playing in the streets, quaint cafes where we had croissants and coffee in the mornings, Gaudi memorabilia in every nook and corner of the street stores, endless rows of trees with the sunlight filtering in, clusters of hibiscus bushes and myriad memories from street musicians who we danced in front of and cranky old men who wanted us to stop kissing under a street lamp!

Last summer we had tried to count the number of lavender shrubs in the windowsills all around the main square, but eventually decided to do something better with our time and hid behind one of the trees to make mad, passionate love before a policeman came. I smiled thinking about the hunger that Ray had for me.

Where had it gone? Was it me? Had I driven him away? He certainly made it sound so. But then if I drove all men away then it didn't make sense for me to be with any other man. Because my heart would get broken again and again. I knew that I didn't need a man to complete me. But it would sure be nice to have one to sleep with.

When I reached the bank, I told the cashier to give me all my money in travellers' cheques that I could cash in India and close my account. Then I took a tram to go to my favourite cafe for a last cappuccino. Arc Café was a quiet little restaurant hidden in the corners of the Gothic quarters of Barcelona. Inside, it had beautiful paintings of different sunsets across Spain hanging on its white walls. The chairs were white as well, and each table had a small white flower arrangement. The cappuccino was perfect and the ambience was soothing and quiet. I loved this place. It was where I could always clear my head—the whiteness eased my mind and the sunsets reminded me of days gone by in my life. But today, as I looked at the cafe, I found myself remembering Coffee De, the cafe below my old house in Mumbai, which had bright walls, mismatched chairs and a mean hazelnut latte. The madness was exactly what I needed. I had started craving it.

I was done with Barcelona. I had studied Barcelona in every miniscule way and was now teaching art. I knew the language, I understood the people and I knew the city. It was warm, friendly and the best place in the world to go for a break. But my break was over. And I needed to head home. To India.

Suddenly I didn't mind that my life would be one big chaos. The chaos of India is a part of you. You become the chaos and life becomes of finding meaning in that chaos. You see struggle around you. You are stuck in traffic for hours. And you'll hate it in the beginning because in Barcelona and most other places in the world traffic and chaos are manageable. In India you just don't know how to cope with it if you don't let it in. But you do know that there are one billion people who would be in the exact same situation as you at any point in their lives. Give or take a few. Yes it's an organism. But I wanted to be part of an organism now and not this lone electron that was moving beyond the ordinary space. Carving a niche in India is a challenge. And that is what I needed right now. A challenge. To find myself again. To know I could survive anything that life had to offer.

I didn't feel so bad anymore. I went back to my apartment and counted all the boxes I had collected over the last year and a half and decided to take only my suitcases. I didn't need the extra things that made up my life here. Those belonged to the old me. The new me would travel lighter, live lighter and know that men were only going to bind me down. From now on I was going to be free from love and all those dumb ideas.

I was going to start afresh!

3

Best Friends Last Forever

I arrived in Mumbai in the middle of summer. I had just celebrated my thirty-fourth birthday with Ray a month ago and looking back I could see that the relationship had been crumbling since then. But women are always more likely to jump to conclusions when there's a possibility of a romance and utterly blind to the details when things are going wrong. Now that I was home, I decided to first get a job and find a place before I went to visit my parents in Bangalore. They seemed disappointed on the phone, but when I assured them that I had moved back to India just for them and would be spending plenty of time at 'home', they were appeased.

Mumbai had changed in the three years I had been away. The buzz seemed sharper and louder; it was as if the drone of toil and struggle had somehow crept under everyone's skin and made them tick at all times of the day and night. The heat seemed unbearable even while I was travelling in an auto with the breeze blowing in from all directions. Even my hair had begun to get frizzy and my skin had begun to blemish. I had stayed through the summer in New York and Barcelona and hadn't experienced anything so extreme. Was it just the city that had changed or had I changed too? What if cities are people with distinct personalities, I suddenly thought. New York would probably be a glamorous, aging movie star clinging to her vibrant past, charming and graceful, with an indomitable spirit that draws hordes of people to her. Barcelona would be a young, carefree woman in a light summer dress living it up in style, drinking wine, flirting with the arts, comfortable with who she is. Mumbai would be the tattooed grunge rocker determined to show her conservative family that she means business, but with a soft side that longed for love and fun. Thus far, she was being difficult, but I knew that if I stuck around long enough, she would open up to me, and eventually become my best friend.

Since I had no place to stay when I arrived in Mumbai, Aditi invited me to stay with her till I could find my bearings. She had recently separated from her husband and had moved back in with her parents who were visiting relatives in Pune. She was contemplating filing for a divorce, had even visited a lawyer who had laid out her options, but she hadn't really made up her mind.

Did I think what Aditi was doing was right? No. Did I think she was brave? No. Did I think that she would survive? Yes. We all had our choices to make and she had made hers. I was determined to stand by her no matter what she decided to do. Just as I hadn't questioned her decision to get married, I wouldn't question her if she chose to get a divorce. It wasn't my business to question. It was my business to support.

And that's what I did. Day and night she spoke about her marriage and what she had gone through and day and night I sat by her, making us endless cups of tea or pouring out many glasses of wine and listening with a patient ear.

'Shall I make some chai?' I asked one evening as I stepped into the kitchen.

'Hmm . . . whatever,' she mumbled while surfing the net on her Blackberry for any new information on her husband. According to her, if he had acquired any new business she could use it in court and say she wanted a bigger alimony.

A few minutes later I emerged with two steaming cups of tea and a plate of cookies I had brought from our favourite bakery, and walked back into Aditi's room hoping she was in a happier mood. She'd pretty much been following me around since I had moved in, unable to understand if she should give me space or cling for my approval.

'Now tell me,' I said as I sat down and offered her a cup, 'what has happened?'

She took a sip of the tea and looked at me, 'This is pretty good!'

'I know. I learnt how to make chai latte in Barcelona,' I replied. I knew we were totally off track, but that was us; these moments of erratic, nonsensical conversation were what made us special.

She then went on to tell me what her husband and his family had done once she walked out of their house. They went from begging, pleading, cajoling and trying to have long rational conversations to being bitter, abusive and downright nasty.

'Divorce is not easy,' she said finally polishing off the last chocolate chip cookie. 'I mean, I have no money if the alimony doesn't come in.'

'No money at all?' I asked my forty-year-old friend incredulously. 'How can that be? Everyone has some savings.'

'I had a joint account with him. He has frozen that. I had a bank locker for all my jewellery, but his mom has the key and she's not giving any of it back. It's all up in the air.'

'What about your job?' Aditi was a fashion designer, a damn good one too. She had sent me pictures of a top film star sashaying down the ramp for her latest collection a few months ago. 'The shows that you were booked for?'

'That was in Rajat's name. The film stars were his connections. The designers were his friends. The people who bought the outfits were mostly his partners. Everything was his. I just designed and got a name for myself.'

'Okay . . .' I said, slowly trying to gather my thoughts and come up with solutions for her. 'So we can use that name and try and get you back on your feet.'

But she shot the idea down immediately. 'That's impossible. Because as soon as those people find out that we're not together, they're not going to raise a finger to help me. They did it for him. Why should they do it for me?'

I guess it's different when ordinary folks get married and when rich industrialists get hitched. They have a reputation to maintain in society and a wild wife walking out would not have gone down well in their cliques. She had a point for which I did not have a counter argument at the time. Then I meekly thought of something else. 'What about your friends? Can't they help you?'

She shook her head and said, 'My friends are like you; they sit around, having coffee and gossiping. While that may be very good for the soul, it hardly does anything for the pocket!' Bitter, but true. All her friends belonged to the same rich circle she had when she married—bored, rich housewives who did some charity work occasionally and travelled the world. A few of them had become designers as well, spending their husbands' money in setting up interior design studios or fashion labels. They would be nothing without the support of their partners' bank balances. All of them had told Aditi to change her mind when she had announced she was getting a divorce; none of them had supported her. A few had even suggested that eventually all marriages ended up being boring and tedious with either or both partners straying in private, but staying together in public. But Aditi didn't agree. She actually believed in love, and she wouldn't stay in a loveless marriage for the sake of appearances. She declared that she had one life to live and she would live it being honest to herself.

'Natasha told me that most husbands don't make time for their wives, or at least as much as the wives want. But then they make up for it with money. And once in a while if they all went for a family vacation to keep society and the kids happy, what was really wrong with it anyway?' Aditi said, trying to mimic Natasha. And though I had never met the other woman, I was sure she didn't sound quite so shrill.

'But isn't it better to be married and old, than be single and old?' I asked.

'Are you calling me old?' Aditi asked looking me straight in the eye with this stern expression. God! Where had all her humour gone?

'I didn't mean *now* silly. I meant at like sixty or seventy when we're *all* old,' I replied, desperately trying to make her feel better with all the fun I could muster.

She suddenly flashed a smile and giggled. 'God! You take me so seriously nowadays.' And then added seriously, 'No, I don't think we should be afraid of old age. I think we should be afraid of being *unhappy* in our old age. When we're young we still have a chance to meet someone who can make us happy. But if we're unhappy now, we'll be unhappy when we're old and then there will be no chances left.'

Aditi had always understood men better than me. And it was clear that despite her separation, she still did. Somehow, even with all my worldly experience, I felt at a loss in that department. Aditi had warned me about Arjun, the married man, years ago. But I had not listened. Then she had warned me against getting involved with a younger man. I hadn't listened then either. I didn't regret those two decisions in my life, but sometimes I wondered what it would have been like if I had listened to her. Would I be with the man of my dreams today? In any case, we cannot turn back time; it is the decisions we make that shape who we become. And we should be proud of who we are.

For Aditi, her marriage had shaped her into a stronger and more creative person. She had a thriving business and had matured into a classy woman. She had come a long way from being an assistant director when I had first met her. I was sceptical if she should give this up and try something new all over again. Our society wasn't favourable for women divorcees hitting forty years old.

I tried to convince her to reconsider her decision, 'If you wait it out a bit more, things between you and Rajat might improve. I don't know much about marriage, Adu, but I do know that there are good times and bad times and sticking through them is what makes a happy marriage,' I reasoned while lying on her bed. I was beginning to feel tired. Conversations about someone else's love life when your own is in a mess can be quite draining on the nerves.

She shook her head emphatically. 'Time together makes a *long* marriage. It doesn't necessarily make a *good* one. Or a happy one. How many years do women still go on with a marriage thinking things are going to change for the better?' She waited for my answer and when I didn't reply, she continued, 'Too long. No one changes in a marriage. Situations might change, but people don't. They might behave differently according to the circumstances, but they don't *change*. And then after many years of hoping and trying, both the man and the woman end up unhappy and old.'

'Why is everything about your happiness and not *our* happiness?' I asked. 'A marriage is supposed to be a partnership, isn't it?' I asked, probably sounding like her parents whom she had banned from talking to her about it.

'No! It *is* about *my* happiness. When *I* am happy, I can make you happy. I can return all your love, understanding and sympathy, and listen to everything you go through and try to make it better. If I am unhappy, I won't care if you are too. Besides, when I'm sad for too long, don't you see it and try and do something about it? How can men go from saying that they understand the woman so completely to ignoring her so defiantly when she is going through this depression?' Aditi spoke as though she was addressing her husband. I knew she was hurting. I knew she didn't want this to fail like the other things in life. But I couldn't help her too much. I had failed too. And I desperately needed some relationship to work so I could believe in love again. Even if it wasn't mine. Otherwise I would be doomed to go through life cynical and disillusioned.

'What if he tries now?' I said quietly, playing the devil's advocate.

I felt that if we take control of one small part of our life, the rest would mould itself to take care easily. If she managed to succeed at her marriage, her career would fall into place as well. Alternatively if she managed a successful career, she could manage living alone too.

'It's too late. He had his chance. I've made up my mind and I don't want to waste another year of my life in trying to make it work. Besides,' she said, 'I don't know where you're getting all your go-back-to-him ideas from when you've just been dumped yourself!'

I gave a wry smile and replied, 'I'd rather wait my entire life for the best than settle with the mediocre for now.'

'Are you planning to meet Arjun again?' she said softly and looked at me suspiciously.

'No, no!' I exclaimed. 'I'm quite done with men. And I have no idea where Arjun is and what he's doing and frankly I don't care. That chapter was over years ago,' I said trying to understand the implications of my own statement. Granted that I had not thought of him as much when I was with Ray, but I had loved Arjun so deeply that a part of me still remained with him. A part that I had partially let go of. Little did I know that taking his name would spark an incident in the near future.

'What do you mean you're done with men? Do you mean after staying in Europe for so long you've decided you want women?' she asked, raising her eyebrows.

I shoved her playfully and laughed. 'Mad or what? I'm tired of giving my heart to men. From now on I'm going to focus on my career and earning pots of money. Pots!'

We went on to discuss what I was going to do and what she should do next with her life and another night of chatting, laughing and gossiping went by. But I felt extremely sad for Aditi and her parents. She had agreed to work on her marriage for her parents' sake and I knew how upset they were when she decided she could not anymore. In a divorce each party only thinks of their own feelings of hurt, betrayal and anger. They never turn around to look at the other person, and realize that they're feeling hurt, betrayed and angry as well. Just as a marriage is about two families bonding, a divorce splits many people as well.

I knew that I had to try and help Aditi get back with Rajat. Their differences could be sorted out. Divorce was not something that would suit my friend at all!

4
Ghosts from the Past

While Aditi was trying to figure her life out, I was trying to find a job. I went to various art galleries asking about openings, but all I could get from the management was that they already had their people in place and since it was a lean season they weren't hiring any new staff. There went my dream of earning pots of money!

Then I decided to apply to colleges as an art history teacher, but there were only four colleges that actually had the class and they already had teachers for it. They told me that I could be a substitute or a guest lecturer and they could pay me for every class I taught. I would earn a measly amount, that too occasionally, not nearly enough to get by in Mumbai. Still I agreed. Something was better than nothing to start with.

I had also overstayed my purpose with Aditi. Her parents had come back from Pune. With Aditi and I sleeping in one room, her parents in another and a full-time servant in the kitchen, the house had become cramped. I was beginning to feel unwelcome and her parents, I sensed, were feeling claustrophobic. So I started looking for an apartment, hoping to get one before I finalized on the job. But that was easier said than done.

Two weeks, ten brokers and forty places later, I was so

despondent that I was ready to run back to either Ray or my parents. I hadn't visited them since I had come back. I guessed it was okay since I had seen them just six months ago. Besides, having them hound me with questions about my love life, my career or my financial situation was not something I was looking forward to just then. I had to sort out my life before I visited them, otherwise they would want to sort it out for me and that was not a pleasant thought at all. What I really wanted was to settle down in the place I called home, Bandra. But, like everything else, the rents in Bandra had skyrocketed and my old apartment was going for three times the amount I had once paid! I begged and pleaded with my old land lady but she was a shrewd, money-minded woman who had neither time nor sympathy for memories and paupers.

After a very gruelling day of looking at over-expensive houses, I decided to go to Coffee De where I knew I would feel welcomed and the couch would be comforting. But as soon as I walked in, I saw that even Coffee De had been renovated! The once bright walls were now white with photographs of film stars hanging on them. It immediately reminded me of the Arc Café in Barcelona where I had spent the last evening before flying out. A wave of nostalgia poured over me. For a moment I wished I had not left a perfectly good job in a beautiful city where I had an apartment overlooking the sea and a man who just needed a little more space. It all seemed surreal. In Barcelona, I had felt the need to belong to a larger community and be surrounded by familiar things and faces. And now that I was home, everything seemed unfamiliar. Suddenly, I found myself feeling completely out of place in my homeland and longing, instead, for 'home' in Barcelona! Ray's words came back to haunt me: You won't belong there anymore Kaveri. You might not have changed. But everything else would have.

And he was right. Nothing was the same. The regular, fun coffee shop with its mismatched yet comfortable seating and bright walls where I had once come every morning now looked like a cafeteria with hard chairs and bright, glaring lights—a large open space where people sat and smoked, drank from tiny cups and had important meetings. Even the name had changed. It had become De Café. Remarkably, it had worked. Like most restaurants and cafes in Bandra, this one too was filled to capacity with people chatting loudly, trying to be heard over the blaring music that was trying to outdo them at another decibel level. Gone was the quiet, mostly empty, little place with gigantic coffee cups I had called my second home. I sat down at a recently vacated table and ordered an outrageously expensive cup of cappuccino feeling more miserable than usual.

I had come back to India with such a positive attitude. I was . . . am an Indian. I belonged here and thought I would be welcomed back with open arms. I was used to the traffic, the overcrowded places and the endless processions on the street for something or another. I thought I understood it all. But after just a few weeks I couldn't put up with it. The traffic was unbearable. People were stuck on the road for hours, no one followed any rules, and the potholes had become wider and deeper, causing accidents with sometimes fatal results. There were newer, bigger slums, and a heap of garbage on every street corner—the stench was overpowering. The quality of life had dissipated but the prices had escalated. I guess I was used to the mildness of Mumbai. And here she was, in all her aggressive force, making me reconsider my decision to move back.

I had just opened my notes and was going through the list of semi-decent places I had seen, one of which I would probably have to settle with at the end of the day, when the ghost of my past walked in. Sometimes saying 'hello' to your ex is far more difficult than saying 'goodbye' to a friend.

He had greyed around the edges and walked more slowly now, but he still looked just as dapper as he had when he walked into my shack in Goa all those years ago. What was different was the young, thin woman hanging on his arm. He immediately saw me and walked towards me. I had nowhere to hide and no time to rush to the restroom to freshen up. Oh God, I thought, how things had changed. The last time I saw him was when I dumped him and was looking my absolute best in gorgeous designer clothes. Now I was barely recognizable— I looked like I had survived a hurricane that had left me with bad hair and crumpled, smelly clothes.

'Kaveri?' he said coming up to me and looking at me more intently.

'Arjun, how are you?' I said getting up and trying to gather whatever dignity I had remaining. He leaned in and kissed me lightly on the cheek. God, he still smelt so good! Aqua de Gio. He turned to his partner just then and I came to my senses. He was no longer my Aqua de Gio. He was now *her* Greek God.

'Tanya, I want you to meet Kaveri, an old friend.'

I smiled. Old *friend*! Really?

'Kaveri,' Arjun continued, 'this is Tanya, my fiancé.'

Emphasis on fiancé. Crap. He was engaged. My smile froze. The bastard! He hadn't wanted to get married when we were together because he believed marriage was a 'mental institution where souls died'. And now just because this leggy lass had convinced him, he was getting married again. I knew I had to stop smiling and say something, anything, before he saw through my smile and realized how not happy I was for them. 'That's superb!' I finally said with fake enthusiasm. My day was not going well. At all.

I leaned forward abruptly and hugged the woman. I couldn't even remember her name just then! I didn't have to fake so much excitement, but I mustered a toothy smile and said, 'I am so happy for you.' And then I hugged Arjun. Oh God, it felt so good to hug him. Stop it, Kaveri, a voice in my head screamed, you're over him. You haven't thought about him in two years while you were with Ray. He has a right to move on. True. Arjun did have the right to move on. Except I had never imagined he would move on so damn fast and introduce me to his future. A part of me had always wanted Arjun to pine for me. Forever. I didn't want to be with him, but I didn't want him to be with anyone else either. He was my favourite toy. Mine! And even though I wasn't playing with him, I didn't want anyone else to have him. It was a selfish thought and I didn't even recognize myself as I thought it.

The waiter came with my cappuccino just as I was turning around and spilt the entire cup on my t-shirt. It was clichéd but the Kodak moments in life are always clichéd. I immediately ran to the restroom where I could pour cold water on myself and calm down. Fortunately, I had not been burned. I sat down and finally gave in to the tears I had been keeping at bay all day. It was all too much for one day. I felt as if I was being punished for something. I must have been gone a long time because I heard a knock at the door, followed by Arjun's voice asking if I was okay.

'Mmhmm, all cool,' I replied, trying to sound cheery. I dared not force anything else out of my mouth since it would sound more artificial. I took a deep breath, turned my t-shirt around so the coffee stain would be at the back, washed my face, and walked out. Arjun and Tanya were sitting at my table waiting for me. I really didn't want to face them right now. So I made my way over to them and said, 'Hey, don't worry, apparently I am made of thick skin,' and raised my arms and continued, 'no burns!'

'Thank God! We were worried. We've ordered you another cup of coffee and a sandwich,' Tanya said sweetly and smiled. Damn it! She was being nice. That made me feel even worse for wanting her dead.

'Thanks, but I am apartment hunting and I've got to run to meet another broker now,' I said coming up with a logical excuse albeit a false one.

'Oh, you're back in town for good?' Arjun asked, making sure not to show too much enthusiasm lest his fiancé get the wrong impression. Oh he was good like that. He didn't have too much to say, but his tone was always correct.

Before I could reply, Tanya got up and, to my surprise, said, 'I'm sure you can meet the broker later. Please eat something. I'm sure you guys have some catching up to do. I'll leave you two alone.' When Arjun tried to protest she brushed him off with a gentle arm on his shoulder and a soft smile, then turned to me. 'It was lovely meeting you, Kaveri. Goodbye!' And with that finality she was gone.

Since she hadn't extended the invitation to 'meet again soon', I figured Arjun had told her about our past and she was giving me a chance to say whatever I needed and then leave her fiancé the hell alone.

I took a deep breath. And exhaled. Why was Arjun engaged? Why did Ray have to cheat on me? Why was I still alone?

Stupid. Stupid head.

5

Coffee and Awkward Conversations

There was an awkward silence for a few minutes while Arjun and I waited for the other to say something. I remembered all the good times Arjun and I had had together, the reasons for our break-up becoming faint in my memory. He had been a good man. It was not his fault that he was a commitment-phobe. Wait a minute! That was exactly what his fault was. He had never wanted to marry me. He had given me long explanations on how to avoid it, corroding my soul in the process. And now he had changed. For all I knew, I had polished this rough diamond into a sparkling gem and another woman was going to show it off! Life was so unfair.

I took a sip of my coffee. Oh, that felt so good. I had desperately needed my caffeine fix. It calmed my nerves and soothed my irritation. A flood of reason washed over me: So what if Arjun was engaged? If he and I had got married, I might not have met Ray, I would not have got the wonderful opportunity to experience New York and Barcelona that I had for the last two years. Life is always giving you signs. You just need to pick up on the signals and work them to your advantage.

'So, engaged huh?' I said, smiling genuinely for the first time that evening.

He nodded and blushed a little. He seemed happy and in love. Then he said something that made me feel queasy again. 'I waited for you, Kaveri. You didn't reply to my emails and after a while I had to move on.'

'I'm sorry. I know. You're right,' I replied in a fast staccato. When I had said goodbye to Arjun in New York I wanted to cut him off completely so I could move on in life. So I had deleted his numbers and blocked his emails. But I didn't want to be a step mom at 31. Reminded of which I asked, 'How are Maria and your daughter?'

'They're doing well. Maria and I've been divorced for some time now. She has a boyfriend. We don't discuss our personal lives with each other. I don't want to talk about mine, so I don't ask about hers except she knows that I'm engaged. I have my daughter on the weekends. There are still some problems with the custody agreement,' he said. There it was. A bit of confusion and doubt. This was why I had left. I didn't want to be in a custody battle for someone else's kid. If he had lost the fight he would have blamed me forever. Besides, I was too immature then to even know how to deal with it. Even now, I was sure I had a lot of growing up to do before I could get married. Maybe I should have told Ray that. But he had already made up his mind.

'I met Tanya at an office party,' he continued. 'She had been invited by a common friend who wanted to set us up. We both thought the idea was ridiculous. But as soon as we met and got talking, we realized we had a lot in common. She's also from the television industry. Except she's in front of the camera and I'm behind it.'

Ah! That explained why she was so thin and pretty. Her job demanded it. She was probably a floozy on some Indian soap opera.

'She's a senior news anchor for CNN-IBN,' Arjun said, almost as if he knew what I was thinking. I nodded in response. But he continued, 'We've been dating for a year. She is very independent, like you. Very artistic too. The two of you have that in common.' It was as if he was trying to compare me with her and assure me that it was okay for him to be with her since she was a paler version of me.

I wanted to scream, 'It will never be okay! She is not me.' Instead, I smiled and said, 'I'm really happy for you Arjun.'

'I really want you to be okay with this,' he blurted out. 'You were an important part of my life and I truly loved you. But, circumstances . . . it's just that we were together at the wrong times in our lives . . . right place, wrong time.'

'I'm okay with it,' I said rather abruptly. I really was. A part of me resented the fact that he had moved on, but a saner part of my brain didn't want to repeat my past mistakes. Sometimes the best thing a woman can do for a man is to walk out on him and give him a chance with someone he truly deserves.

'That's great then,' he said and smiled, probably relieved to be done with the topic of his fiancé. 'So, what have you been up to?' he asked casually.

'Well,' I spoke, 'I was looking for a place, but this city is just unrelenting to newcomers. What has happened to it? The rent has gone up everywhere. Jobs are difficult to find. The friendly faces in trains and taxis have been replaced by scowling, irritable people who don't care if they help you or not. This was not the Bombay I knew!'

'It is *Mumbai* now and it's tougher than ever to get a foot in the door,' he said. Moments later, he added, 'I have a lovely two-bedroom place which you could rent from me.'

I looked at him sceptically.

'I've bought a new place in Bandra,' he explained, 'but I didn't want to give up my old apartment. You can stay there if you like.'

'I can't accept that,' I said, not very convincingly. It was a tempting idea though. I could stop thinking about getting a place and finally concentrate on finding a job. But I realized I could not rely on yet another man to 'rescue' me. I had to become independent. I had found a place for myself in New York and Barcelona and *then* let men enter my life and share my space. Why was I feeling so helpless in a city that was my own? I needed to toughen up. So what if the monsoons were coming? I was not made of soap. So what if I didn't find a house? I would go stay at the YMCA till I figured it out. So what if I couldn't get around all the new things that Bombay had acquired in the last three years? It was still my home and I would love it with all my heart. I didn't need a man to help me figure out my life or find a roof over my head. I would not only survive, but also be the best at whatever I chose to do.

'Thanks, Arjun,' I said with finality, 'but I'll be fine. You've been very sweet to me. You need to start your own life. And I'm happy for you. Keep my number and maybe we can bump into each other again soon.' I was moving on too. There was no point in living in the past and trying to ignite the spark of a memory when I knew that there were no embers of love for a future.

This was called being grown up.

6

Alternative Beginning

Miraculously, several things happened the very next day. One of my brokers called and said a new place had just opened up on the market, and though it was in Santacruz West, not Bandra as I had wanted, it was in my budget. He asked if I wanted to take a look. When I went and saw the apartment, I knew instantly I wanted it. It was a small one-bedroom apartment with off-white paint peeling off the walls but a decent bathroom and marble kitchen in an old building that overlooked a large lawn. The location—slightly away from the main road, but close enough for easy access—was perfect. I decided to sign the lease right then.

I finally had a roof over my head.

Later that day, Aditi went through her phone directory and found the number of a close friend of hers who used to work as a producer but knew the entire media industry and could help me connect to some people. It was a great idea. The more people I met, the better idea I would get of the types of jobs out there for an art enthusiast.

His name was Scunjay Panjwani. The 'c' was silent; he was not. Scunjay was in his late forties, tall and trim with a warm smile and a cloudy head. We met in his office—a dark dungeon with black walls, a black marble desk, a grey executive's chair for him, and a matched pair of smaller chairs in a different shade of grey for visitors. He spoke nineteen to a dozen and ended each sentence with 'I don't speak too much'. When I asked him how he knew Aditi, he told me his entire life history, detailing all his achievements. And when I nodded in appreciation he would say, 'That's nothing. That was like doing it with my left hand.' After hearing descriptions of the many things he had accomplished 'with his left hand', I began to wonder if he was actually left handed!

He had a tiny Sony Vaio on which messages popped up every now and then, much to his annoyance. He said to me, 'I don't know how to shut this down. I can't see this bloody screen!'

I nodded sympathetically and asked, 'Are you planning to change it?'

He shook his head vigorously and said, 'Oh no! I just bought it. I think it's very sleek.' And then he snapped his fingers and bellowed, 'RT!' Instantly, a little man—short, with hair that was slathered with some strange-smelling oil, wearing dark horn-rimmed glasses, a chequered full-sleeve shirt, trousers and shiny shoes—entered and tapped on some keys on the Vaio's keypad and hurriedly walked away. This silent, swift, eighties debonair man, as I later learnt, was Rakesh Thanki, a Gujarati who relished dhoklas and was always in deep trouble with either his boss or his wife. One of whom would leave him soon enough. And since he didn't seem too concerned about his marriage, it wasn't hard to guess which.

'So what can I do for you?' Scunjay asked after his hour-long dissertation about himself.

I took a deep breath. I thought I would start by introducing myself since he hadn't asked a single question about me and didn't have a clue why I was there. 'Well, I am an art teacher. I was living in Barcelona the last two years. I . . .'

Scunjay interrupted. 'You were living where?'

'Barcelona.'

'Where is this? Near Pune?'

'It's in Europe, sir . . . not many people have heard of it,' I said stammering a bit to make it easier for him.

'Aah. No wonder. Is it close to Switzerland? Most of our Hindi films are shot there.' He snapped his fingers and bellowed, 'RT! Look up Barcelona for me.' RT entered, Googled it on Scunjay's Vaio and left. Scunjay waved his hand as if to indicate not to bother with this tiny five-foot man coming in and going out so noiselessly, 'I'll read about it later, you carry on.'

Since I quickly realized his attention span was as short as a buzzing bee in a valley of flowers, I told him I had taught art history at the university in Barcelona, and was wondering if he knew of some job opportunity for me in Mumbai. He closed his eyes for about a minute with his elbow resting on the desk and his fingers covering half his face pondering deeply to what I hoped was a job opportunity for me might as well have been how to tick RT off. Just then a woman knocked and entered his office, bearing a box of kaju barfis. At first he declined meagrely but then he took five pieces and wolfed them down. She offered them to me but I politely refused.

He then looked at me and spoke about Barcelona. 'I don't go to these places where they don't speak English,' Punjwani said with raised eyebrows in all seriousness. 'Too tough to understand what to order. What if they give me some dead animal to eat that I haven't heard of?' he asked with a shocked expression. 'You know I'm a vegetarian on Tuesday. I only eat fish.'

Before he embarked on another story about himself, I quickly butted in, 'I know seven languages, sir. That why it's easy for me to understand them.'

He suddenly sat up and stared at me with what I thought was respect, but would later realize was just food poisoning. He closed his eyes and held his head in his hands once again.

I asked him gently, 'What is it, sir? Are you unwell?'

He shook his head slowly and pointed to the ceiling. I didn't know what to look at. So I asked, 'Ceiling?'

He sighed and said, 'Top lighting.'

I waited for further explanation.

Still holding his head in his hands, Punjwani said, 'Top lighting gives me a headache. I don't know why they don't keep lamps in this goddamn room! RT!' The moment RT entered, he hollered at him, 'Tell them to keep lamps in this room and get rid of these above type of lights. Bloody fools!'

I didn't know what to say so I just cleared my throat, smiled and nodded.

'Can you speak Russian?' he asked me unexpectedly.

I nodded, 'Yes.'

Scunjay leapt out of his chair and shouted, 'RT!' and the tiny man was inside the cabin a second later as if he had been waiting right outside.

'RT, I think I've found our answer,' Scunjay said as he sat back down, completely ignoring me. 'She can help us with Bela.'

'Bela?' I asked, unsure if he was actually offering me a job.

'Bela Bandhan. She's half Russian and half Kashmiri. But she knows no Hindi. And she's the next top actress of Bollywood,' Rakesh explained, while his employer stood by, looking as if he was going to faint.

'It's all settled then. RT, take care of it,' Scunjay said feebly, clutching his head once again.

I began to get worried. Was this man having a heart attack? 'Sir,' I asked with concern, 'are you feeling okay?'

His eyes closed against the glare from the 'top light', he nodded and said meekly, 'It's the kaju barfi. Tell her, RT.'

RT leaned towards me and whispered, 'They make him sleepy.'

'Sleepy? As in drowsy?' I asked incredulously. I had never seen that happen with a man. But RT nodded in all seriousness and led me away. But hadn't he taken the sweets himself? And if he knew this was the effect why would he do it to himself? RT answered with a straight face as if he had read my thoughts,

'Kaju barfis are his weakness.' The last image I had of Scunjay Punjwani was his head down on a table muttering away how people were determined to poison him.

Once outside Punjwani's office, Rakesh explained what the 'job' for me was. He said that they had been searching for a translator for Bela who could travel with her and translate her scripts from Hindi to Russian so she could understand them and help her learn Hindi so she could learn her lines. I would be paid handsomely for my tuition, translation, and would be given extra if I were travelling out of Mumbai with her since I would have to be with her all the time. By the time shooting ended on her current film, they wanted her to know Hindi fluently. So far they had shot only one schedule which was some ten days of shooting in Mumbai and they weren't planning to use most of the shots. So I would have plenty of time before the film was released to have her speak Hindi without an accent. Rakesh added that not only would I be with her for the entire length of this movie, but, if need be, future films as well. And with my talents and the industry importing these foreign 'actresses' who neither spoke nor understood Hindi, I would be a permanent employee with them.

I was thrilled. I could finally visit my parents, now that I'd sorted out my life. Perhaps even do up my apartment and invite them over for a short visit. The only problem was that it took me very far away from art, which was my core skill and passion. But it *would* bring a host of new experiences. God doesn't give you everything you want, but he does give you exactly what you need at the right time.

7

Bela Bandhan

I had decided I was going to be two things once I came back to Mumbai—self-sufficient and open minded. Keeping that in mind, I went to meet this new Bollywood actress who was supposed to be the talk of the town. She didn't have a single release in India yet, but she was already being courted by a few directors. She was a former Miss Russia and had been on the modelling circuit abroad for a few years, lately as a Victoria's Secret angel, before she decided to become an actress.

Bela Bandhan was renting a posh three-bedroom apartment in Bandra, and had a full staff. And by this I mean a watchman to get your signature and open the door, a maid to usher you into the private office, a butler to bring you water and ask if you want tea or coffee and another maid to clean the house and dust the office while you are sitting in it. Precisely fifteen minutes later, a tall and milky fair woman with long, dark-brown hair and dark eyes entered the room. She was wearing tight white capri pants that showed off her slim frame and a dark blue polka dotted silk blouse with a red belt. She looked like a million bucks. She smiled at me and extended her hand.

'Hi, I'm Bela. You must be Kaveri. How are you?'

I could instantly make out why I was hired. She spoke with

a heavy Russian accent. For Bollywood to accept her she would have to speak fluent Hindi *and* less accented English. When we began chatting I got to know a little about her. She had four brothers and three sisters who were still living in Russia. Because she came from such a large family, they all had to start working very early on in their lives. She had begun her modelling career with small campaigns until she participated in and won the Miss Russia pageant. Thereafter, she had travelled to the States where she had been working as a Victoria's Secret angel when she was noticed by an Indian film director. He had urged her to move to India and be a part of his movie. It had seemed like an interesting opportunity, so she agreed. She said something about having some ancestors who were Indian, but that she had never felt the urge to come back to India since she didn't know anyone here.

Once she came and settled down in Mumbai, she had begun shooting. One ten-day schedule had already been completed when the director had said they needed to dub her voice. Being the hard-working girl she was she had decided she was going to learn Hindi. No self-respecting actress had anyone else dub for her. And that's where I came in.

'I hope you can work with me to improve my language,' Bela said sweetly. She seemed very down to earth. I felt this would be a comfortable enough job for the money the producers were paying me and I would soon be able to get back to my art world. With correct patronage from the film industry, I might be able to set up a gallery. Perhaps Bela Bandhan would inaugurate the opening exhibition! My head was in the clouds as I envisioned my future.

Her phone rang just then, and she excused herself and went into another room. I could hear snatches of the conversation and understood that she was trying to cajole the caller—a prominent actor—to get her out of having to attend yet another birthday party. But apparently he was refusing to listen. I heard words like 'image', 'social' and 'career' and I figured the actor wanted to help her with all three. Finally, she sighed, 'All right. I'll go into hair and make-up now and be there by eleven.'

When she entered the room again she said, 'I have an engagement that I must attend and it will take me a few hours to get ready. Do you want to do our lesson another day or do you want to wait here?'

I offered to wait in case she needed any help. I was trying to be polite and hoped she would see me as more of a friend than an interpreter so we could get along better. Bad idea to begin with. I would realize that the first rule of the film industry is no actor is your friend. Not even if they appear so. We started chatting in Russian. Soon enough her stylist and her make-up person arrived. Carl, her make-up artist, was a tall, burly man, incredibly fair with warm brown eyes that seemed immensely alluring and lively. I couldn't believe such a man could be a make-up artist until Bela left the room for a bit and he said in the most damsel in distress voice, 'Oh God!' and sighed very deeply like a sixties' heroine. 'Why don't these people tell you earlier where you need to go? I had to cancel another shoot to be here. The things I do na!' I didn't know which people he was referring to so I kept quiet and smiled.

The stylist, Shyamolie, was a little less dramatic. She was short. In fact several inches shorter than the average height of five feet two inches for an Indian woman. She had honey-coloured skin, a striking body, lovely black eyes and a mass of black curls that fell to her waist, but the effect was ruined by the extremely scornful look on her face. She wore a diamond nose ring and several semi-precious stone rings on both her hands, which had probably been recommended by an astrologer. Her clothes were ordinary—an A-line dark red skirt and a white sleeveless top that brought out her dark and petite frame quite agreeably.

Bela got up, gave them a hug each, and then introduced me, 'This is Kaveri. She will help me speak fluent Hindi and by the time shooting ends I'll be able to give all the press interviews in

Hindi and floor the media!' She said this with a flourish as if it was going to be the greatest achievement of her life. I seemed to be the only one who understood what she said since the other two took a few moments to get the gist of her statement beneath her thick Russian accent. Carl and Shyamolie smiled and nodded their head with vacant eyes at Bela and me. It was in conjunction and seemed so artificial as if all they could do was just agree with whatever she said. So I quickly said, 'Well, I can only try.'

For the next two hours, Bela ignored me while she got her make-up done—Carl had set up an entire range of the Mac department store on her dressing table—and argued with Shyamolie about what to wear. She didn't want it to look like she had taken the time to get dressed; it had to seem effortless but smashing. Shyamolie assured her that she looked great in everything but Bela fussed over everything that Shyamolie showed her from the suitcase she had brought. Finally, Shyamolie sat down in exasperation after having shown her every piece of clothing and accessory she had.

'This is the best I could do in half an hour's notice, Bela. Rocky and Manish are not available right now so we'll pick something up from them for another event.'

Bela looked at her in disgust and said, 'Then where did you get these dresses from? Local boutiques? Do you want me to look like an extra or a superstar?' Shyamolie convinced her that either of the two styles that she had chosen would go well on Bela and the suitcase was full of other options just in case she wanted to mix and match. Bela sighed dramatically and before Shyamolie could answer she added, 'Well then, we'll go with the white dress with the brown belt and I'll wear my leopard skin Louboutins with that. Next time Shay, be more careful. I have an image to protect.' I watched the drama unfold in silence, not knowing if I should leave or just stick around since I had told Bela I would be here in case she needed me. I thought it might look rude and my job would be in jeopardy if I walked out. In any case I had nowhere else to go.

Shyamolie sat down next to the things that Bela had picked out and summoned her assistant who took the dress to get it ironed. A maid walked in with two cups of tea for us. 'Aah!' Shyamolie exclaimed in relief when she saw the tea. She thanked the maid in Marathi as she took a cup, and the turned towards me. 'I really hope you can do something about her English more than her Hindi. I can barely understand her. When she said she had a casual birthday party of her boyfriend's sister to attend, I thought she would go in jeans and a nice top. Instead, she wants to go as if she's attending the freaking Oscars where she's been nominated in the best actress category.'

I burst out laughing.

She smiled and continued, 'Seriously though, I can barely understand what she's saying on the phone. No wonder I have so many fights with her. You've got to help me more than her.'

'Why do you work with her then?' I asked, taking a sip of the tea.

'The pay is great. And she asked for me.' My interest was now piqued. This unassuming woman was famous? My expression probably gave me away, because she continued, 'I've been working in this industry since I was born. My granddad was a dressmaker for stars like Madhubala and Nargis. Not a stylist, but he was what you call a "dress dada". Then my dad took over the business and expanded it so that there could be many dress dadas in the industry working for him. When I grew a little older I began to understand colours and fabrics and would even tell my dad what combinations worked and what didn't. Then I got into styling. My break came when the stylist on a film set had a nervous breakdown and quit and the director asked me to figure out costumes for a hundred and twenty people that day.'

I looked at her wide-eyed and mouthed the words *a hundred and twenty*.

She nodded. 'Yup. And I did! It was a great achievement and the director loved me. I've been styling the stars since then. All the designers in the industry know me,' she said triumphantly.

It was quite a life. But she seemed so young; her skin was radiant and her manner youthful. With experience like that she could easily have been in her late thirties, but she seemed as if she had just graduated from college.

'I've been working since I was sixteen,' Shyamolie explained. 'I began immediately after I finished junior college. I didn't do a graduation. There was never enough time anyway, and the money was pretty good. Why should people have to study if they're already working in an industry they've always wanted to be in and earning the same amount of money, if not more, that they would after they graduated, right?' she asked nonchalantly.

I had a preconceived notion that if one didn't study till their mid-twenties and got a PhD, they were fools. Yet, here was a woman who was debunking that belief in its simplest and most cutting way by proving it wrong.

'Anyway, tell me about yourself,' she invited, and I did.

A little later, Bela emerged from her room with rollers in her hair and her foundation and eye make-up done. It really seemed as if she had put nothing on her face, but when you looked closely you could see her eyes had opened up and all the blemishes on her face were covered.

'Back to the dragon lady!' Shyamolie muttered as she got up.

Another hour later and Bela looked absolutely stunning. Shyamolie had picked the outfit so correctly for her and Bela had given her so much grief for it! The white dress fit Bela perfectly, accentuating her curves without making her seem gauche, and the accessories were just right for an evening out with friends and a few pictures for the paparazzi. It was amazing how good make-up and correct styling could change an unpretentious girl into a striking woman.

Bela waved goodbye to us as she got into her fancy car and we all gave her fake smiles and a thumbs up sign. Then Carl, Shyamolie and I went to a bar where we had a few drinks and gossiped about film stars and the filmy life.

I was officially part of Bela Bandhan's coterie now. And I knew I was going to enjoy this new stint in my career.

8

Shyamolie

Over time Shyamolie and I became close friends and spent many hours together. Since trying to be the best at whatever I did was ingrained in me, I chose to spend as much time with her to understand the film industry that I was now a part of, even if it was from the fringes. I followed Shyamolie to all the designers and even went to a few sets with her to see what actually happens on a film set.

I also went to Bela's house every day to teach her Hindi, but invariably she would be exasperated and throw me out an hour later. Learning a new language was as difficult for her as it is for a fish that must learn to walk. As a result, after our sessions every morning, I was free for the rest of the day to do as I pleased, and often Shyamolie and I would do something together.

I learned more about this charismatic woman who, despite her diminutive size, commanded a tremendous amount of respect. She would get a call from Hrithik Roshan in the middle of something she was doing and she would drop everything, go to a store, pick up a few outfits, and rush to his house to deliver them for him. She said it gave her a high to be able to work through people's 'clothes crises' as she called it.

I thought it was strange that grown men and women did not

know how to choose a simple shirt and jeans, but Shyamolie explained that each star had to be careful of the image they projected. 'If they all wear what they like, it might be a complete disaster since they'd probably wear something too tight, too loose or decide to ape a global trend they've seen on a runway that might not suit their image or their personality. Like if Kareena wore a loose multicoloured print sack, then she would be laughed at. Or if Hrithik wore a see-through shirt thinking he'd look cool, he would be mocked. And they need to be careful because they are always being photographed and one fashion faux pas could cost them endorsements or films. And, the worst thing is that that will be the one picture that will be printed in the media for eons. The media is like that. If they don't like someone they'll carry the same drab photo of you even if you have a hundred better ones. The pen is truly mightier than the make-up; never piss off a journalist.'

Okay, I suppose that made sense.

Shyamolie continued tutoring me, 'Besides, stylists, designers and everyone in the fashion industry also want to generate more income and publicity for themselves. If all the stars actually did something right, then we all would be redundant. We need to create a myth and reiterate it that they cannot do it themselves. That they cannot go to stores and pick up clothes and accessories . . . that they do not know what will look good on them. If we keep telling them that again and again, they begin to believe it. And if they veer off the path and wear something on their own and are not laughed at, we say it's luck and that they should be extremely careful in the future. A fear rises in the community of the stars where we perpetuate the insecurity. Then we stylists have power. With that power we can use it to demand things from stores, designers, and so many more brands, labels, etc. It creates work for more people. After all we're a very large nation of people who need work. Each of us needs "others" to do something for us. Like a cook, a driver, a maid, a milkman and so forth. We Indians think we need them to make our life easier. Similarly we need stylists. Essential.' She said all this with such confidence, that I could not doubt that she was a very intelligent human being.

But I had one question. For a woman who was so smart and confident, why was she wearing so many rings?

She looked down at her hands and explained each one's significance to me, 'Oh, this one is a pokhraj worn for good luck, this one is a metal worn to ward off evil and this one is a moonstone worn to control my temper or I would have slapped Bela "Pseudo" Bandhan by now,' she replied while we sat at a designer's studio waiting for the designer to arrive.

With Shyamolie, we never had time to just go for a coffee or catch a drink. She was always working. She was always on her Blackberry or flipping through magazines to catch new trends, or answering emails or talking to people or sitting in stores waiting to pick up things from designers. Even I couldn't keep up with her dynamism. In the beginning, I had hung out with her till two or three in the morning and then tried to wake up a few hours later and be on the set with Bela by eight. But I soon realized Shyamolie had far more energy than I did. Mid thirties might not sap your enthusiasm, but they definitely sap your energy. I'm sure with all those rings she wore, she had one for strength as well because I had never met a woman like Shyamolie.

'Why do you call Bela pseudo?' I asked her. I didn't know if it was a stupid question or not. Here I was, a post-graduate who could speak seven languages and had travelled the world, but somehow I still felt inferior to this tiny ball of vivacity.

'Because that's not even her last name,' she stated.

'What?' I asked incredulously. 'What's her last name?'

'It's Krakowski or some shit like that. She's not even half Indian. She was sleeping with this director when she was in the States and begged him to get her into Bollywood. She literally had him by the balls! And since men only think with their dicks he brought her here and gave her a break in his movie. She met one of the top actor-producers of Bollywood at a muhurat party, where she flirted with him. It was he who told her she had to change her image, have a more Indian name, and hence be more likeable. *He* changed it to Bandhan since he wanted her to be "tied" to the industry. It had a nice ring to it. He helped her get many more offers, and in return she became his slave. His sex slave. And now, even before her first film has been shot completely, she's been signed on by three very reputed producers.'

'What happened to her director boyfriend?' I asked.

Shyamolie took a deep drag from her cigarette while watching the cars pass by on the Juhu Link road stretch and replied, 'She hardly cares for him now. She sleeps with him once in a while to keep him happy, but she's firmly linked with the superstar 'cos that's where her status can grow.' She finished her cigarette and stubbed it out on the pavement. 'The men get what they want from her, and she gets what she wants from them. Everyone is happy.'

I stubbed out my cigarette too. Aditi never smoked and I hated smoking alone, but with Shyamolie I had found a partner in crime.

'I think that completely sucks,' Shyamolie said. 'I mean love is supposed to make you whole. It's a natural and good feeling. I mean I want to be in love where if I feel like kissing my man, I will do it right here and now and it will be considered beautiful.'

I had a strange and awkward déjà vu moment and I blurted it out, 'Are you a virgin?'

'Oh God no!' she said as if it was a fatal disease. 'I had one guy a long time ago. He was my best friend since we were kids. He's gone to the US now to do some shit. I was heartbroken for some time. But then I realized I had no chemistry with him anyway. I mean he wasn't even good in bed.'

'How would you know?' I asked sceptically.

'I just do. I wasn't consumed by him. Love is meant to consume you. It should take your breath away. You shouldn't

have to think about being in love. It's supposed to be mad and
passionate and extraordinary. There are too many mediocre
things in life for love to be one of them.'

'Shy,' for that was what I called her, 'that thing does not exist.
All relationships begin that way but the passion and excitement
fade away. A compatibility remains. Love is non-existent. There
are no perfect men. In fact, even ordinary men do not aspire to
be perfect. You are talking about stuff that happens in romance
novels.' I realized I was beginning to sound like Aditi, the voice
of reason in my life who had imparted some of her cynicism to
me.

'Whatever dude,' she said nonchalantly. 'That's the only thing
I believe in. And trust me, I will get it. 'Cos the minute you
stop looking for it, it won't happen. And as long as you keep
believing, the entire universe will conspire to make it happen,'
she said in Hindi which was a dialogue from a film she had
worked on and was a massive hit.

A few minutes later, the designer came back and Shy and he
began a heated discussion in Bengali. Shyamolie was a Bengali
who had been born and brought up in Mumbai, but loved
Kolkata with a passion that left me wondering why she didn't
settle down in Bengal and work in Bengali films rather than stay
on in Mumbai. The fame and money, she had said once, were
much better here and her home was the gullies of Mumbai
rather than the lanes of Kolkata. Marathi came as easily to her
as Bengali, and between these two languages she conquered the
hearts of many. However, she tried to go to Kolkata once every
year during Durga Puja and seek Ma Durga's blessings from
every pandal she visited.

Being with Shyamolie and hearing about her views on love
and life brought back memories of another era. I had been like
that a decade ago—a virgin in love, hoping a knight in shining
armour would sweep me away and promise to look after me
forever. Then life got in the way and after a string of bizarre
relationships and broken hearts I became wiser. Now I knew

that love didn't exist in this pure form. It was a matter of convenience for the human race. We all got married for the sake of society, had children because we wanted to propagate the species, had affairs to satisfy our sexual urges, and ultimately died talking about this elusive thing called love that was like God whom one could not see, hear, or understand but needed in our daily life.

I would show Shy what the world was made up of. She might know Bollywood better than me but in matters of love, I was the wise one.

9
Of Men and Matters of the Heart

After working with Bela for four months and traipsing around the city with Shy, I had a deep urge to go back to my roots and discover art all over again. Lately, I had been feeling that instead of progressing in my career, I was going backwards. I had never imagined myself as an interpreter and translator for an actress. I had worked as one in the beginning of my career for foreign delegates and dignitaries who visited India. I had even translated brochures, manuals and books for people. All intellectual stuff with a great growth curve for someone in her early twenties. But after branching out on my own, and studying art at prestigious universities around the globe and even teaching art history I was now reduced to being a translator once again for a woman who could easily have someone dub for her in her films. It was all vaguely depressing.

One afternoon when I was feeling purposeless and didn't know which direction my life was heading, I decided to get an 'art fix'. There was a Picasso exhibition at the Cymroza art gallery and I trudged all the way from my Santa Cruz flat to town just so I could sit in front of something I knew and understood. The exhibition was from the Blue period of the painter's life and it was truly what I was feeling today. I sat in front of 'The Absinthe Drinker' pondering on Picasso's work and wondering if I should get some Absinthe myself when I heard a voice behind me say, 'I would almost say that Gauguin made this and Picasso just signed his name on it.'

I turned around and saw an elderly gentleman speaking to himself. I didn't want to intrude on his thoughts, so I took another, longer look at the painting in light of what he had just said. It did seem like an imitation of Gauguin's work and I probably had mentioned this in one of my lectures, but I had been out of touch with examining art for so long that his comment felt like I was learning something new.

'You're right,' I said. He came and stood beside the bench till I waved my hand at the empty seat next to me. In fact the whole room was empty. No one wanted to come see an exhibition in the middle of the week in the middle of the day when they were busy making money in the commercial capital of the country. I wondered for a second why this man wasn't doing the same, but I let the thought slide, eager for a chance of some art-related conversation.

The man sat down and crossed his legs. 'It's quite a languid depiction of Pablo's worst phase of life. I mean artists are supposed to be at their very best when they're most depressed.' The man spoke as if he knew Picasso personally, and judging by the grey hair around his temples, it might not just have been a vague possibility. 'Anyhow, it did sell for only 35 million pounds so I could be wrong,' he said with a hint of a smile.

I giggled. It was a different and refreshing take on it. And it was a refreshing way to start a conversation with a woman.

'I'm Kaveri,' I said and offered my right hand.

'Siddharth,' he said, shaking my hand.

We talked a little about ourselves. He was a forty-six-year-old businessman—a divorcé with no children—who lived a life full of travel and was acquainted with more boring hotel rooms than he cared to count. What struck me most about Siddharth was the way he was dressed. For most men, an afternoon off in the middle of the work week meant wearing shorts, an old shirt from their college days and heading off to eat something or sitting on the couch and watching television. But this man was impeccably dressed in a crisp white Prada shirt, dark brown blazer, and dark blue distressed Gucci jeans with shiny Paul Smith shoes. I wondered if the whole look had been put together by his stylist! After living in Europe for many years, first with my parents and then alone, I had begun to identify fashion and brands really well. I might not have known Indian designers as well as Shyamolie, but I could tell the difference between Prada and Gucci. And Siddharth wore both of them effortlessly.

He saw me noticing his shoes and smiled, 'I love picking up things for myself.'

'Obviously from abroad,' I smiled wryly. 'I love Gucci and Prada and brands and stuff. I'm not dismissing you at all,' I added hurriedly, lest he think I was an impudent brat. 'I meant to say you have impeccable taste and tremendous knowledge about clothes.'

'And art?' he asked slightly flirtatiously.

I felt myself blushing. I shrugged and replied, 'I can't judge you on the art bit yet. I will need to know what you think of many more artists, paintings, sculptures before I do. I was an art professor, so you wouldn't want to question me!' I said cheekily.

He laughed. It was a mellow bass sound. For a man who was so slim, I wondered where he got this deep voice. He was unlike the other men I knew. He was tall, but didn't tower over me. He was well built, but not overly muscular. He had a few crooked teeth, but he also had the most amazing eyes I had ever seen—light brown that twinkled with immense charm and oozed intellect. Completely mesmerizing.

'Okay, then let me take you to another art gallery and you can judge me there,' he said looking at me intently. I wasn't sure if I wanted to go off with this man. He could be a murderer for all I knew, said a little voice in my head. And immediately another voice piped up, why would he murder you and get blood on his four-hundred-dollar shirt? I was hearing multiple voices! One was even in Russian. Maybe I did need an outing and some new friends. My thinking was beginning to get warped with too much estrogen in my life.

'Sure.' I responded. 'Where do you want to go?'

He got up and reached a hand out to me, 'I know just the place. You leave it to me, Ms Professor.'

For a fraction of a second, as I looked at his hand, I debated the wisdom of taking him up on his offer. I had just got out of a relationship and had no intention of being in one again anytime soon. What would . . . Oh! There I went again, over thinking everything. The man was merely having a conversation with another person about a subject he really liked. But the problem was that it was the first time in months that I truly felt alive. And my gut instinct had never been wrong. I could feel something brewing.

Good Lord! I was in for trouble!

10

Fantastic Dates and Worrisome Natures

And so I went on my first date after months. I didn't even know if it was a date. All the while he never tried to hold my hand, or kiss me or flirt with me or even try to get me into bed. That was the strangest thing; nearly all the men I knew had tried some gimmick or the other to show me how smart, funny or romantic they were to impress me. But Siddharth was different. He just wanted to take me to a place which would enrich my soul.

He took me to Colaba where a four-bedroom apartment had been converted into a beautiful art gallery. All the pieces on display were exclusive and by renowned international artists whom everyone tried to get their hands on. The whole apartment had central air conditioning and was kept at a low temperature so the art would not be damaged. Admittance to the exhibitions was by invitation only. This was what I had wanted to do when I had moved back but was unable to. One of the rooms had been converted into an office and the rest of the space had false ceilings with mellow lighting with individual lights on all the pieces that were hung.

Mamta, a statuesque woman with chestnut-coloured, short

cropped hair, ran the gallery. She seemed to be well known to Siddharth and immediately welcomed him in. She hugged Siddharth and smiled at me warmly with her twinkling brown eyes. We were the only two people there that day. She took us around the gallery and gave us a brochure of the current exhibition. The artist was Dganit Blechner. I knew how well respected she was in the art world across the globe. It must have been impossible to ship her works down here, and yet here was Mamta, showing off at least fifteen Blechner prints.

'Her unique style and new technique combine many different visual sources into a very colourful and personal composition,' Mamta uttered as if she was quoting from a book.

'A very vibrant palette,' I contemplated loudly.

'Yes,' Mamta agreed.

I had never seen such a beautiful combination of art and photography. I had been teaching the old masters to my students and seen much of post-modernism stuff that leaned towards dark sentiments of the artist. Here there was a bright interplay of colours that immediately lightened my mood. I felt after many months I was in the company of like-minded people. We spoke exhaustively about different painters, sculptors and artists from Monet to Munch, Amrita Shergill to Siona Shimshi. I described how I used to study for a lecture and felt like an artist myself when I took classes in Barcelona; I was moulding the minds of students and it felt quite powerful. It felt wonderful to discuss my true passion after all this time with people who understood it. All this time I'd felt as though I was taking a sabbatical from art. I was avoiding dealing with the emotions of a break up by cutting myself off from things that reminded me of Ray. And that included art.

After our tour, Mamta took us into her office. It was large room, done up in soft tones that contrasted with the dark wood floors. A plush cream sofa stood on one side of the room with a low coffee table in front of it. On the other side was a large mahogany desk with a Macbook and some papers. A large bookshelf covered one part of the wall where there were hundreds of books about painters, sculptors and artists from across time and space. Cream coloured Venetian blinds at the windows were half raised for the light to enter. Once we had sat down, she offered us the most delicious red velvet cupcakes I'd ever eaten and steaming espressos. The coffee maker in her room was very similar to the one I had had in Barcelona. I remembered with a pang how long it had been since I'd left Spain and the dreams I had then. For a moment, I wondered what Ray had done with the cappuccino maker we bought together. The raw wound of the break-up suddenly opened for a moment. A flood of pain, anger and sorrow felt like it would overwhelm me in that office of a stranger where a mere smell of coffee brought these feelings back. I took a deep breath and released the negative energy. It was a time gone by. I didn't need to dwell on it anymore. And suddenly I began to focus again on the current moment and how wonderful it felt.

As I listened to their conversation, I realized that Siddharth must have bought a few pieces from Mamta and may even have had something special with her in the past. They spoke fondly of each other, lightly teasing but never crossing any boundaries. He seemed at ease, reclining on the sofa, sipping his Brazilian espresso. We chatted for a bit longer. Then Siddharth said we needed to move along to our next destination and we left from there. Mamta promised to invite me again for further exhibitions and I felt most privileged. I had felt a connection with her and hoped that someday we would become good friends.

From the gallery, Siddharth took me to lunch at Fenix in the Oberoi Hotel. It was a late lunch and even though I was ravenous, I decided to be prim and proper for his sake and not wolf down the food when it arrived. He told me about his work as we ate. He ran one of the top software companies in the country. And, he added with a cheeky grin, he was now valued at one point two billion dollars.

My jaw fell open and my eyes popped out. I tried to get some composure and asked, 'How did you do that?'

'Well my father was wealthy and he passed it on to me,' he said taking a mouthful of his watercress salad while I stuffed myself with chicken risotto and some cold, lemon ice-tea.

'I'm so sorry to hear that. When did he pass away?' I asked in all earnestness.

'He's not dead,' Siddharth said with a smile.

I was horrified. 'I'm so sorry. I thought . . . oh God!' I said with deep embarrassment. I didn't know how I managed such goof ups in my life!

'That's okay. He is still alive. So is my mother. They live in Bangalore. I manage the business now. But I've branched out on my own with my investments so I'm not all a spoilt rich brat as they would call it.' He said it with élan. So he had been born rich and then became richer. Right. How would I describe my life to him? Poor and now pauper.

'My parents live in Bangalore as well,' I said finally.

He asked me more about myself. He seemed genuinely interested in my life and my dreams and what I was currently doing which was so far removed from what he did and who he was. He offered to help me set up my own gallery and put me in touch with people from the art world, but I remembered what Aditi had told me about how her husband had helped her set up her business but once they separated she had to start all over again since none of his contacts would want to endorse her fashion brand anymore. Even if Siddharth and I never dated, and simply stayed friends, I would be stuck in a similar situation if the relationship ever soured. I didn't want to end up feeling sorry for myself in five years that I hadn't built anything on my own. So I didn't pursue that line of conversation and said I would think about it once I completed the current project of sprucing Bela Bandhan up.

'So art and software are polar opposites!' I said once our plates had been cleared and we ordered a fine Belgian dark chocolate mousse cake.

He nodded his head and replied, 'I know. I was always

interested in art but with a family deep in software I never got the chance to explore the creative side. I'm not much of a painter or anything,' he explained casually though I thought that he might be underplaying that as well, 'but I was fascinated by paintings. I started studying them by myself at Brown University while I was doing an MBA and then travelled many continents to see different artists' works. I slowly started understanding them and now eventually can collect a few.'

The best education, the best travel and the best pieces of art right at this man's feet and yet he seemed so unassuming and sweet. I was flabbergasted. I would never match up to this person. For a moment I thought of what his mother would say when she met me. She would probably look like Meryl Streep in *Devil Wears Prada* and ask her son, while looking at me down the length of her nose, 'Who is this ragamuffin you've brought into our house, Siddharth?'

I don't even know why I let my thoughts wander that far. This was the first time we had met! But he was an extremely interesting man and we had a most pleasant afternoon. He didn't push me to have dinner or drinks with him. After another round of espressos and scintillating conversation he dropped me back home.

It was gentlemanly and endearing. It was also unromantic. All my dates had ended way past midnight with me trying to get into the guy's pants or vice versa. At one point I had considered the idea that he may be too old for me, but I never realized that he might consider me too young for him! A part of me felt slightly rejected. It was a strange feeling. I really wanted a chance to get to know him better. But he was gone without us exchanging numbers. One point two billion dollars had just driven his Maserati right out of my life. Aditi was going to kill me.

11

Aditi's Reasons

It had been four months since I had moved into my new flat and I had done up the place rather nicely. Although it was small, it looked pretty. The walls were an eggshell white. I had placed a small beige couch in the drawing room at one end and a bookshelf on the other. Blue paisley Fabindia curtains adorned the windows and a multi-coloured rug on the floor covering a large portion of the ugly tiles that lay beneath. In the bedroom I had painted one wall an ocean blue to remind me that the sea was always around me, and help me stay calm. My king-size bed, which almost took up the whole room was placed against this wall. There was a row of dark built-in wardrobes along the wall on the right side of the bed and big windows to the left. The TV was mounted on the wall opposite the bed. A large chair stood at the foot of the bed and that was where my laptop usually rested. I had thrown cushions in different colours and patterns all across the house so I could still keep a semblance of my old self and a little nostalgia of Coffee De with me. For the kitchen, I had got curtains to match the pretty rose and lime-green tiles. In one corner stood my gleaming coffee maker that I had bought as soon as I had moved in, so I could enjoy my steaming cappuccinos at home instead of heading off to one of the insanely expensive coffee shops nearby. The shelves were lined with glass jars full of coloured pasta in different shapes, spices, dals, and crockery and flatware. The fridge was stocked with fresh produce and other groceries. I had started eating more at home and had got myself a cook who came and made healthy food for me. Shyamolie had been over many times and since she was an excellent cook, she would usually whip up some dinner for us.

Aditi and I had drifted apart since I had moved out of her parents' house. With new developments in her divorce proceedings she had been too occupied to visit my new place. And in my quest to become healthier, I had been avoiding her as well. With Aditi I knew we would always be eating out or ordering in; she hated having anything from home. But just because she had superb metabolism and could inhale food without ever putting on weight didn't mean I could too.

But then one afternoon she dropped by unexpectedly, and seeing her I realized that bad influence or not, I had missed her.

'What a quaint place!' Aditi chirped as soon as she entered.

I took two chilled cans of Diet Coke from the fridge and reached for two glasses.

'I'll just take the can,' Aditi said.

I opened a can for her and said, 'You know you should always wash and wipe these cans before you drink from them. If they've been in a shop or warehouse, they could have rat droppings and other rubbish on them. You might contract some awful disease.'

Aditi grimaced reaching for a glass from the cabinet. 'You read too much. I'll never drink from a can ever again.'

We took our drinks into the drawing room and got comfortable on the sofa. We had nearly four months' worth of catching up to do.

'So, how was the meeting with Arjun? You never told me if you're still in touch with him? Are you getting back together?' she asked taking a sip from her glass.

'Nothing!' I said not wanting to give out too many details. 'He offered me his place. I told him no. I found this. Haven't spoken to him since that evening. He's probably busy with his wedding preparations,' I said.

'And you're okay with that?' she asked with concern.

I took a sip of my drink and said very confidently, 'Oh yeah. It hardly matters.'

She looked at me sceptically, to which I replied, 'Well it's not great. But it's okay.'

She understood what I meant. We always had an understanding. She didn't probe into what I felt. I didn't offer any further explanation.

'So have you met any interesting men?' she asked.

I considered telling Aditi about Siddharth, but then decided against it. She might misunderstand what I had with him. In fact I wasn't sure I understood it either. The whole day kept playing in my mind over and over again; I had loved every moment of that day. Siddharth was constantly in my thoughts, and I knew I wanted to spend more time with him. But I didn't know how to explain feeling like this about a guy I had only met once, so all I said was, 'Not really.'

'Are you getting any sex?'

Trust Aditi to never beat about the bush. She had had a new guy on her arm every week before she got married and had enjoyed every single sexual encounter she had.

'No! And I don't know where to get it from! What about you?' I retorted, and then, a sudden thought came to me, I added, 'Aditi, are you getting divorced because the sex died?'

'No, yaar,' she said lazily lounging back on the sofa.'The sex died because there was no conversation left. And while I enjoyed sex before I got married, it just wasn't me post.'

'You didn't like sex?' I asked incredulously. This was a woman who couldn't remember the names of some of the men she had slept with because she never bothered to talk to them!

But Aditi had changed. And so had I. Aditi was a woman

who was living exactly as she wanted. And somewhere it pissed me off. She got married because she wanted to, she was getting divorced when she wanted to. She stopped having sex because she didn't feel like it. It all seemed very selfish to me as I thought more about it. Yes, we all need to live our individual lives. We all need to look out for our own happiness. But somewhere we also need to care for the people who've helped us along the way. I felt bad for her parents who must be completely heartbroken at seeing their daughter who they thought was 'settled once and for all' back home with them. I felt sympathy for her husband who must have tried to please her in his small way but couldn't live up to her expectations. I didn't know whether my resentment came from the fact that I had been dumped and maybe some of the residual feelings were stirring up again hearing about how Aditi had chosen to dump her married life without really trying.

'Aditi, what really happened with your marriage?' I asked with a raised eyebrow.

'Rajat and I had a lot in common. And after we met a few times, we did fall in love with each other. Or actually I thought I fell in love with him.'

But Rajat had just wanted a glorified trophy wife who didn't do much and who didn't need much from him. She had tried for two years to integrate herself into his world. She cooked his favourite meals, spent hours trying to understand his business and then talk to him about it. She would dress up and go with him to the A-list parties he was invited to and be the perfect hostess at their own parties. Aditi had made her entire life about him. Rajat, however, never had time for her. He would work till two or three every morning and when he did take time off from work on the weekends, he would play golf or hang out with his friends. At first she had confronted him and demanded that he spend time with her and take her places. And he had relented a few times and taken her on vacations. But when they got back he would again disappear for days, leaving her with his mother who lived with them. Slowly Aditi became close to her and started looking after her. This was exactly what Rajat had wanted, a companion for his mother rather than a woman for himself. Apparently, he had had plenty of those.

'I'm not so sure if he was ever in love with me or he was just playing his part,' Aditi said contemplatively with tears welling in her eyes.

After a long pause Aditi admitted that their marriage had become something that constricted her. There were moments that were memorable and passionate. The sex was absolutely fabulous. Rajat was a great lover and wonderful in bed. They had had sex at least twice a week, but it was always when he chose, not when she wanted it. Soon she began to realize that he didn't respect her. She didn't do as much as other men's wives did. Apparently, even if you were a trophy wife, you needed to be seen in society as doing something like running an empire or starting a magazine or a boutique or dabbling in art. Aditi didn't do anything like that. She had been an assistant director for so many years. All she knew were films. She knew where to get a hat for an actress and a hat stand for an art director, the best angle for a shot, how to deal with a pampered star throwing a tantrum. But in the world of money and politics, those skills were useless; in a completely different society she couldn't match up.

'All right, you've justified it this far. But that doesn't mean it should lead to divorce,' I said wanting the story to move along faster. But Aditi wanted to take a break so we decided to eat lunch. I offered her bhindi and dal, but she grimaced and ordered a Subway sandwich for herself. She made some cold coffee for us while we waited for the sandwich to be delivered.

'An arranged marriage is never easy for any party,' Aditi said. 'You try to adjust to your spouse, to a new family, an entirely new set of friends, hoping all the while that they will like you and accept you.' Sometimes, in trying to make these adjustments, she added, you might lose your own identity and after a few years you might realize that you've changed. That's when you want to go back and search for the person you were and reclaim your identity. One doesn't realize that marriage is also a process of change for an individual. It's a part of growing up. And the person that you were before you got married needs to be left behind. Instead, people lament the loss of that part of their youth and try to recapture it. Who you become after your marriage or having children is also a part of the growth. A good part. But if you start believing that you've changed and it's because of your spouse then whenever something goes wrong with your life you're going to blame him for it and not understand that adversity is a part of life. Alternatively, you can find an amazingly caring husband and a very accepting family who love you for exactly who you are and encourage you to do what you like, who do not expect you to adjust. The two sides of a marriage are as tricky as two sides of a coin.

Aditi had got a mixed bag. While she had an amazing mother-in-law who pampered her and showered her with gifts and lots of love, she had found a husband who had absolutely no time for her.

'But I thought she kept your locker key?' I interrupted remembering that Aditi had told me her mother-in-law was a supreme bitch.

'Yes. But after Amitabh, my brother-in-law told her to give it she said she was holding it in the hope that I was coming back and not for any malicious reasons,' explained Aditi clearing my doubts and reinforcing me to believe that she should stick to her marriage. But soon enough she was lonely in her marriage. Although she had a few friends before marriage, they had also got married and started living their own lives. And inevitably, they attended parties and get-togethers with their husbands. Aditi was the only one by herself, and when asked where her husband was, she would always say 'at work'. Soon enough it became so awkward for her that she stopped going to the parties altogether. She began spending more and more time at home, and didn't make any new friends.

It was then that her brother-in-law Amitabh entered her life. Aditi and Amitabh had become great friends during her wedding. He was fun loving, enjoyed reading and watching Bollywood films. He spent a lot of time with her, talking to her for hours about her experiences and accompanying her on shopping expeditions. Two years after Aditi's marriage, Amitabh completed his MBA from the US, and came back to India for a break. Beginning to get disillusioned with her marriage, Aditi poured her heart out to him and he gave her practical advice, and instead of letting her mope around he decided to play saviour and took her to all the places she loved to go to. The attraction was inevitable. Aditi adored him, but she wasn't in love with him. She still believed she was in love with Rajat. His break over, Amitabh went back to start a job. Aditi missed him a lot, and eventually they started chatting via Skype.

Engrossed in his job, Rajat continued to ignore Aditi, just glad that there was someone looking after his mother. But Aditi wasn't looking after the old woman for him; she was looking after her for Amitabh.

'I don't know when it became love,' she said with a sigh. 'I knew it was wrong but I couldn't help myself.'

I took out a packet of cigarettes and lit one while processing what she was saying. I didn't really want to know the answer to my question, but I asked it anyway, 'Have you slept with him?'

Aditi was silent. And I knew. She looked down at her empty glass and didn't say anything. She didn't even move her head. She looked up and asked me instead, 'Do you think I'm morally reprehensible?'

I already had the answer for that. 'No. I'll never consider you morally reprehensible, Aditi. I will never judge you. That's not what friends do.' And I meant it.

In all the anger and frustration I had felt in the afternoon towards her I realized that 'I' had featured prominently in it. How selfish had I become? After living alone for the last three to four years of my life I had become so independent that I had gone back to square one in my judgements. When I was going through a rough period Aditi had never judged me. I had been in love with a married man and all she said was, 'Be careful.' She had been there to pick up the pieces when my heart got broken and she was there to support me when I went back to him time and again. She had just been supportive of my decisions without *judging* what I was doing.

I stubbed out my cigarette as soon as she made coughing noises and commented how she was dying of passive smoke. I smiled and continued speaking, 'Sometimes you need to avoid the people you miss the most to keep the people who love you for now.' We need to remove certain people from our life no matter how important they feel to our heart at the time to clear our head. An infatuation can give us what we want but a true love can give what we need. It's important to know the difference and not get carried away.

Just then her sandwich came and we sat down for lunch.

'How long has it been going on with Amitabh? Does anyone else know about it?' I asked coming back to the topic that was pressing at hand. Affairs were easy to manage. I had become a pro at it!

'Less than a year. Before that we were just friends. I really wanted things to work out with Rajat. We've been married for three years now.'

I couldn't believe it had been three years since I attended Aditi's wedding and had been on a reality show! How time flew. There had been a time when I had desperately wanted to be married. But looking at Aditi I began wondering if it was such a sane institution to enter into after all.

'I told Meghna once that I was attracted to my brother-in-law and she was completely shocked,' Aditi confessed, bringing me out of my reverie.

Meghna was a friend of Aditi's from her film days. They had been assistants together until Meghna had switched to a corporate job. She had been married for a long time and was very much in love with her husband; the couple had two boys. Meghna was also the greatest gossip in the world.

'How could you tell Meghna?' I asked in disbelief. 'She will spread it all across the town.'

'I know! But I didn't know what to do when it was happening and it seemed like you were very busy and happy. This was not the kind of thing I could tell you over the phone or on Skype na?' she hurriedly explained.

It didn't matter why she hadn't told me. What I needed to do now was damage control so her reputation wouldn't suffer. A married woman who was having an affair is considered a tramp. A married man, on the other hand, is easily forgiven. It is unfair, but we live in a flawed society, one unlikely to change any time soon. People never see how lonely or depressed the wife is. They only believe that since the man is providing for her, he should have the liberty to do as he pleases.

'Whatever is done is done. Now how do you plan to fix it?' I asked.

Aditi shrugged and smiled. I figured that she wasn't planning to do anything about it. 'You're not sorry are you?' I asked her.

'Hey, I do feel liable for this entire mess, but I can't help it. *The heart wants what it wants.* Isn't that what you told me when you were with Arjun?' she retorted, as if I should take some of the blame for affairs that she had.

'Aditi,' I started softly and more maturely, 'you can't continue this affair with Amitabh. It will shatter too many people—Rajat, your mother-in-law, your parents. Even your friends, regardless of the state of their marriages and their morals, will not want you anywhere near their husbands for fear that you might seduce them. And all for what? A rebound relationship!'

I continued, 'I know you're madly in love with Amitabh right now, but I think you should give it time. If you're certain that your marriage cannot be salvaged, then divorce Rajat, wait for some time, and then reveal the fact that you're in love with his brother . . . if you still are then. Distance might help you understand your feelings better. And you need to heal from a divorce as well. In the meantime, stay away from Amitabh, and don't say anything to anyone else.'

Either Aditi was listening very keenly to my ideas or she had already made up her mind about what she was going to do and was just nodding to indulge me. But I chose to continue since it was my right as her best friend to give her my opinion and let her make her decision. 'Or you can let it blow up in your face and all of the above will happen,' I said with finality.

Aditi thought about it and asked, 'Isn't there a third option? Both of these are equally fucked, you know.'

I shook my head. That was the way I saw it.

'I know what you're saying,' Aditi finally conceded, 'but it's going to be tough.'

'It's got to end Adu. You know it as well as I do,' I said and lay down to close my eyes for a bit. I was feeling completely drained listening to her.

Aditi was quiet for some time. She probably felt extremely dejected that I hadn't taken her side. What I had said was the truth and what I truly felt was a logical thing to do. I hadn't seen Aditi's side in it. Even though she had tried to defend her affair I refused to see it. Women always got themselves in precarious situations. They feel that love should be a challenge. It should be exciting, adventurous, and new. They never realize that love is a staid old man who gives you a roof over your head and enough space to do what you want in life. If women don't get enough space from a man, they call him 'clingy' and leave him. If they get all the space, they say they want him to be jealous. If they find a man who is stable they call him boring. If they find a man exciting, they want more stability. It is never ending.

Sometimes love is just a screwed up game.

12

Call Me Papaji

'Fuck man!' Shy said as soon as I answered her call.

It was not the usual response one expects when answering a call, but then Shy was not a usual type of girl.

'What happened?' I asked.

'That Panjwani asshole has become the producer of the film,' she said, not bothering to conceal her disgust.

'Scunjay?' I asked not understanding the full importance of her displeasure. 'So?'

'Yes. Now that fool will want to be part of more than just Bela's acting assignments. He'll want to look into every aspect of the filmmaking process even though he knows diddly squat about it. Anyway, he wants to meet you. He's lost his phone and called me to tell you to meet him today at four.'

'If he's lost his phone then how did he call you?' I asked.

'Because Panjwani has two phones; one for people he thinks are important and one, the one he's lost, for people he couldn't care less about. I wish he would lose the one that has my number. Anyway all the best,' she said hurriedly and added, 'And whatever you do, don't call him Papaji.'

'What?' I asked, slightly miffed that he didn't care to store my number in his 'important people' phone, 'Why should I call him that?'

'You'll see,' she said and hung up.

And I did see. And learn. And laugh.

When I entered the office, Scunjay was sitting on a couch outside his office. RT sat at the desk beside him, typing furiously. Strains of some new remixed music could be heard from the darkened office.

'Sir, you wanted to see me?' I asked.

'Yes, yes, sit down and please don't call me sir. Call me Papaji. I want to be a father figure to all you bachchas,' he said pointing to a chair far away from him.

Since I had been warned about this I didn't reply. I smiled and addressed Rakesh instead, 'Hi RT.' He looked up for a second, gave a brief, superficial smile, and went back to his typing.

Punjwani glared at RT as if there would be some radioactive waves that could emanate from his eyes and burn RT down. 'He forgot to type out the minutes of three of my meetings and I need them filed immediately,' he explained. 'If he's going to be an assistant to a producer, he had better get his act together.' I noticed beads of sweat forming on Rakesh's forehead.

'Congratulations on becoming producer of *Aap Meri Zindagi*,' I said to Punjwani. He nodded nonchalantly, as though he had expected it all along. 'Now you will have many actors wanting to get a hold of you, sir.' There was enough butter in my voice to make a kilo of dal makhani. I had learnt that flattery played an important part in this industry that was filled with fragile egos and shaky friendships.

'I know. What to do. It's a curse,' he said shaking his head. Humility was clearly not his strongest quality.

'You're right, sir,' I said, not wanting to argue.

'Papaji,' he corrected. Just then his phone rang. He looked at it and sighed. 'It's the slave.'

Before I could ask what he meant by 'slave', RT leapt out of his chair and offered to take the phone from Scunjay, but the latter shook his head. RT returned to his desk and resumed his work. Punjwani sighed again and explained, 'There is this fellow who calls me every day and asks for a job. I make him sing to me.' I didn't believe it, but he took the call and put it on speaker phone.

A meek voice at the other end asked, 'Have you found anything for me today, Papaji?'

Scunjay gave me a pointed look and replied, 'First you sing that song from *Hare Rama Hare Krishna* for me.'

'Yes, Papaji,' the voice said, and proceeded to give such a tuneless rendition of *Dum maro dum* that I wouldn't have been surprised if R.D. Burman came back from the dead just to strangle this 'slave'.

But Papaji closed his eyes and swayed along for three verses and then suddenly interrupted and said, 'Enough! I have to go for my meeting. You speak to RT about the job on the company landline.' And with that he hung up, muttering, 'Where do these people come from!' I stood there in silence, wondering if this was an office or a circus. RT continued typing with one hand, picked up the phone with his other one, dialled a number and barked, 'Two coffees. Now!' Perhaps this was why he was so useful—he could multitask and was ambidextrous. Not that I cared. I cleared my throat and asked sweetly, 'Papaji'—everyone else seemed to be calling him that, I might as well—'why did you call me?'

'I wanted to know how Bela's progressing? We are leaving for Milan soon and there is sync sound on the set of the film. While we are there we need to do press interviews and she can't sound like a squeaky Russian cat.'

I wanted to say she was doing well, but the truth was that she wasn't. She hadn't been paying attention in our sessions and I could hardly push her. Once when I had scolded her for not taking our classes seriously, she had sulked and not returned my calls about scheduling our next session for two weeks. I had coaxed and cajoled my way back into her good graces since then, because if she didn't like me I would be out of a job and, between the rent and the EMIs on the new car I had just bought, I couldn't afford to be unemployed.

'It's progressing well, sir . . . umm . . . Papaji,' I lied. 'But you asked me to make her fluent.'

'I don't care anymore about her being fluent. As long as she doesn't sound like a villager from Siberia. If she's ready then I'll settle your account and we'll see if you can do something else.'

That was when I realized that he had no other plans for me and if I didn't hold on to this job, I would be soon unemployed.

'No, no, Papaji,' I said with a very silky confidence in my tone. 'Let me work on her a little more. She will be perfect when I'm done with her. And your film will sound much better. Why do you want to spend so much money on dubbing with another artist when you can spend only half on getting Bela's accent right?'

At the thought of saving money, Punjwani's ears pricked up. If there was a way to save even two rupees he would go to any lengths to save it, and I used that to my advantage. He nodded and said, 'All right then. But then you will have to travel with us. I can't afford to waste one month while we're shooting. And you had better train her on the sets then. No wasting time on my outdoor shoot!' I nodded. Just then the coffee came and he offered me a cup. He got another call on his phone and he yelled at RT to quickly get him a number from his 'other' phone.

'I think I need to go for a drive now. RT, I'm going to Pune. Don't call me if you need anything,' he said without rising from the couch.

'Pune sir . . . I mean Papaji? It's Wednesday. And it's almost seven in the evening.'

Scunjay nodded. 'I should be there in one hour,' he said still not rising. 'I need a drink.'

'It takes three hours sir, doesn't it?'

He shook his head. And raised his index finger. One hour. I looked at RT who nodded, a terrified expression on his face. Obviously, he had been on such drives.

Scunjay took a sip of his coffee and closed his eyes. I figured that was my cue to leave. Besides, I was too psyched to stay and extend this bizarre evening. I had too many things to do. I hadn't visited my parents yet, and if I took off for a month on a shooting schedule without having visited them, I would never hear the end of it!

13

Just Because You're Older Doesn't Mean You're Wiser: Mom

I spent a week with my parents. That was five days too many for a normal person and an agonizing one hundred and sixty-eight hours for me. Nevertheless, I attempted to be happy eating my mom's cooking after ages and going for walks with my dad.

My mother had already planned a family get together on the day I arrived in Bangalore to welcome me back. She had done this behind my back since she knew I was so averse to meeting any of my relatives that I would have flatly refused if she had asked me. But since she had already planned it I had no choice but to go ahead with the party arrangements and grin and bear the conversations on the topic that would take centre stage: my love life.

After a few pleasantries were exchanged and snacks devoured, one aunt, who had probably left her dentures at home, asked, 'So, beta, when do we hear the good news?'

'Yes,' chirped another ancient monolith in a green sari with fat spilling over the edges of the chair she was sitting on, 'you know, your biological clock is ticking!'

I really didn't want to discuss my biological clock with old women who had done nothing in their lives but raise children.

Children who, although considered the brightest gems the family had ever seen, were quite possibly the most boring pieces of furniture the world had ever been subjected to. I smiled and kept quiet, desperately hoping to sneak outside for a walk and a cigarette.

'You know your parents would like to see you settled down and happy, beta,' the aunt continued. Her husband, who had no intention of participating in 'women' talk said to my father, 'Let's go out for a smoke, Kishore!' I silently begged my dad not to leave me alone with these women, but he winked at me and walked out into the lovely garden my mother had planted.

All seven aunts immediately pulled their chairs closer to mine and began interrogating me about my imaginary wedding. There was no way I would survive without more alcohol. So I got up and said with a smile, 'Be right back.' It was going to be a long night.

I toyed with the idea of telling them that I had almost married an Italian man several years younger; I knew that would shut them up. Or I could tell them about Siddharth, the much older man I had one date with, and was dying to see again. But their momentarily horrified expressions would not be worth the tirade I would be subjected to about not finding a good, young Indian boy.

'Beta,' the thin, blind aunt shrieked from the corner of a sofa and broke my reverie, 'you have to tell us if you like anyone. We don't have a problem with any caste, or background. If you love someone, we are happy for you.'

They made it sound like they were doing me a favour. Why must all relationships lead to marriage? Why can't the happiness of singledom remain? If I was going to end up like them after I got married, I definitely did not want to be in the institution.

'Otherwise let us know and we can start looking!' exclaimed another aunt who was closest to my mother in age and nature.

I rolled my eyes at my mother who immediately got the hint and said, 'Now now, let's not bother her about such trivial things like marriage and kids. When the time is right, she will let us know herself.'

'But what's the harm in seeing a few boys?'

After I gulped down my second drink I had a revelation. Maybe this whole 'arranged marriage' thing might be fun, I thought. I was going to stay in Bangalore for some time anyway. I might as well have an entertaining evening with the IT chaps who were looking for a bride. In any case it had been some time since I had any sex and I was getting very strong urges to screw Carl, Bela's gay make-up artist. That was not a good feeling! I needed a straight man. And I needed him soon!

'Okay, I'll give that a try!' I said suddenly. My mother was completely shocked and gave me a very suspicious look.

'Done! We'll show you some photos,' said the fat aunt who didn't notice my mother trying to figure out what I was up to.

'Actually,' the thin blind aunt dragged out the word in a long breath, 'I know a lovely boy.'

And so it began.

14

Bonding over Preparations

My first meeting with a 'boy' promised to be fun. It was set up by my aunts and my mom who seemed super excited for me. The phone rang off the hook all of the next day as they finalized the details of the meeting.

'Dad,' I said in the evening when he and I were having tea, 'you know I'm not going to marry this guy, right?'

'I know,' he said, reaching for one of the khari biscuits on the plate. We looked at each other for a moment and then smiled. I was so happy that I had a parent who understood me. We really didn't need to say more. We were happy to not chat, to just *be* in each other's company. 'But have fun,' he added with a grin.

'Dad!'

'It's fixed!' my mom announced as she came from the garden where she had been walking around with the cordless phone, talking to her sister. 'We're going to Savitri's in the evening and the other family will come there with the boy.' She sat down with aplomb and reached for a khari biscuit as if it was the one thing that would complete the circle of joy. I asked, 'How old is he? Twelve?' Seeing her puzzled look, I added, 'Why is he called a boy and not a man?'

'Because anyone who is younger than us is a girl or a boy. You'll never be anything but children for us oldies. So obviously you'll remain our little girl and the person in question a boy.'

'Okay, Mom. Whatever you say,' I said. 'I suppose I'd better get to a parlour then so I can dazzle this lovely boy,' I added with a wicked smile.

Bangalore had not changed much even though everyone said it had changed drastically. They complained about the traffic and the commercialization of the place, but honestly beyond a few extra shops here and there, I didn't see too much of a difference. It was the same pleasant place with friendly people, rows of green trees, flowerbeds in gardens, filter coffee and idli chutney served in small pockets of the locality and a wonderful climate. I had done my early schooling here and when my parents started travelling the world I completed my education in different countries. I wondered how my life would have been had I just stayed in one school all my life as had most people. The travel bug had bit me very early on in life. After staying in one place for some time, I would fall prey to the 'itchy shoe' syndrome and leave. I always thought of my parents at times like those. I was their only child. It must have been hard on them to not have a hold on me. The main thing that bothered them was who would look after me when they died. It is a strange thought parents have. As if people can't look after themselves. And as if in our old age, my husband would be able to look after me. I mean, he would be old too!

I decided to wear black trousers and a lovely pink, paisley chiffon top that evening. I accessorized with diamond hoops and a small bracelet, and then stepped into my six-inch Manolos. I might look demure, but I wanted to be way taller than him. Plus heels make your butt look sexy. One last glance in the mirror and I was ready for my arranged date.

15

The Arranged Marriage Meeting

We reached Savitri auntie's house. After the initial greetings and exclamations about how wonderful we all looked, I reached for the homemade snacks that were kept on the table.

'Yum, what is this?' I asked, munching enthusiastically.

'Can you stop eating till the boy gets here?' my aunt demanded and then glared at my mother as if she had brought up the most uncouth person in the world. My mother just shrugged and went off to greet her brother-in-law. They had one son who was married and working in the US in Silicon Valley. Why he couldn't work in the IT capital of India and be near his parents was a question that plagued my mother incessantly. Apparently he was absolutely brilliant and had to be abroad. That just left two old people in Bangalore who had nothing better to do than try and get their nephews and nieces married off.

'When is the *boy* coming?' I asked grinning widely with food in my mouth.

'Is she going to be like this?' Savitri auntie asked my mom, already horrified with what I may do. My mother shook her head and lightly patted her sister, assuring her that I was just teasing and would be very well behaved. Then she shot me a pointed look. Parents can say so much with a look. A child, no matter how young or old, will understand exactly what their parents are saying to them.

Fifteen minutes later, the doorbell rang. My aunt who had been sitting down, shot up like an arrow and said, 'They're here. Quick. Go hide.'

'Huh? Why?' I asked, completely baffled.

'So you can make an entrance and he'll fall head over heels in love with you,' she said, rolling her eyes as if I had missed the obvious.

I burst out laughing. 'You've got to be kidding! Don't worry Aunty, he'll fall in love with me anyway, especially if I do the snake dance in front of him!' I mocked while going to open the door and swaying to a 'nagin' song I was humming for them.

'Stop!' she screeched. And I really stopped in my tracks. 'What are you doing?' she asked.

'Opening the door, Aunty. Relax!' I said.

God, my family was weird! They were all acting as if I had never been with a man in my life. Oh, actually maybe they *did* think that I had never been with a man in my life. Okay then.

I opened the door and found a man standing there. He was short compared to the men I had been with; I immediately regretted wearing my heels since I really towered over him. If we became a couple I would look like Katie Holmes in heels to a short Tom Cruise. He had a thick mop of black hair and lovely olive skin like mine. He smiled at me, displaying a row of perfect white teeth. He was wearing Georgio Armani perfume, like someone else I knew. Someone who was probably married for the second time by now. Next to him stood his mom, as slightly older version of my aunt, but in a different sari and brighter lipstick and a tallish gentleman at the back with white hair and a pleasant face. My prospective in-laws!

I welcomed them in and sat down. The old people—I was going to call them that since they were calling me 'girl'—started discussing the traffic. This was the one thing that all Bangalore people liked talking about. The couple was most apologetic about being late. I thought they were early; being late by a mere fifteen minutes in a Mumbaikar's clock would mean he would be apologizing for being early to a party. All of them had a very strong accent and broke into Kannada quite frequently. My dad never understood the language so most people spoke English around him. The parents had made room for two seating arrangements close to each other so that the 'boy' and I could converse.

His name was Prashanth. Everything in Bangalore has an 'h' attached to the end. Even if it is never used. The conversation started with the usual—what we did and where we stayed. He, like I had presumed, was born and brought up in Bangalore. And while he had travelled a little to meet his relatives abroad, he had never found the urge to live there citing it was too hard.

'Who wants to do all that laundry and cooking and everything da?' he asked, his speech heavy with the typical south Indian accent. He lived with his parents since they preferred it that way; he could look after them and they were happy to have someone around whom they could bully. He chuckled.

'Let's get something to drink,' I said and walked into the kitchen. He followed. I could see the glances the elders shot us and at each other. I didn't know if they were wondering why I wanted to drink on our 'first date' or if they had made up their minds what to wear for the wedding.

'What would you like to drink, Prashanth?' I asked, taking out two glasses and looking at the alcohol collection my uncle had laid out.

'Um . . . I don't drink.'

'Are you a teetotaler?'

'Yes, I only drink tea!' he said, grinning.

I smiled in response while I poured myself a drink. A man who didn't drink was a first in my life. I thought it was a bit strange that a man who was in his thirties, single and living with his parents never drank alcohol. If it had been me, I would have been a loony drunk by now. But he seemed nice. He was definitely intelligent. I couldn't make out his sense of humour yet. Maybe if he had a drink he would have loosened up.

He declined my offer to make him tea, so we walked back to the living room. We decided not to sit next to the parents and listen to their rants about astronomical electricity bills and problematic servants. I took him to the balcony instead where my uncle kept a rocking chair and a small sofa. It had been my idea last time I was here and he had completely loved it and got it for the house. Prashanth offered me the rocking chair but I decided to sit on one end of the sofa. He took the rocking chair and exclaimed he'd never sat on one before. I was surprised; there were so many things I had done that he hadn't experienced. I was well-travelled and more learned in the arts than him. If he couldn't sustain my interest for one evening then how would I ever spend the rest of my life with him?

'Think like Aditi!' a little voice in my head said. 'You need him for one purpose right now. If he can live up to that, then you can take one day at a time.'

As we talked I learned that Prashanth was extremely good at his job and was, in fact, the group head of his company. Since most of his time was spent at work or in attending family functions he never got out much to date. And since he didn't drink going to a pub with friends to meet women was pointless. He had dated one or two women but it hadn't worked out; he didn't elaborate further. He was extremely shy. I could see why he was still single.

'So finally my mother pressured me into considering an arranged marriage and I agreed. I mean I do want to settle down with a nice wife and start a family . . . kids.' I gathered from the look on his face that I, he hoped, would be that nice wife. And then suddenly it hit me, he was probably judging me as much as I was judging him.

'Prashanth, what did you think of me when I opened the door?' I asked him with a smile.

He looked at me and tilted his head. I felt unexpectedly self-conscious. 'I thought you had very pretty eyes,' he said and I nodded and replied, 'Thank you.' 'And,' he continued, 'I thought you were probably a very spunky, outgoing girl who was doing this for her parents' sake.' He seemed pretty perceptive.

'Girl!' I teased.

'I meant woman!' he said with a laugh.

I decided it was time to have a bit of fun with him. 'How many women have you slept with?' I asked.

He started blushing. 'I don't think that's an appropriate topic for a first date.'

'Oh, come on! You can hardly call this a date!' I said, gesturing towards the parents in the other room.

'Most of my first dates are like this,' he said quite solemnly.

I was horrified. *This* was a first date? No wonder he hadn't found a woman. He needed to break out of this mould.

'Hey P,' I said familiarly, 'you need to take a woman out to know what a first date is. You need to woo her. Take her to a bookstore and buy her a really nice book you like. Or take her to a nice restaurant or to the races and give her money to bet on horses so she can have a real fun time. And then you can take her someplace nice and do her!'

'Do her?' he asked, confused.

'Have sex with her,' I explained. Damn! Instead of flirting with him, I had become his tutor.

I continued, 'It's fine to meet the woman with your parents, but you've got to make the effort to do more than that.'

'I have made the effort,' he said with a pause, 'sometimes. But I've never gone to someplace nice. It's not easy you know. We live in a very conservative society. My parents might not be as liberal as yours might be. It's not a done thing in our community to *date* or live in with someone or sleep with someone before you get married. It might be easy for you because you live in Mumbai. But most households in India are very conservative and it's not looked highly upon to go party with a girl you aren't betrothed to.'

He did have a point I thought. 'So how many times have you gone for this arranged match thing?' I asked suddenly feeling as if I was in a line of women he went through.

'This is the seventh time,' he replied. 'But only because I thought the first six women weren't good looking. I think you're really pretty!'

He had rejected six women before me because they weren't pretty? That was kind of shallow. I had to admit I was beginning to not like him all that much.

'Are you a virgin?' I asked incredulously even though I didn't believe it.

He shook his head, 'Not at all. I've had sex with one woman.'

I waited for him to continue and he did when I raised my eyebrows at him for more explanation. He said softly, 'But my friends got her for me.'

'You mean a prostitute?' I asked in disbelief.

'Shhh. Keep it down. Do you know how difficult it is for a guy like me to date and take it all the way? When I turned 21 and was still a virgin my friends decided to give me this gift.' He was speaking in a terminology that was left behind in the 80s. I could see why he wouldn't get laid easily!

I could hear my mother calling my name and it seemed like a blessing in disguise. I had said all I could to this man who was truly a boy and I knew we didn't connect at all. The rest of the evening was spent in having dinner and making conversation with his parents and discussing politics. A topic that could last for hours around a table full of intellectual people.

Most men knew what they wanted from a woman by this age just like most women knew what they wanted from a relationship. It was clear that Prashanth wanted a nice pretty wife who would look after his aging parents, settle in Bangalore with him, and have pretty babies since the wife would have to have good genes. And he was trying to find women who would fit into his mould. I guess that is the problem with arranged marriages.

Everyone comes with preconceived notions of what they want and they don't want to relinquish the ideal in the hope that the next match would fit their criteria. It isn't as if they are willing to settle for less now.

With love marriages, it's more of what you see is what you get. And since it is so difficult to find the correct person, fall in love and want to stay in it, one feels the need to work at it since you don't want to go through the entire process all over again.

There was no point in knowing why he had slept with a prostitute. But I did tell him one last thing before we went back to the parents, 'Hey Prashanth. A word of advice. Never ever tell a girl that you intend to marry that you've slept with a prostitute. It creeps women out.'

On the way home, while I was driving the car my mom asked me the inevitable question, 'Well, how was he?'

But before I could answer my father said softly, 'She didn't like him.' My mother looked from me to him and before she could ask either of us what that meant, he answered with, 'He was too short!'

And with that no more meetings with 'boys' were arranged for the remainder of my visit.

16
A Surprise Named Siddharth

When I returned to Mumbai, I saw a receipt from Blue Dart asking me to get in touch with them regarding a package. I was very intrigued. When they came to deliver it the next day, I saw it was from a Siddharth Mafatlal. The package contained the most gorgeous calf-skin, midnight-blue Salvatore Ferragamo bag I had ever seen, and a card that said: 'Some blue periods must last forever. Call if you like it.' There was a business card attached to it.

I sat down on my sofa, clutching the bag to my chest. It was magnificent, and incredibly expensive. I simply could not accept the gift, no matter how much I wanted to. I looked at my mobile not knowing what to do. I mean I didn't know this man. At least not enough. Why was he buying me such an expensive gift? Immediately my antenna was up. I took another look at the bag and made the call.

He answered on the third ring, just when I was about to lose nerve and hang up.

'Hello,' came his baritone. I could easily imagine that head cocked to one side with an eyebrow raised and speaking at an unknown number.

'Um . . . Hi . . . This is Kaveri . . . I got the bag . . . thank you . . . you shouldn't have . . . This is so out of the blue,' I said stuttering and feeling extremely unsure about what to say next.

'Did you like it?' he asked, and I could tell from his voice that he was smiling.

'I love it! But I can't accept it Siddharth,' I said.

'Why not?' he demanded. I could sense his displeasure; his earlier joviality had evaporated.

Because it is expensive. Because I didn't know you well enough to accept a gift from you. Because I didn't know what, if anything, you expect in return. There were too many answers, but I replied with a question, 'How did you get my address?'

'Oh, that's easy,' he scoffed and added reading my mind, 'Listen, Kaveri, I don't want anything from you. I think you're smart and beautiful. I saw the bag and remembered you. I knew you would like it, appreciate it since you like brands. I'm in London right now and will be back in a week's time. Can I save your number and call you then if you don't feel I'm imposing?' he said all this with supreme confidence as if he already knew what I was going to say. For a moment I wanted to tell him he didn't know me and I really couldn't accept the bag. But then I thought of all the men who had never given me a Ferragamo bag. And all the men who never would. Besides, it was a really pretty bag. I chose to be shallow for a change and told him he could call me whenever he wanted.

In the course of the week we spoke every day, almost three or four times a day. There were no 'hellos' or 'good byes'. We started conversations as if we were already in the middle of them. He would be somewhere and call and spout quantum physics, 'If particles can move backward and forward in time, and appear at all possible places do you think I could be there with you right now and simultaneously attend this boring meeting I need to be in?' Or he would call while I was eating lunch and say, 'Dark Belgian chocolate coffee mousse pastry with a shot of espresso. That's what I'm having right now. What are you eating?' And I would tell him about my sorry meal of curd and cabbage since I was being a health freak.

I was so distracted during that week that I barely gave Bela or Shyamolie any time. Siddharth and I spoke for long hours during the day and at night. He called me one night and said he wanted to be next to me while I slept and he read a book. So I went to bed with the phone next to me, and when I woke up a few hours later and whispered a 'hello' to see if he was still there, he said gently, 'I'm here, babe, go back to sleep.' Even though we were millions of miles away it felt beautiful to be part of a man's life again.

It's far more difficult to evade love than to search for it. As soon as you tell the Universe you're perfectly fine with where you are, you can be sure it will try and do something dramatic to change it. The Universe threw me a curve ball in the form of Siddharth Mafatlal. When the week was over and he asked if I could pick him up from the airport and spend time together, I immediately agreed.

Waiting outside the international airport at 5 a.m. the next morning, I really didn't know what I was doing picking up a man I had met only once. But I felt I knew him already. His words to me before he got on the flight were, 'Please don't react to me because I don't know how I would react to you.' This seemed extremely strange since I now definitely didn't know how to react. When he walked out I smiled and said, 'Shall we go?' And he nodded. I drove him to my apartment. I had hardly slept the previous night and was extremely conscious of the dark circles under my eyes that I had tried to hide with a little concealer. Later he would tell me that I looked absolutely radiant and he had fallen deeply in love me on that quiet ride home. But for now, I didn't say anything. And it was all for the best because after a week of endless conversation, I really couldn't think of anything but cheesy lines to say. And I didn't want him to suddenly fall out of fondness for me, for my stupidity.

The first few minutes at home were awkward. I asked him if he wanted coffee, and then took out towels so he could take a shower. Basically I needed to do something so I wouldn't say or do something silly. And then suddenly he turned around and said, 'This is weird isn't it?' and smiled hesitantly.

I turned around and said, 'What the hell are you talking about? You were the one who told me not to react?'

He took two strides towards me and wrapped his arms around me in a hug. 'I know how to react now,' he whispered. And then what felt like ages, he said, 'Can I ask you for something?'

I looked around and responded, 'I've already brought you back to my home and offered you the use of my shower. I think I'm pretty much done with the giving, dude!' I said with a smile.

'Can I kiss you?' he asked gently. No one had ever asked me that before. It was understood most times, and implied the rest. So I nodded and we kissed. Honestly, I didn't know where the time went. Because the next thing I knew, I had opened my eyes and the clock said twenty minutes later. And before we knew it we were in bed.

The sense of touch, the movement of his hands, the feeling of his body on top of mine. He was an extremely giving lover. It was intuitive. He knew where he needed to be. He understood my body better than I did. It wasn't short and rushed. It wasn't as long as a tantric session. It was just enough for me to be brought to a brink before he made his next move. He knew that. He didn't have to wait for my moans to be told. Our lovemaking was less about passion than it was about feeling complete. It was less about having an orgasm than about giving to each a part of ourselves. It was as if I was a virgin all over again. But this time it was an emotional one.

We lay there for a long time just looking at each other. Thinking how different things had been twenty-four hours ago. Caressing each other's fingers. Feeling as though we were connected. It was a spiritual connection that I had never had before. All my life I had thought about the perfect relationship. I had dreamt about it since I was sixteen. But with each relationship that failed in the years since then, I came to believe it didn't exist. Eventually I had made my peace with the fact that there would never be a relationship like I imagined. And now, all of a sudden, I found myself in it.

This relationship, if we could call it that since we had only been together a few hours, was so new and yet so familiar. It wasn't like the romances we read about in Mills and Boons. It was unlike any relationship I had ever been in. With Arjun or Aaron or Ray, I had known there was something missing, and yet I had been willing to sacrifice my being to be with them. But here there was no sacrifice. Because Siddharth was what I wanted and I was what he needed. Siddharth was different. He had the thing and hence he could give it. It's as if someone knows that you want to eat avocados but can never get them for you. So he understands that aspect of you but can never give it. Siddharth was the tree that bore avocados.

It was a strange feeling since the last time we met there was no physical intimacy at all and suddenly it felt as if we hadn't parted since that day. It felt as if there had been no distance between us. Had our phone conversations made us so close? I wondered if the Ferragamo bag was a way of getting to know me better. Couldn't he just have called and chatted? I would have willingly spoken to him in any case. I asked him this.

'Why did you wait two weeks before you sent me that bag? And why didn't you just get my number and call me instead?' I said while I made him some toast with jam.

He happily accepted this from me sitting on a stool in my kitchen and answered, 'I couldn't get you out of my head for a week but I didn't have an opening line. I have never dated as such. And I'm much too old to pick up a phone and say *hey do you remember me?*' I looked at him then. He was older. A whole lot older than me. From a man six years younger to a man twelve years older, my love graph was phenomenal. Was the Universe telling me that there were no men around my age that I could fall in love with? In love. In a few weeks. My heart suddenly beat louder.

I knew I had to be cautious. If I let myself slip in too easy it would land up like all the rest of the relationships.

After we both got dressed, he held me tightly and looked down at me. He was tall. But not so tall that he overpowered me. His eyes were full of depth, and whenever he spoke, it was with meaning, with reverence, with love. He was passionate about his work and he had become passionate about me. He took a taxi back home and promised that we would meet soon. I told him vaguely that I had work and might be flying out soon. I didn't want to seem too eager.

But my heart already knew that this could be my One True Love.

17

The Romance Continues

Siddharth wooed me as if I was a princess. He would pick me up everyday and we would visit different art galleries and eat at all the fancy restaurants I had ever wanted to go to. He was unrestrained with his gifts that ranged from lavish coats and sparkly diamond earrings to Turkish carpets and beautiful art for my house. I was having the time of my life! I felt pampered, cherished and worshipped. It was what all women dreamt of.

One evening he took me to his penthouse at Worli that overlooked Haji Ali. We were sitting in his balcony enjoying the cool breeze and admiring the view. It was a dazzling panorama: the iridescent moon shimmered on the dome, the inky black waters of the Arabian Sea lay peaceful and the bright stars twinkled in the clear night sky as if they knew a secret but refused to tell the people down below. I had a glass of Chardonnay in one hand and this handsome man by my side. This is the life, I thought to myself and sighed deeply. Siddharth noticed.

'What happened, love?' he asked me.

I was quiet for a moment. He never pushed me to speak. He just listened when I did. 'I'm the happiest I've been in a long time,' I said.

'I'm glad. I want to make you happy,' he replied with tremendous warmth. This was a respectful relationship. This was what I had needed for so long. All these years I had been going after younger men or men who didn't understand how to pleasure a woman. Maybe an older man was exactly what I had needed. I didn't want to ruin it by asking the mundane questions about marriage and children. I had learnt the hard way that those topics scare away men. I needed to live in the moment. He loved me. I loved him. Nothing else mattered; neither a paper to make our love legal, nor a child to cement our devotion. This was what it should have been in the first place I thought. But then one has to kiss a lot of frogs to find one's prince. And one needs to have one's heart broken for it to become wise.

'Sir, dinner is served,' Siddharth's servant came and informed us.

We walked back into his penthouse. It was a gorgeous three-bedroom apartment with a large drawing room and personal music room in one of a set of red brick towers that had been built a decade ago. The property had been extensively refurbished with incredible flair and character and came with a state-of-the-art integrated AV system in each room. It was carefully designed with a harmonious mix of tough, attractive materials including wood, glass and gloss lacquers just the way Siddharth liked it. The kitchen came with a wonderful white island with a walnut countertop where we had spent an afternoon cooking. Actually, he had cooked us lunch while I had sat on the countertop drinking a very expensive wine from his collection. We had eaten lunch much later that day since we ended up making love on the countertop. It was risqué knowing that there were several servants who could pop in any moment but the thrill made it an afternoon to remember forever. The generous and continuous living space was arranged alongside a secluded terrace with sweeping views of the mosque on one side and the Worli skyline on the other which was where we had spent the maximum portion of this evening. All around were expensive and exquisite pieces of art from a range of artists and sculptors. Rich Persian carpets adorned the teak wood floors. A magnificent chandelier hung over the dining area and a full bar that boasted glassware from Norway and liquor from Turkey adorned another part of the room. Tall palms in hand-crafted pots dotted the corridors and empty spaces were filled with fresh flowers and miniature paintings. It was the most beautiful penthouse I had ever seen, not that I had seen too many. I wondered if he had done the entire designing himself and asked him as we sat down at the Italian marble dining table.

'I had a designer who helped my ex-wife set it up. I told her I wouldn't give her the house when she decided to leave. She didn't care. She wanted to move out with her boyfriend. That didn't last long since he was more of a wastrel than the actor he claimed he was. But then she found someone in the theatre industry and moved to Illinois. She's very happy there and has a child of her own. I put in a lot of thought into the apartment after she left. Re-did a lot of things. Bought all the paintings myself. Chose a lot of pieces with the designer even when she was doing it up. I'm a very involved man, Kaveri.'

I could tell he was. I was happy I would never have to deal with Siddharth's ex and he didn't have the baggage of children either. I didn't want to bring it up but before I knew it, the words slipped out of my mouth: 'Why didn't you want kids?'

'Kids were never a priority. I was hardly married. I was too busy making a name for myself and earning money,' he admitted, tasting some of his mushroom risotto. He was a vegetarian. That could be a problem. I was a hard-core non-vegetarian who loved her chicken as much as her job. As far as I was concerned, chickens were put on earth so life would not be so dreary and I would never give that up for the world! But we only ate vegetarian food at this house because Siddharth believed that non-veg food corrupted the 'thought' process. Our thoughts make up who we were; essentially we were what we ate. And to kill and eat another living being was not just cruel, but a blemish on your mind. While he worked like mad and had all these beautiful things, Siddharth was a gentle soul who believed in living well. He frequently went to Igatpuri for Vipassana, to centre himself. He was definitely an 'older' man. He didn't have the hang ups of what love should be and would never go into raging flare if something annoyed him. He meditated every morning and went for discourses on Buddhism.

I was vastly different from this man. While I was okay about living the good life with him, I definitely didn't want to go for Vipassana or chanting. I wanted to live life to the fullest. He was always measured and correct. I let him be the way he was and he let me be too. It was a wonderful combination.

But as usual I had a bug in my head. It would come wandering about every now and then and plant a thought that would nag away at me till I verbalized the question: *Could this last forever?* Did he want to marry me? But I never asked him right away. That would come later. There were other things to discuss.

'I must tell you about Bela,' I said suddenly. 'She is the most quirky woman I've met. I mean next to Shyamolie, of course.'

He nodded while I prattled on. I didn't know what it was, but I wanted to prove as if I could be more to him. He was this extremely distinguished man who had impeccable taste and was good at business and cooking. And here I was, an 'order-in' woman with a career serving a movie star. There was definitely an imbalance in my life when it came to him and to make up for it, I would tell him about my work or my dreams exhaustively to prove I was a better person. Deep down I knew it didn't make sense. But the feeling was there and I just couldn't shake it away. He always dropped me back home at night instead of letting me stay with him. He was very particular that the help in his house view me as a 'lady' rather than a disreputable woman. He could send the help away for the afternoon while I was there but since they all had a routine in the morning he couldn't stop them from coming. I was quite flattered, but a little taken aback as well. How did any of that matter if you were horny? You should have enough passion to want to have sex anywhere and everywhere no matter what people thought. Even Shyamolie said so. That was what should have been. Besides, we were in his house, not some hotel he owned. Who cared what the help thought? But Siddharth did and I had to be respectful about it. He even refused to do any more than just give me a peck on the cheek in the car. It was considered correct decorum.

While I loved it all, I was left a bit confused. My hormones were raging and there wasn't enough room for decorum in my life!

18
Two Sides of the Same Coin

While my romance was blossoming, I couldn't neglect my job. So I went off one morning to meet Bela at her gym. She had said that she felt most invigorated after a workout and wanted to do some lessons at the hotel itself. When I got there Bela was headed towards the showers and told me to wait in the lobby of the gym.

She emerged almost an hour later in tiny, ripped denim shorts, a baby-pink ganji, flip-flops and a pair of dark Aviators. A few bracelets jangled at her wrist as she tied her long hair into a high ponytail. She looked stunning in this simple attire and I could see why the director and her star boyfriend were so taken with her. They probably couldn't take their eyes off her!

We sat in the hotel's coffee shop having breakfast and picking up the lesson from our last session. I went through proper accents of words while she picked at some fruit and sipped her black coffee. Bela was always watching what she ate. I had cribbed about wanting to be thin for a long time, all the while eating muffins and drinking double-shot mochas. But the fact was that if women wanted to look a certain way, they had to work at it every day. Good genes also helped. And age. Women in their twenties can burn off whatever they eat with very little effort, but those of us in our thirties have to struggle twice as hard. I had learnt that the hard way. I used to be thin when I was in New York. But ever since I'd returned to Mumbai, my willpower had sauntered over to other pastures while I grappled with a career. Losing weight was the last thing on my mind even though I tried to eat healthy at home. Besides, when I was with Siddharth, I hardly ate. We were so wrapped up in each other when we were together that hours would go by without either of us sparing a single thought to something as mundane as food. As a result, my body had started craving food when I was away from him, and I greedily dug into any rubbish without giving it much thought. So I ordered some blueberry pancakes with whipped cream and maple syrup and was happily chomping on it while Bela went through the workbook I had made for her.

Just then Shyamolie entered the coffee shop and sat down at our table. She seemed agitated. I smiled at her but she ignored me and turned to Bela. 'You fired me? How could you? Punjwani called me and said you told him to fire me! Is this about the IIFA awards party?'

'Where were you?' Bela demanded angrily. 'Styling some other actress, I bet! You didn't show up, and I had to wear something I already had. And then Kangy and I landed up at the party in the same outfit. It was a complete disaster, Shay. The media was all over it the next morning, comparing the two of us, asking who wore it better. And guess what they said, I lost! How could you do this to me, Shay?'

Shyamolie had hot tears forming in her eyes. 'Bela,' she began gently, 'you didn't tell me you intended to go, otherwise I would have been there. I would've told you that Kangy was wearing the same dress to the party, and picked out something spectacular for you.'

I could see that she was pleading with Bela. 'Personally, I think you looked far better than Kangy in that dress,' I said, giving my two cents though I did not know which outfit they were talking about. But seeing the dirty look that Bela shot me, I hastily returned to my pancakes.

Shy continued pleading with Bela, 'Please give me another chance. I promise to make you look amazing for all your appearances from now on.'

Bela took a deep breath, softened her stance a little bit and said, 'All right! But from now on I want you to bring all your best clothes to me first. And I need to know what other people are wearing so it doesn't look like I'm a fashion disaster.'

Shy tried to protest; that would be unfair to her other clients and quite against her work ethic. But before she could say anything a young girl came to the table asking for Bela's autograph. While Bela was talking to the girl, I shot Shy a look that said 'agree with her now, later you can do your thing'. Shyamolie nodded. When the girl left, Shy said, 'Okay. I promise. The other fashionistas won't know what hit them when I'm done with you.'

Bela nodded dismissively and said, 'I have a script reading to go to. I will catch you later.' With that she got up and left. A few photographers, who had spotted her earlier, snapped pictures of her as she walked past them.

I turned to Shyamolie and asked, 'What happened? Why were you so upset? I thought you didn't want to work with her in any case? So if she fired you, isn't it a good thing?'

Shyamolie nodded her head and replied, 'Ya I don't really want to work with her but she has many connections. And those connections keep my business going. I can't annoy her. She can tell all her filmy friends how I'm useless and they'll stop working with me. In this industry, word of mouth works. And film stars believe other film stars. They hardly care if they replace the staff. *Ek driver gaya, toh naya aa gaya.* One stylist leaves, another one can come. *I'll* only lose work. If I have to leave her, it'll be on my terms. Not because she's upset with me.'

Seconds later the bearer came and gave me the bill. I was shocked.

'Hello! I didn't want to eat here. Why am I stuck with a bill?'

Shy shrugged. 'This is what happens with these people. They

want to be seen at the best, most expensive places in the city, but are not ready to foot the bill.'

'But they have so much money!' I exclaimed in shock taking out my credit card with a racing heart. Two coffees and some breakfast had set me back by a few thousand bucks. With that kind of money I could have bought myself a new pair of jeans! I wanted to weep.

'Can I claim it back from someone? What about Mr Punjwani?'

'Scrooge won't even give you vada pao on his birthday, let alone reimburse you for his heroine's breakfast. He'll probably say we need to make sacrifices for the greater good in life or some shit like that and expect you to pay for her dinner as well!' Shy said with disgust. Then she took a five hundred buck note out of her wallet and kept it on the table. 'We'll split it.'

'No, Shy. It's okay. I can afford it. I was just appalled at the way she behaved,' I said, signing the receipt the waiter brought back.

'Then let me treat you to dinner later. You could do with a break.'

'Where is Bela going anyway? I thought we had the whole afternoon to work. Punjwani has been after my life to have her dialogues completely ready before the foreign shoot. It's all sync sound and he doesn't want her to sound bad.' I got up from my table and slung my bag across my shoulders.

'Probably to meet her new crush,' Shy said nonchalantly and walked with me to the elevator.

'New crush? I thought she was doing the director and seeing that actor. Who's this third guy?'

'He's the new hunk of town, the latest heartthrob of the industry. She has a huge crush on him and is trying to woo him. They've been paired opposite each other in her next film and already sparks are flying. Of course, she's trying to keep it quiet because if her actor boyfriend finds out he'll be furious, and she can't afford to piss him off or he will take his connections and kick her to the curb and then all the producers will drop her,' Shy said as we stepped out of the elevator.

I thought that was extremely sexist and unfair and said as much.

She just shrugged. 'That's the lay of the land, babe.' We got into Shy's red Hyundai i10, and drove off. 'They say the world is changing and women are opening doors, but in Bollywood male protagonists still rule. How many films are made with women in central roles where there is not a prominent man in the lead? And how many of those are big budget movies? None. Because producers don't want to spend so much money on women. Even a Priyanka or Kareena or an Aishwarya can't compete with the monies and the roles that men get.'

'What's with all the songs in all the Bollywood movies?' I asked. I remembered going on a date with a man from the industry who was appalled I didn't watch all these films and I had told him that too many songs ruined the plot for me. At that time he had burst into a melody to convince me that songs take the plot forward and I had ended the evening right there. So ironic. I was now moving around with people who made songs, danced to songs and styled the songs.

'Music is an extremely important part for the Indians. They express themselves through music. Sad songs help them when they're depressed and love songs help them when they're in love. Lyrics help them convey what they feel to another person. Bollywood film songs have spin offs for singing and reality shows on TV. Bollywood music helps with sangeets in marriage functions. When people commute for hours in trains and cars to work, this music keeps them going. The music industry sponsors live events, shows, concerts. You download it as a ring tone or caller tune and more people make money. A song can generate so much income for so many people. Hollywood can never have that. We're too cool man!' she said proudly and continued, 'It is entertainment at its best. Without songs people would get bored. We don't have a pop or rock or hip hop culture that caters to different audiences and stuff. We have only one genre—Bollywood. Everyone knows it and loves it,' Shyamolie said with great authority.

I didn't think that was true. There were plenty of rock groups and bands that played their own music and had an audience for it. Coke Studio and The Dewarists on Indian television was a proof of that. Even the NH7, the three-day festival in Pune, India's modern-day Woodstock, had Indian bands and international artists jamming together and was attended by thousands of people from across the country. Not everything had to have a Bollywood spin off. Shy and I argued about this for a while till she got fed up of talking about it and decided to change the subject.

'So what's happening with your love life? Where have you been all this time?'

I told her about the connection Siddharth and I had and how wonderful it felt after so long. I also told her my apprehensions about the vast economic and age difference between us.

'But why? Isn't that what love is supposed to be. A feeling that sweeps you off your feet and you go with the flow? How does age matter?'

'Well, yes,' I replied. It *should* be like that, I thought as we drove, but life teaches you that it isn't. Love is a calculated risk you need to take when you *can* afford to fall in love. It's like the stock market. You need to play it when you're ready to lose and if you win, then it's just a bonus in your life.

'Anyway,' Shy said, interrupting my thoughts, impatient with my long silence, 'I'm really tired of doing this work. I just want to start my own label.'

'Shy,' I squealed, 'that's a fabulous idea!'

She nodded. She started telling me her plans about her designer label and what she needed to do for it. She had been quite irritated with all the tantrums some of her clients had been throwing lately; a veteran like her didn't need to take attitude from the likes of Bela, but she knew that one wrong word in the industry and her career could take a nose dive. 'I mean,' she said spilling gossip to me, 'there are top heroines who lock themselves in the trailers of their co-stars and then don't come out for fittings or shots for hours, keeping the entire production crew waiting. But if any one of their entourage says something to the press or even complains about their attitude, the whole industry bans that person. Ridiculous!'

I could understand Shyamolie's irritation. I had also worked for bad bosses until I became a teacher in Barcelona. And even there I had to deal with faculty members who didn't take too kindly to an outsider who presumed to know more about art and their culture than they did.

I thought Shyamolie had real spunk. She had always followed her dreams and now wanted to do something greater than what she was already doing. Somehow, I had lost that initiative. Breaking up with Ray hadn't just been another break-up with another man. It had really shaken my confidence. I thought I had it all. And then the earth just crumbled beneath my feet. With Siddharth entering my life, my heart had begun to feel whole again, but I could not bring myself to trust him completely. I didn't know why. I really wanted to, but suddenly the walls I had when I was in my twenties had resurrected themselves. I just could not let anyone in again. It was a wonderful feeling being with him, but I was conflicted about our future, our present, and how much I should reveal about my past.

Would Siddharth leave me if he knew about the men in my life? We all came with baggage but would that baggage be too over powering for a man eventually? I was afraid to find out. Yes, I was very different from Bela or Shyamolie. One gave up love to get further in her career and one would give up her career to find love. I believed neither worked.

19

Aditi Moves On

Aditi had started feeling terrible since she gave up her relationship with Amitabh. Love is so strange! It happens in the most unusual places and at the worst times. But it's a force that no one has any control over. Siddharth and I began to meet more often and while I was back in the throes of a relationship, I was advising Aditi to stay away from hers. Honestly, I felt that what Aditi had with her brother-in-law was just lust. And lust never wins. It's a dangerous, seducing feeling that leaves you giddy and broken hearted in the end. Love lasts forever. You might not be 'in love' with a person forever, but you'll always love him somewhere deep down. And this is exactly what I was trying to explain to her one evening. 'It doesn't matter if you change your mind tomorrow or a month later,' I said softly trying to make her reconsider her decision. We had met in a lounge for drinks on a Friday evening. 'It doesn't matter if you reverse your decision to get divorced. You know I will always be there for you and support you. I know that we change and sometimes we choose things we later realize we don't really want. It's okay. With friends it doesn't matter,' I said, taking a large sip of my wine. Ah! That was good! Chilled. Australian. Dry. Just the way I liked it. Just what I needed to give this pep talk.

'I tried to make it work. The things they tell you to do in *Cosmopolitan*, so you can have a happy marriage—taking a vacation or trying to have more sex—I did them. But you get to a stage in your marriage where even those don't work. You just want something more, need something more. Something the other person can't give you.' Aditi looked older to me. She had started showing signs that she was forty. Small signs that only I could see since I had known her for years. Signs that she abhorred about herself since she loathed getting old. But it was the flaws she hated that I found most endearing.

She continued while I sat, silent, 'Last year I sat and watched the monsoons roll in. I sat on my balcony for three hours. I watched every inch of the earth get soaked just as I noticed every pore in my body being drenched. Right there I was complete. I didn't need anyone then. I've never needed anyone Kaveri. I completed myself. I just wanted to share a part of that completeness with someone. But there was no one around. Not then. Not now.'

She took a deep breath and continued, 'I felt alive again with Ami. I didn't need him to help me live every day. I wanted him around so I had a friend to talk to, who understood me, who desired me, who made me feel less lonely. A male friend that makes you feel special and important. And now it's gone. All because we bring logic into love.'

I knew that I should have told her to just go with her heart but this time I wanted her to be cautious. With listening to her head and my advice, I felt that Aditi was doing something positive for herself. It takes longer to heal on your own than with someone, but the healing is more complete and makes you stronger. 'I know that you're a complete woman, Aditi. I know that you do a lot for people. But ultimately you need to satisfy yourself and your individuality. You need to figure out your life by yourself through some introspection. And I'm always here to be a sounding board,' I said, expressing my support.

'I wish there were better reasons for getting a divorce. Society will ask if he beats me, tortures me, they'll want to know if he does not give me money, if he does not care for my needs. And I have nothing to say. Because those are not the reasons. The reason is that I feel there is a noose around my neck,' Aditi said calling the waiter to refill our glasses.

'I can't be in the marriage because his mother is great. Or because I totally love the new house he has bought me. I can't be in it for those reasons. I need to be in it for him. And I don't want to be in it for him! That's the biggest thing,' she complained. 'And things are not going to change. Even if he starts spending time at home and doing chores and taking me out and spending less time at work, it's all going to be temporary. Men can only make one thing their priority at a time. I will be a *project* for a few months. And then when I start expecting love again, he'll go back to his business. It's a neverending cycle.'

'But if that's the case with all men, wouldn't it just be better to hang on to the one who has at least bought you a house?' I asked. In the settlement Aditi had asked for a place to stay and Rajat had said that instead of paying her alimony he would allow her to stay in his house till he decided to sell it and that would not be for another five to ten years at least.

Aditi shook her head, 'It's not my house. It's a house I can live in, because he's letting me. It's still his property, and it is still his name on the door. He's not so dumb. And besides, money isn't everything. Maybe there is a man out there who will get me. One who will at least try. I have a roof over my head for now, but hopefully I'll be able to buy my own house soon and start my own business.' She looked outside, as if wondering if what she had said would actually come true or if she was just dancing with dreams.

I could understand that. I had seen women bow down to society. Even someone like Bela—rich, young, successful— would not proclaim to be in a relationship openly. She had to be discreet for the sake of her career. I knew that sometimes women needed to suppress their individuality to appease the society. If you told the world what it wanted to hear, you would get appreciation and validation. If you tried to be something it disapproved of, you would be considered a 'loose' woman. And in a society where perception was everything, it would become tough for her. However, I had always felt that if women didn't take a stand, and carve a niche for themselves, we and our future generations would live in the sixties forever.

Aditi continued, 'I don't want to have expectations from a marriage anymore. I don't want to live, hoping that things will improve. I don't want to expect anything from anyone except myself. I am happy finally. Once I let go of the expectations, I didn't need to change, control, overpower, nag, shout and hope anymore. It made me calmer. I could just let go. I could focus on me. My future. My dreams. I can finally find my centre again.'

'Are you scared?' I asked Aditi; I knew I would have been. To be in my forties and be labelled a divorcee would scare the living daylights out of me. But Aditi believed in herself and knew that it was better to be alone than in a dead end relationship.

'Yes. I'm very scared,' she said surprisingly, 'but divorce is never a right or wrong decision. It's a chance to escape when you're pushed into a corner. I've been pushed into that corner.'

'Divorce is not going to be easy. It's not going to be a smooth road at all. It's going to be tough, with many battles ahead,' I said before I became too drunk to take anything seriously. 'And the utopian picture that you have painted for yourself will come crashing down in a few months' time. So you need to be very strong from right now to be able to do what you're doing.' The number of divorce cases had risen in India, leaving men and women disillusioned and alone. I didn't want Aditi to be one of those statistics.

Aditi smiled. 'I don't know what I would do without you.' Then added, giggling, 'How could I ever have thought that I would change and be docile after marriage?'

'That's true,' I said with a knowing nod and a twinkle in my eye. 'You tried. You gave the best years of your life to someone who should have treasured them. But you also need to give something to yourself now.'

Aditi nodded. 'Considering I'm probably going to live another thirty years, I want to live them being free from expectations—other people's and my own.'

'You know what people will ask, don't you? Don't you want to grow old with someone? Don't you want a companion in your old age when you have nothing? What will you do once your parents die and you are all alone in this world?'

'You know, people make being alone sound like a disease.'

'That's the other thing—what if you fall sick? Who will look after you?' I knew I was sounding like her mother, but I wanted to play devil's advocate so she would think about every possible scenario. True, the divorce papers had been signed, but there was still a month left of the six-month wait period before the court made the divorce final. She could still withdraw her petition. I didn't want her to think that I hadn't helped her make the best decision.

'A nurse,' she said dryly.

'And what if your parents die and you're still not *settled*?' I asked, not really believing what I was saying but needing to have it out there for her.

'Well, I don't think my marital status is going to bother them much when they're gone,' she replied irreverently. 'In any case, my parents should be proud of who I am and not because I'm married! If they're so worried about society, then it's their problem to find new friends who are more supportive!' Then she added with a pause, 'I've been so lonely for so long that I need to be alone to be alive again!'

'I suppose it's better to be single and lonely than being lonely in a marriage. At least with the former, there is hope, but with the latter, there is effort,' I rationalized.

'I hope I'm doing the right thing in the long run . . .' Aditi said.

'I don't know. All I can tell you is I love you. And I'll be with you.'

'We'll grow old together. Like two old maids. Living together, reading Virginia Woolf and drinking lots of cinnamon coffee,' she mocked.

'Yes, we can do that,' I said laughing heartily. What a picture that would be. We would be cranky and frustrated and keep losing our dentures. But we would be quoting Existential poets and female writers to each other. That would be quite the hoot.

'And we'll need to have a schedule for bringing men home,' she said with a wink, looking more like my old Aditi.

'I solemnly swear never to steal your boyfriend,' I said laughing.

'I can't promise you that,' she said which made me guffaw even harder.

Here was Aditi, a disillusioned old divorcee; I, a slightly tired, semi-attached middle-aged woman; and then there was Shy, a young single woman raring to experience love but with no knight in shining armour around. What a triumvirate we made!

20

What's the Fear of Parties Called? Oh Yes, Not Wanting One!

Love was getting to be very tricky for me. Tricky, because I was already deeply and madly in love with Siddharth! I didn't know if it was because of all the gifts he was showering on me or if it was because I found myself being able to make intellectual conversation with him. Whatever it was, it felt so good after so long. After Ray and I broke up, I had many moments of self-doubt. What had I done wrong? Why couldn't I change him? Had I tried hard enough to keep him in my life? Had I made a wrong decision to leave so quickly? Would he have come back? Did I even want him back? But those thoughts had happened almost a year ago.

And now my birthday was coming up again. And it was going to be a big one. I was turning thirty-five! Just like women all over the world, I was trying to pretend that my age wasn't a number looming over me. So of course I told everyone I was thirty-one! But I could see that no one believed me!

Siddharth and I were having a lovely romantic dinner at one of the posh South Bombay restaurants when he said, 'I want to throw you a lavish birthday party!'

I almost choked on my wine. While that was a generous

offer, I hardly knew enough people in Bombay to invite to a party.

'We'll call all your friends,' Siddharth was saying. 'We'll have it at the new place we went to last time, near the race course. Lovely white chairs, dainty little flowers and lighting, a large decadent chocolate cake. Just the way you like it. I can call a few of my friends so they can finally meet you. It will be terrific!'

I smiled and said, 'Let me think about it. Let's just enjoy our meal right now.'

Siddharth looked confused, 'What's to think about? I want to do something special and we only have two weeks left. I need to start organizing things. I had thought to plan it as a surprise party but I don't know all your friends and would have had to ask you for their numbers, and that would have killed the surprise.' He took a bite of his paneer shashlik.

I knew he felt he was doing the correct thing, what a boyfriend should do for his girlfriend. But I was panicking. Meet his friends? We had been seeing each other for less than eight months, and even though we knew we had a fabulous connection, I didn't want to make our relationship public just yet. And what about my parents? They might have planned something for me as well.

'We'll fly down to meet them the very next day,' he said when I asked him. 'We can meet my parents as well and celebrate with another party there!' Siddharth said, sounding very confident about his plan.

Meet the parents? So soon? And another party? I was already freaking about the first one. This was all too much. I had to put my foot down. I felt like I was having a heart attack. I knew that Siddharth and I could have a future. Even if he was twelve years older than me, I didn't care so much. He was a fantastic man. He had a zest for life that I had lost over the years. But I didn't know how to tell him I didn't want the parties without offending him. This was the tricky part of having an older boyfriend. With a younger one, one always feels superior in some way, and able to tell him anything without worrying about hurting his feelings. If Ray had suggested we have a big party for my birthday, I would have shot him down and suggested, instead, that we go to Paris for the weekend, and that would have been that. But now, if I told Siddharth it was a terrible idea and that I'm not a party person, he would immediately say in his best 'grown-up' voice, 'Now, now, maybe it would be good for your career if you socialized a bit more. After all you need to start doing more with your life.' I could almost hear him say it.

So I didn't say anything. I went along with it. And I tried to reason with myself. Maybe it would be fun. Here was a man who was trying so hard to please me. The least I could do was try and be part of his world instead of being so uptight about it. After all, it was only going to be a party.

But deep down I knew that something bad was about to happen. That was the main reason I didn't want this party. My instincts had yet to fail me. But I didn't know how to put it down in words. Or put my finger on what was going to happen.

21

A Middle-aged Birthday

My birthday—1 April—came much too soon that year. The
dreaded date when we're older, but hardly wiser. I was at home.
No running to Coffee De for an early morning coffee or late-
night alone-time since I was meeting everyone tonight at my
party.

I stared at myself in the mirror. Was that little red bump a
pimple? Seriously, God? A pimple! I was turning thirty-five
today. And He was giving me adult acne now! As though I
didn't have enough problems already. I was feeling old today.
Why, I didn't know. I was in a relationship with a warm and
caring man. I had a well-paying job that required minimal
effort. I had healthy parents and fabulous friends. I didn't show
too many signs of aging. Maybe a few love handles had crept in
but otherwise I was fit. I had no idea why I was feeling so low.

I decided to at least get a facial done so I wouldn't look so
awful for my party which I was dreadfully apprehensive about.
I never liked parties. Large crowds where I had to make small
talk were not my scene. A large classroom or a one-on-one
party on the other hand, now that . . . But what was the point
of thinking about that. I took a deep breath, willing my feet to
move.

The phone rang later during the day. It was Aditi. 'Hellooo,' she crooned. 'Happy birthday! How does it feel to be middle aged?' She always had a way of cheering me up with her sarcasm. 'At least you don't have to worry about losing your virginity!' she said and then laughed at her own joke.

'You're such a ray of sunshine in my life! What are you wearing tonight? I'm so nervous,' I admitted.

'Do you want to go shopping?' she offered, 'I'll buy you something nice.'

But I wasn't in the mood to hear about Aditi's life and ideology on my birthday. 'No,' I said, 'Shyamolie is bringing a few outfits for me to try. It helps when you have a stylist as a friend.'

Aditi moaned, 'But we haven't gone shopping for so long!'

I quickly tried to pacify her, 'Not that I don't want to go shopping. It's just that I don't have time today. I've got a pimple and I want to get a facial so I don't look like a frumpy in the evening in front of Sid's friends.'

'Oh okay,' Aditi said though with considerably less cheer than earlier. 'I'll finally get to meet this Siddharth guy. He sounds interesting!'

I was excited about Aditi meeting Siddharth. It would be the first time that I had introduced any of my men to her. I really hoped they would get along. And I told her that.

'I met the most adorable man when I went to my lawyer's office yesterday. We have to meet and bitch babe! Maybe I can meet you at the parlour later so we can gossip for a bit before the party,' she said much to my dismay. How things had changed; four years ago all I had wanted was her approval and her time. Whereas now, I didn't want to meet her at all. I wanted to be alone. To reflect on the past year, on moving from Barcelona to Mumbai, on Ray and Siddharth; I needed to take stock of my life. I also was quite done talking about men. I needed peace. But before I could say anything to her the doorbell rang and I had to hang up. Shyamolie was standing there with her assistant and two suitcases.

'What's this?' I asked astonished.

'Clothes!' she replied, entering and putting everything down in the drawing room on the lovely multi-coloured carpet I had. Then she told the assistant to go and get some of her chores done since she would be spending time with me today. She settled down on the floor next to one suitcase and opened it up. It was filled with dresses. She took out a deep purple knee-length dress and held it up to me. 'Try this on. I think this might look nice on you.'

I sat down next to her. 'Who are all these clothes for?' I asked.

'You're kidding right? They're for you to try on to see which one you like the most. So that you can go as a super chic girlfriend to your party and stun everyone!' She smiled and added, 'Now please make me some coffee. And get me an ashtray.' She was already lighting up.

After that my mood immediately improved. Peace be damned. I was going to have a fun morning! Shyamolie had exploded into my life and settled down so well in it that I felt she was more a part of it than Aditi—I absolutely loved her. And I was so thankful that she had come over with clothes and a positive attitude. It was just what I needed. I made us some coffee and then tried on dress after dress, in a variety of colours, fabrics, cuts and designs. I was in fashion heaven. She opened up her second suitcase that had accessories from bangles, earrings and necklaces to weird headgear, boots and feathers. All afternoon, I modelled the dresses and accessories for her while we had multiple cups of coffee and cigarettes. I felt like a movie star! And I had Shy to thank for it. I messaged Aditi saying that I would meet her directly at the party since I was stuck with some bank work. I hated lying to her but if she knew that Shy was over, she would have dropped in as well to make her presence felt and then it wouldn't have been the same. I made a mental note to take her out shopping soon so her feelings wouldn't be hurt. But for now I felt like I was on a Hollywood red carpet and I didn't want to share the limelight with anyone.

Through the afternoon I received four bouquets. One from my parents who always sent me lilies and with whom I would have a conversation later about how I was making them feel old as I grew older. Another from Bela whom I would see at the party. One from Arjun who sent a card along with it to have coffee with him some time. And the last one was from Siddharth, which was the biggest bouquet of them all.

Shyamolie had been taking photos on her phone and then typing stuff all afternoon. I finally asked her what she was up to.

'I'm tweeting,' she said and she showed me her phone.

'I've heard of it but I didn't think it was so interesting. I mean there's Facebook to keep track of all your friends and family. And email for work. So what's the need for Twitter?' I asked, shovelling another spoonful of red curry into my mouth. I had ordered some Thai food for us for lunch since she was the only person I knew who loved it just as much as I did.

'It's the most awesome thing. 'Cos you can keep putting up what you're thinking and feeling. If you read something and want to comment then you put it up and you have people who you don't necessarily know who will follow you and talk to you, interact with you and stuff. It's really cool. You should try it. It allows you to get in touch with other like-minded people who are beyond the circle of friends and family you know. It opens up your world.'

I was on a high with all that caffeine and nicotine and so I said, 'Sure. What do I do?'

'First tell me what you want your name to be? That's going to be your *handle*; people will know you by that. And you can use anything, as long as it's not taken. So, what do you want?'

I thought about it and said with a smirk, 'Kaveri Love Guru.'

'Seriously, you?' she asked joking and I shoved her playfully. Then she got on to Twitter and signed me in. 'There you go. Now you can tweet about whatever comes to mind. And you can find people you want to follow and then some people will follow you back. Just make sure you write short sentences.

Brevity is the key here. Express your thoughts in less than 140 characters. There. I'm already following you!'

So that afternoon not only did I pick out the perfect dress for my birthday party, I also learnt something new. I would also learn soon enough that my world was going to crash and that Twitter was going to save me. But I was on too great a high to give a damn right then.

22

Disasters and Parties Make Fun Cocktails

When I walked into the party at eight, not one person could have said I was not qualified to be Siddharth's girlfriend. I wore a long, dusky rose, chiffon dress that had a plunging neckline and showed off my curves beautifully. It was an exquisite dress, reminiscent of old Hollywood, when Grace Kelly would have worn something like it to the Oscars. I'd teamed it up with diamond hoops that Siddharth had given me, a cocktail Swarovski ring and delicate silver Manolo Blahniks. My hair was blow dried to perfection and fell around my face in waves. The smoky hues of the eye shadow accentuated my green eyes. I had topped the look off with a Mac pink lip gloss that gave me a sultry pout. I thought Shy had done a magnificent job in styling me and the look on Siddharth's face was confirmation enough. His jaw dropped and he quickly came to my side, and whispered that he wanted to whisk me away from the party so he could stare at me all night. I giggled. This was exactly what I needed! I needed to feel like a princess before I met all his influential friends.

The venue looked gorgeous. He had shifted it from the race

course to the rooftop of his apartment building where he had made arrangements for a dance floor and a DJ. There was a bar at one end with waiters handing out delicious snacks and exotic cocktails. Mini tent-like structures had been erected all over the rooftop under which stood circular white sofas with matching white tables bearing white flowers and white candles for intimate gatherings. It was a beautiful setting with cool breeze and just the right atmosphere for romance and fun.

Siddharth introduced me to a friend who had already arrived and we started chatting. During the next half hour, more people arrived—Bela, Aditi, Shy, Carl, more of Siddharth's friends and some other people from the film industry whom I knew well. Everyone was amiable and seemed to get along with everyone. The alcohol was flowing and Siddharth was the perfect host. He made everyone feel comfortable by talking to them and he never left my side. He would take me along to meet friends, and he would sit and have lengthy conversations with mine. I felt fabulous. The party was a grand success.

When I finally had some alone time with Aditi the first thing she said was, 'He's really cool, Kavu. When are you getting married?' I laughed. It did feel perfect. She added, 'You look amazing. I've know I've already told you, but you do. Love suits you.' I gave her a big hug. To have your best friend approve of your boyfriend means the world to a woman. But before I could say anything we were interrupted by Bela, who had come to say goodbye since she was leaving early. I decided to see her to her car.

Bela spoke to me while we were going downstairs, 'I don't know if you've been told but Kaveri, we're planning to leave for Milan in a week. We have a schedule there. You must tell Punjwani to get your tickets and visa done.'

I smiled and said, 'But you're doing so well, Bela. I don't think you need me anymore.' Things were going so well with Siddharth that I wasn't sure I wanted to leave him and travel all the way to Milan for God knew how long.

'No no,' she said as her driver came around to open the door of her white BMW, 'it's always better to be there. It's a sync sound film and the entire portion needs to sound perfect. I don't want to goof up on my dialogues at all. Besides, I've never been to Milan and it will be nice if I knew someone who could speak Italian there as well. So you can translate all that I need. Between me trying to tell the production crew what I need in my suite in English and what they will tell the hotel people, it will be a complete disaster. So come. Take a break! I'll see you day after in any case for our session in the morning. Ciao!' She blew me a kiss and left.

Once I saw Bela off I turned and headed back to the party. It was just around midnight. I took the lift to the top floor— it didn't go all the way to the rooftop—and got out and walked towards the stairs. I climbed the first flight of stairs and took a turn to the second shorter flight when I heard Siddharth's voice. I don't know why but the instinct to not call out to him and instead remain silent pushed heavily down on my heart. I took a step back into the shadows and stood still. He was talking to someone.

'How could you not tell her?' he said.

'Arrey! I didn't remember you at all till she introduced us this evening! How could I have told her?'

'What do we do now?'

'Nothing. Absolutely nothing. What she doesn't know won't harm her. She's in love with you.'

'And I'm in love with her. But this is all wrong. This is like deceiving her.'

'It was a long time ago. And we weren't serious. We were just fuck buddies. I barely knew you.'

'Yes, that's true. So, we don't tell her anything? We keep pretending that we met for the first time tonight?'

'Yes. Besides everyone has a past. She knows all about mine. I want to keep this our secret. Please.'

I was aghast. This could not be happening. I had heard

enough. I emerged from the shadows and stood before them—
Siddharth and Aditi; my boyfriend and my best friend.

Siddharth immediately tried to come towards me.

'Fuck you. Fuck you both!' I shouted.

And then I ran. I almost twisted my ankle as I made my way
back to the lift. Luckily I found a taxi as soon as I stepped out
of the building. Thankfully in Mumbai there is a cab at any time
of the day or night to take you anywhere. I told him to drive
straight to Shyamolie's house. I knew Aditi and Siddharth would
try to follow me and explain themselves, but I didn't want to
see them. I borrowed the driver's mobile and called Shy who
was still at the party, and in between sobs I told her to meet me
at her house.

And then I cried. I cried as if my heart was shattering with
every breath I took. And I cried as if my body was being torn
apart. I could not go through another heartbreak. I just couldn't.
I hated them both for doing this to me. For ruining what could
have been one of the most memorable birthdays of my life.

23

The Aftermath of a Disaster

For a week after the party I didn't talk to Aditi or Siddharth.
I didn't even go home fearing they might land up there. I
needed to sort out my head and figure out my life. I stayed at
Shyamolie's place, leaving only to meet Bela for work. I also
told RT to get my tickets for Milan. The sooner I got out of
Mumbai, the better I would feel. I didn't want to visit my
parents and hear another lecture on my unmarried state. I had
almost introduced Siddharth to them. We had planned to fly to
Bangalore together and meet our parents—an informal proposal
of sorts before the actual proposal. But I didn't go; I told my
parents some important work had come up, and that I would see
them after I returned from Milan. I sent messages to Siddharth
and Aditi asking them to let me be for some time and not to
hound me with calls. They stopped.

I had been staying with Shyamolie for three days, and had
cried constantly. She hadn't asked me any questions or given
any advice. She gave me time to deal with my grief, knowing
I would seek her out when I was ready to talk. In the meantime,
she cooked delicious food for me. I tried to help with whatever
I could so I organized her house and bought tons of the
imported groceries I knew she favoured from the neighbourhood

vendor. It was my way of saying thank you for everything she was doing for me.

Shy stood at the stove and was stirring something when I entered the kitchen one evening.

'What are you making?' I asked.

'I'm making chingri maacher malai curry,' she said with a smile. Prawn curry with rice. Yum. I went over to her and gave her a big hug.

'I don't know what I would have done without you,' I said emotionally. She just waved back and told me it was okay.

'Seriously, Shy, I never imagined Aditi would betray me like this. I don't know how to get my head around this fact that my boyfriend has slept with my best friend. It makes me so sick. I can feel the bile rising up even now when I think about it.'

'Hey, watch it. I'm making something nice and I don't want it ruined!' she said with a smile.

I sat on the chair in the kitchen that was made out of a tin bucket with photos of film stars on it. It was very kitsch and cute. Just like Shyamolie. She added, 'Continue. Just don't mention sickness.'

I sighed. I had given it a lot of thought. I could never go back to Siddharth. He might have been the perfect man but I just couldn't get over the fact that he had a past with my best friend. And I could never forgive Aditi! True, I knew about her past and had even joked about it with her, but right now it disgusted me that she had behaved like a whore. I hated using that word for her but then she herself had called herself a 'fuck buddy'. She had been fuck buddies with my fiancé. Fiancé. Fiancé. God! I couldn't get that word out of my mind. Siddharth would have been my fiancé. We would have got married eventually and I would have had my happily-ever-after living in a large sea-facing apartment with my own gallery. My dreams would have finally come true. But that idiotic woman ruined them for me.

What would the two of them have done if I hadn't come across them in the staircase that night? Had quiet dinners with me at the table, keeping their affair a dirty secret forever? My blood boiled even more. Did they think I was stupid that I would forgive them for their past? I didn't know why I was so enraged. After all, everyone did have a history and I knew somewhere deep in me that Siddharth must have had many women. For God's sake he had been married! But I always felt that those women were faceless and nameless. But now that I knew about Aditi and Siddharth, I couldn't get the image out of my head. Aditi had described how her men were in bed so many times and somehow an image of both of them lying there naked and having sex flashed through my mind. I knew why I was angry. It was not that they had a past with other people; it was that they had a past with each other.

Forgiveness is an over used virtue. I wasn't going to be naïve and forgive this. But as the rage abated, a deep sense of loss permeated my body.

'Why does this happen to me?' I asked finally while Shy continued watching me in silence. 'First there was Arjun. All he ever told me was that marriage was a dead institution. It was where souls went to die and shit like that. And then he went and got married to someone else. Then there was Ray, who said he would never adjust to who I was. Then there was Siddharth. The one man who I thought understood me. All I wanted to do was adjust to him. I never spoke about marriage and babies, topics that had turned Ray and Arjun off. Maybe it's not the men. Maybe it's me. Maybe I repulse men!' I said woefully.

Shy looked at me sceptically and said, 'You can't honestly believe that! Come on! They were dufus douche bags and you deserve way better.'

I shook my head, 'I don't. I don't deserve better. I don't deserve anyone. All those other men I slept with were purely hormonal. My true loves are over!'

'What do you mean?' she asked as she served us some rice and curry on two plates. I picked up my plate and took it to the small round dining table she had in the living room. Shy believed food must be eaten on a table and given the proper respect it deserved. That's why she was so thin. She respected food while I thought it was a wonderful substitute for the hole in my heart.

'I think we only get three chances at love. You can only give your heart thrice. Then the opportunities are over. From now on there won't be any *love*. Only sex, maybe. At best!' I said stumbling for the words before I dug into the piping hot malai curry.

'That's bullshit,' Shy said. 'All those men were stupid. And you *will* find love. You will Kaveri. You've got to believe in it for it to happen.'

I shook my head. 'Not anymore, Shy. I'm done. I'm going to ask my parents to set me up with someone—even a short, ugly IIT guy who can't find a woman for himself—and marry him. I'm done looking for true love. I'm thirty-five years old, damn it! How much longer will the Universe keep asking me to be patient? I've given everything of myself to these men. What more could I have done? Nothing! I am not giving into this shit of trying to date again. I'm done,' I said emphatically.

Shy let me be. She didn't want to oppose me yet. But after we had cleared our plates and we sat on her windowsill that had been converted into a seating area with plants around, she lit up a cigarette and said, 'Love is the most over used word in the dictionary. If we think about it, we have too many expectations from it.'

'You mean people. We have expectations from people,' I said correcting her. What did she know? She had hardly seen love or the world. I had a lot more experience than she did.

'No. I meant love itself. When I say *I love you*, it's *my* interpretation of what I feel for you. But the other person sees it as how he wants it to be. Like when a guy tells me he loves me, maybe he loves my body, or my personality or the way I speak or how I am with his friends. But actually he probably means he loves me for the way I make him feel about himself.

It's complicated, but think about it.' Shy took another drag from her cigarette while I puffed away on mine silently. 'Everyone's interpretation of love is different. If we allow room for the other person's interpretation to be more than ours, maybe we would all be far more at ease with relationships than we are today.'

'Are you saying I'm uptight? Are you saying what I did was wrong? That I should take Siddharth back and give Aditi a chance?' I asked directly.

Shy could see that my aggressive mood was not going to help her cause so she said calmly, 'Not at all. What you want to do with those two is entirely up to you. But just remember there is no relationship that has not been taken for granted at some point. The good ones rectify it immediately. The bad ones let it slip.

'And always keep room for someone falling in love with you with their definition of love instead of yours. And then maybe you'll feel true love again!' She stubbed out her cigarette and announced that she was going to bed. I smiled and thanked her for a lovely dinner and words that made sense to me.

I didn't go to bed immediately. I sat on the windowsill for a very long time playing her words again and again. I read all my SMSes from Aditi and Siddharth as well. I knew I could not forget what I had heard. And I knew I didn't want to forgive so easily. But I had to stop being harsh on myself and them. I needed to go back home and face them. I couldn't escape from life anymore. What they had done was in the past. Did it matter anymore? I had to be the bigger person. I weighed the pros and cons of having Siddharth in my life and realized that I was a far better person with him by my side. I liked who I was. I shouldn't give that up. But I needed my heart to heal a little bit. And I needed to start by having a conversation with my boyfriend.

24

Confrontations Are Never Easy

I went back to my house after a week and decided I wanted to clean it thoroughly. I changed the sheets and did a load of laundry. I sorted out the kitchen that hadn't been used for so long. My maid had come and cleaned the place since she had her own key, but I needed to put a few things in order. Then I took a long shower and wore some fresh clothes. I made myself some breakfast and a fresh pot of coffee. Then I called Siddharth. I needed to speak to him and find out his reasoning. I was feeling calm and collected. I wasn't going to let him hear my tears and my pain. I would talk to him as an adult.

'Kaveri! Thank god!' he said as soon as he answered instead of the standard greetings.

'Tell me what you need to tell me,' I said crisply. I needed to hear how wrong he had been. How he should never have slept with Aditi over and over again. And how he planned to worship me for the rest of my life by making up for this fatal mistake in his past. Yes. That's what I hoped.

'Let me start by saying I'm sorry,' he said calmly. 'I'm sorry I slept with Aditi. It was foolish of me. It was a long time ago and I was stupid back then. I was shocked to see her at the party. Neither of us knew how to react to each other. I swear

I was going to tell you about us in due course, but you stumbled upon us having that conversation before I could. I know we shouldn't have gone behind your back. But honestly, we cannot change our past. I hope you find in your heart to forgive me so we can move on. I do love you tremendously.'

That was it. His cool, rational approach annoyed me a little. But I didn't react to it. I wanted him to feel more apologetic. Although I understood the logic in his little speech, I couldn't wrap my head around it. How would he see Aditi when we were together? If they interacted I would always worry that they might hook up. I would never be able to banish that image of them in bed together.

'Kaveri,' he said before I could say anything, 'I need to call you back. I am in an important meeting and the clients are waiting for me. Can we meet this evening?'

No, I wanted to scream. I want to talk to you now! But instead I said, 'Sure. Come over.'

'Thanks, love. And just remember Kaveri . . . don't give up what we have for something that happened in the past. What we have is special. Don't do something foolish that you will regret later.'

I replied, 'Siddharth, this is *your* fault. Not mine. I will have to live with something stupid that *you* did for the rest of my life *if* I'm with you. If I had been a kleptomaniac and had a police record would you stay with me? Wouldn't you wonder what it would be like every time I went into a store?' I asked, giving a very ambiguous example.

'Not really,' he answered, 'because I trust you.'

'That's not the point,' I flared up. 'You know what I mean.'

Siddharth was quiet for a moment and said, 'I'll see you at nine; we'll talk then.'

My argument bordered on the ridiculous. Trust me never to come up with the right words when I needed them the most. Fortunately, I knew exactly what I wanted to say to Aditi!

I took a deep breath and went out for a walk. I was high on

insomnia, nicotine and anger. It was a perfect combination to walk to my former friend's house and give her a piece of my mind. I didn't even know if she would be home. But I didn't care. I would wait for her. I had to teach her a few things about manners. When I reached her house the servant told me that she was out. So I went to her room to wait for her. I sat on the bed and before I knew it I had laid my head on her pillow and fallen asleep. I woke up several hours later when it had already turned dark. I could hear people bickering in the drawing room.

I dragged myself out of bed and walked into the drawing room where Aditi was watching a soap opera. Instead of screaming at her for ruining my life, I heard myself saying, 'When did you start watching Hindi soap operas?'

She shifted on the couch and patted the spot next to her in invitation. I sat down next to her and started watching with her. She started explaining the story to me, 'It's about a marriage between this fat guy and this woman. It's about love when you're middle aged. It really relates to our generation.'

'Are you calling me fat?' I asked dryly.

Aditi giggled. 'No, I'm calling you middle aged!' she said and I giggled with her.

Aditi called the servant and told him to serve some poha that he had made. He returned moments later with food and hot coffee for me. I took a sip and smiled—it was perfect. Chotu obviously knew what I liked. He was the only man who ever got me. If he wasn't so ugly I might have been in a relationship with Chotu. By the time I had eaten and watched the entire episode, my anger had abated and I was actually beginning to find the story interesting. Two revelations for me in one day.

Aditi finally turned to me and said, 'I'm going to go get my gun now so you can shoot me.'

I smiled. Maybe I had been stupid to react like that. It was their past. And I was a present and a future. Everyone's entitled to mistakes. Mistakes like sex with their best friend's boyfriend.

'I don't even want to know about it,' I said.

Aditi nodded in understanding and she stayed quiet. She didn't say another word about it. It was actually better to get it out of my head. I wondered why I had found it easier to forgive her than Siddharth. Why couldn't I let things be with Siddharth as well? Maybe because he thought he knew me when actually he didn't. Maybe because I wanted Aditi's friendship more than his love. Maybe because there had been a nagging sense that he might not be the one and I just needed an excuse to end it? That thought left me a little worried.

'I know you don't want any explanations, but all I want to say is I'm so sorry. I promise to become celibate if you truly want me to from now on!' Aditi said with her hands folded.

I smiled. Aditi celibate? Well that was asking for a lot! But if she meant it, it was a good apology and I let her be.

'Chill madi,' I said getting up and collecting my things, 'you are and always will be my best friend. And besides, I'm better in bed than you are!' And I laughed. It felt good to laugh after being overwhelmed by grief the past few days.

She came over and hugged me. 'Why are you leaving so early? I thought we could hang out like old times for a change. I barely get to see you anymore, now that you have new friends!' she remarked.

'Once I'm back from Milan, we'll hang out, I promise. But tonight I have to talk to Siddharth,' I replied. 'Tomorrow I fly off for a month!'

I was so looking forward to my trip. And dreading the evening with my boyfriend. I hoped that we could sort out this mess before I left.

25

Where Do Memories Go When the Relationship Dies?

I wish I could say 'no' to people. That was my biggest flaw. I'm the type of person who needs to please everyone, to find appreciation from the most innocuous of situations and inconsequential of people. I would be gentle with the vegetable vendor lest he think I'm a bitch. I would rather not call a person back than actually have to say that the relationship is over. I didn't like nasty rows and unpleasant conversations. I would rather ignore the situation, bury my head in the sand and let people take their own decision rather than be the one who would end things. I had done that once with Arjun and sometimes, just sometimes, I regretted it. Since then I was inclined to let relationships take their own course. I hadn't wanted to break up with Ray but I had no other option. I didn't want to break up with Siddharth either but I didn't know where we were heading. Siddharth made me feel far more alive than I had in quite a while.

He was waiting for me in his car when I got back. I had taken an auto home and got stuck in the traffic. He had called me when he reached at nine sharp and said he would wait for me in his car. By the time I got there I was half an hour late and he was pretty hungry. So instead of going up for a long chat he decided we would go out for dinner to a nice place where we could unwind and talk. I looked like a mess but agreed. I didn't want to say no!

I quickly went up and changed my shirt and put on some make-up and came down within minutes, not wanting to keep him waiting. We went to the Marriott where he was a regular and the waiters knew what his order was. They immediately brought him a single malt and a glass of white wine for me. After a few sips I felt warm and calm and capable of having a decent conversation with him.

He started with, 'Routine gives us structure, structure gives us discipline, discipline gives us success. And here's to success!' he said raising his glass. I wondered if he had gone completely mad. 'Young', I realized then, need not necessarily mean foolish, just as 'old' did not always mean wise. I might actually be the wiser of the two of us even though he was the more successful partner.

'Does the routine imply me as well?' I asked dryly taking another sip of my wine.

'Relationships are not supposed to be exciting. They are meant to be routine,' he said. Before I could protest he continued, 'Once upon a time I didn't understand that. I wanted newness in everything. I had sex with random women thinking it would give me great pleasure to conquer more and more women. At the same time I was working on everything my father gave me and partying like mad. I was young, foolish and reckless. I lived like that for a very long time. Then my father had a heart attack. And I needed to sober up. Fast. I realized I needed stability. I got married. And though I was not in love with her, I would still be married if she hadn't fallen in love with someone else. A marriage is routine. Relationships are routine. Routine is good. It is what makes us successful in our personal and professional lives. I like the fact that you and I can be routine.' He paused and drank from his glass while the waiters arranged the appetizers on the table.

There were prawns for me, I noticed. But I didn't feel like eating. Had he just called me boring? Routine? Had he just said that he wasn't in love with me, that he had gone along with the flow because it was the right thing to do? I didn't know how to react to that. All I knew was that I needed to be with a man who truly wanted to be with me because he couldn't imagine being with anyone else, not because it was routine. We spend so much time, energy and money in proving a point to the world. And so little in making the one we love happy. Siddharth was so bent upon making everything a success that he did not even stop to think if the right way to do things was really right when you're in love.

But suddenly I had one thought, if my heart was telling me it was over: Where will the memories go when the relationship dies?

If I walked out right now, where would this memory go? Memory cripples us more than circumstances. If we can't let go of the past, we can't tackle the present and can't move on with a future. I had so many memories of so many men in my life. And at all times they would come flooding back. Days I spent with Arjun, or the moments I had with Karan or even the nights lying in Ray's arms. And now, the times I had spent with Siddharth. I could not forget any of them. What do I do with them? Did we all just hang on to the men since our suitcase of memories was already overfull? Did I want to let this relationship just be and go with whatever he was saying? I felt confused. I sat quietly through dinner letting him speak and explain himself. But slowly I was getting a sinking feeling.

Siddharth's words resounded in my ear. Was he saying there was no love between us? That any show of affection had just been a routine? No one owes love to anyone in this world. You give it because you choose to. Only then is it honest and pure. And with Great Love comes Deep Sorrow. But without true love, life is empty. Surely Siddharth knew this since he was 'older and wiser'.

I felt something going amiss but I couldn't actually say the words. A relationship comes to an end when two people stop relating. The words die between them and the silence is never comfortable. I knew I couldn't be influenced by the world and its opinions. I needed to be influenced only by my heart and my opinions.

I cleared my throat and asked, 'Do you think that we need some space to clear out our thoughts?' hoping for a completely negative response.

'If that's what you want,' he said rationally.

What did I want? Were all relationships so twisted or did I attract only the ones that were. I knew that I had always wanted to be with a man. Even when I thought I could be alone, I would meet men and find my resolve wavering. There was not a single day when I could say a man hadn't occupied my thoughts for even a single minute. But had I attracted all the wrong relationships? I presumed I needed to take responsibility for this. After all I had asked the Universe to help me find my True Love and all, but had I forced that label onto every man who came my way? Maybe the Universe was just sending me men for other purposes in my life and holding out for the real one. People who don't learn from their mistakes deserve to have them repeated. And I was a prime example. Maybe it had been a Mistake to fall in Love with an older man.

'Siddharth,' I began, 'we think we need the love of someone else to anchor us. But true love is simply knowing deep in your heart that it needs no anchor. When you walked into my life I needed that love. And an anchor. Today, I am free to choose to love. And so are you. We are not the sum of all that we expect from each other. We are not routine. We are more because our relationship gives us the opportunity to go beyond that what we ordinarily see and surprise each other to see anew. That's who we are.'

He put down his glass of scotch and looked at me in complete awe. He had never heard me speaking like this. I knew what I

had to say. I knew who I needed to be. Knowledge is knowing
you've changed. Wisdom is understanding you never want to be
the old you.

'I am not scared of being alone, Siddharth. But I am scared
of being lonely when I am in a relationship. I do not find
humour in routine. I had always thought it's not about how
much you can give me because you love me. It's about how
much you love me so that you give so much. That's how I feel
about you. And I hope that is how you feel about me. What
happened with Aditi was unfortunate. It's okay to forget the
past, as long as we remember the lessons it taught us. I don't
regret the mistakes I have made in my life, just as I don't expect
you to regret sleeping with Aditi. For it is those mistakes that
have made us who we are today. You can't move on in life if
your past holds you back. We are constantly evolving as human
beings. Our relationships are constantly evolving as well. If it
doesn't give you stability or make you passionate, it's time to let
it go,' I said, and added defiantly, 'I am not interested in
routine.'

I asked the waiter to fill my glass again. I knew it wasn't the
wine talking but I sure needed it to keep my head balanced for
what he might respond with.

He cleared his throat but didn't say anything. He looked
deeply into my eyes for some time and finally said, 'You are
right, Kaveri. For the first time I'm seeing you in your true light
and it shines. The problem is that everyone wants their
relationship to work. But no one wants to work on the
relationship. And you're the first woman who wants to make it
work despite the odds stacked against you. I like that. I like your
spunk.'

I wanted to slap him then. What odds? I had never felt there
was anything between us till he just spelt it out. But I gulped
down my glass of wine instead. Food was served moments later.
I wasn't hungry at all. I was far more concerned now about
packing my clothes for the next day's trip and finding a

resolution to this conversation. Relationships are supposed to be quid pro quo. From family, spouse, friends or colleagues. If you're not getting what you need, it's time to move on!

'How about this,' he started after our table had been cleared. 'Let's say we love each other but we need to figure out what the future of this relationship is. We can't go on being so vastly different from each other. Let's try and see what we can mould about ourselves to suit the other and what we choose to hold on to so that the other compromises. Deal?'

I nodded but my mind wasn't working. I guess relationships needed a refresh button every once in a while. It puts things in perspective. And this month-long vacation was exactly the refresh button our relationship needed.

Yes, I attracted weird relationships. There was no other explanation for it.

Sometimes you need to be your own beacon of light. No one else will shine it for you. I planned to be that light from now on.

26

Outdoor Shoots

There was enough excitement at the airport to light up a city. Some forty people were travelling to Turkey and Rome and Shyamolie and I were a part of the group. Apparently the director, producer and a whole unit had left a day earlier. Bela and Rajvir, the hero, were leaving a day later. They didn't want to travel with the rest of the crew. Shyamolie had been to hundreds of outdoor shoots and she had vowed that this would be her last shoot. After this she was going to start her own boutique and design clothes herself instead of trying to find clothes for actors. But she had been saying that for a while. The thrill of meeting actors and being on a film set was what kept her going. A part of her wondered if she would get bored just sitting in a shop all day.

'There's no place to smoke around here,' she grumbled.

I didn't care. I had decided to cut down on my smoking. It was not doing anything for my skin and I was beginning to look old. It hadn't even helped address my hunger cravings; my 'muffin top' had crept in again. I had pointed it out to Shy a few weeks ago when she had loaned me a pair of designer Cavalli jeans. She had immediately taken away the jeans and told me that unless I lost weight I would not be allowed near designer wear. So I decided I would first quit smoking, then the sandwiches, and then all the mithai I was eating. But so far nothing had helped.

'We have a little while to board, let's go to the smokers' lounge,' Shyamolie suggested. 'Ah!' she said, a few minutes later, taking a long drag of her cigarette.

I ignored the temptation to smoke, and fished out my Blackberry and signed into Twitter. Shy looked over my shoulder and commented, 'You're hooked aren't you?'

I nodded, 'I love the fact that I can say whatever I like on this forum and if people like it they respond and follow me and if they don't then they go screw themselves.'

Shy laughed. 'I've created a monster,' she said. 'So how many people are following you?'

'Oh, I don't really care. There's this one person who keeps commenting about my tweets though.'

'Oh ya? Who?' Shy asked taking another drag and checking out the men in the smokers' lounge. She knew the best way to date a man was to break the ice with another smoker.

'This handle called SomewhereFarAway,' I said.

'You know, it could be a lesbian chick who is in love with you and wants you to go over to the dark side with her! There's no way of knowing if handles like that are men or women!'

I laughed at her ridiculousness, 'Why would anyone go through so much trouble? Though, now that I think about it, maybe I need a woman for a change. All the men in my life have been quite useless so far.'

'Oh ya? Isn't that a good thing?' she said naughtily, with one eyebrow raised. I laughed just as there was a boarding announcement for our flight.

'Crap,' Shy said stubbing out her cigarette, 'I didn't get to flirt with the cute guy in the yellow tie.'

'Maybe you'll meet him in Italy!' I muttered as we left the lounge.

It is true that some things are meant to be, for Shy would find someone in Italy, just as I would, too. And though we boarded the same flight, our lives were about to go in different directions.

We decided to have lots of alcohol on the flight and watch the same movie so we could comment on it loudly for other passengers. But as soon as I settled into my seat, I fell asleep— the exhaustion of the last week had taken a toll on me. I woke up six hours later for our stop over in Dubai feeling refreshed. I was looking forward to shopping with Shy at the Duty Free in Dubai and then being in Milan for a month. And even though it was going to be a work trip, my mind was feeling like it was going on a vacation!

Although I had been to Milan briefly the previous year, this time I actually noticed the beauty of the city and was enchanted by its cobblestone walkways and quaint neighbourhoods. It was as if I had been transported back to the time of Leonardo da Vinci. The beautiful cafes, the Piazza del Duomo, the immaculately dressed men and women were a breath of fresh air from the hustle and bustle that was Mumbai.

The crew had checked into a three-star hotel, twenty minutes from the five-star hotel where Bela and Rajvir were staying. Apparently they didn't want to mingle with the crew. Of course, later they would tell the press how they had a wonderful time shooting with the crew and were all a big happy family but that was all nonsense. Directors and actors rarely ever stayed with the crew, probably because they could do as they pleased without the danger of it being leaked to the press.

I met Bela later in the day though, since she wanted to have a lesson. Strangely enough, it had nothing to do with her dialogues or the scenes she had to shoot the next day. Bela was lounging on the open air terrace in a micro white bikini with a Diet Coke by her side. She waved to me as soon as I entered. After I had sat down beside her, she looked around suspiciously as if ensuring no one was within earshot, and then said in a whisper, 'I want to you to teach me dirty things.'

I was taken aback. 'What?' My trip would have to be cut

short here since this was not part of my contract. 'What do you mean?'

She tried to explain it to me in Russian. 'You know, saying things to a lover in bed.'

Oh! She had meant dirty pillow talk.

She continued, 'I have a boyfriend and he wants me to speak dirty to him. But whenever I open my mouth I don't know what to say. Last time I tried, I said something foolish and he burst out laughing. I was most embarrassed. After that things weren't so good.'

I desperately wanted to burst out laughing as well but I knew that the conversation would not be so good either after that. I took a deep breath and found myself at a loss for words. She immediately understood and asked me, 'Do you want a drink?' I nodded. Yes, a drink would help. I had never been very good at dirty talk myself, and it had been ages since I had been with a man who wanted to talk dirty. I tried to recollect all that Arjun used to say to me. Or the things that Aaron had muttered when we were having tantric sex. We chatted about other things like her scenes for the film while waiting for my drink. Half an hour later, I gulped down the dregs of my Sex on the Beach before I started tutoring her on the art of dirty talk.

'First of all, you've got to be relaxed in your own head when you speak to him. Don't get uptight. Take a deep breath. Let all this feel natural . . . warm . . . sensual . . . Always keep it simple. Tell him how much he turns you on . . . look into his eyes . . . tell him how attractive he is and how you feel when you see him.' I tried to keep it basic, and stay away from murky waters. But she wasn't buying it. She needed details. So I ordered another drink and continued, 'Say things like how you love his body, how his skin makes you tingle, how the sight of his smile makes you want to kiss him.'

She nodded. In between she asked me to repeat myself again so she could pronounce it correctly. Then she asked me to go on.

'You have to flirt with him, you have to tease him. Start by doing things to his body and asking him if he likes it. Be careful of your tone. Don't be squeaky. Be soft, have a low pitch. You have to be confident. Tell him how you love his gorgeous skin against your body . . . how your mouth searches for his every time he smiles and how his rock hard shaft pressed up against your thighs is making you tingle with deep wanton lust. Take things slowly, with your touch your words, your intimacy . . . tell him how horny he makes you, how you love touching yourself while thinking about him, lying in a warm bubble bath with soap suds gently caressing your breasts, and you rubbing liquidy soap all over your bare flat tummy and letting your fingers slip to other areas. Tell him you want to spell out dirty words with your tongue on his inner thigh. Tell him you want to cook naked for him, your bosom heavy with sweat as you slave away wearing nothing but an apron. And when he comes home, you want him to take you right then and there in the kitchen. Then ask him if he's ready. Slowly climb on top of him. Ask him if he likes being inside you. Tell him he feels so good inside you. Say his name. Moan loudly. Tell him how wet you are. Move in a rhythmic motion. Slowly. Steadily. Then faster. Harder. Shout it to him. Tell him how he's so deep inside you. Tell him how your body has been waiting for him. That you've been touching yourself all morning thinking of him. Show him. Caress your breasts. Let him come on top of you. Be a beast. Raise you arms up so he can suck your breasts. Groan. Oh how you love that. Stroke his ass. Moan, bite your lip. When he says he's coming, breathe deeply and moan you're coming too. Let his body blaze down on your passion. Make it raw, sexual and passionate.'

The lesson over, I took out my packet of cigarettes from my purse, flicked open the Zippo for a smoke, and took a long drag. Thankfully I had not completely quit yet. This was definitely more than I was being paid for. Bela thanked me and I left. I had no more energy to teach her dialogues. I would see her the next day for the shoot. Till then I desperately needed a man to have sex with. It had been too long!

27

Smokes, Shoots and Leaves

The next day we were shooting a whole scene at the Basilica of Sant'Ambrogio in which Bela would be praying when Rajvir arrives to tell her that he was in love with her, but she would say that she had vowed to be a nun and there was nothing more they could do about it. I knew it was going to be a long day. There was no way an audience was going to buy Bela's portayal of a girl caught between the man she loved and her vow to God. Especially not when she was busy arguing with Shy and demanding to wear a low cut white blouse to show her heaving bosom when she ran. Yeah Bela, I wanted to tell her, that looks very virginal. But I kept my mouth shut and just went over the dialogues with her in her vanity van. Even here in this remote location, Scunjay Punjwani had arranged for a vanity van for the heroine to change and relax in. Rajvir, on the other hand, had to make do with a room close to the location which had been converted into a makeshift make-up room for him.

Punjwani caught hold of me when I came out of the vanity van. 'How much longer will she take? I want to finish a song also today,' he bellowed. 'We need to shoot one of the songs in Milan. Or at least parts of it so we save on the location cost. At least one mukhda and one antara needs to be done here,' he said looking around and then with an afterthought, 'But obviously not here. We will need to move to Porta Venezia gardens and maybe even that whatchacallit castle.'

'Sforza.'

'Bless you.'

'No, sir,' I said trying to correct him. 'It's called the Sforza Castle.'

He nodded. 'Correct! That's where we have to go. We have only four days in Milan and we need to finish all this. And that stupid RT hasn't come back yet, and I won't know how to move my crew,' he said trying to call someone on his mobile.

'That shouldn't be a problem sir. I know how to get there,' I said smiling. 'I've been here before and know Milan like the back of my hand,' I said trying to impress him. I could look it up on Google maps since I remembered it vaguely from the brief visit I made a year ago.

Scunjay looked at me with more respect than ever before. 'Wah child!' He called everyone he was truly fond of 'child' otherwise he referred to them by their name. That was a sign that I was in his good books. 'You have turned out to be so resourceful. First you teach my actress to speak and then you become my location manager. From tomorrow you can tell me where all to shoot and save my budget. Oh and while you're at it, tell that stylist we don't have any more money for more costumes. Whatever she has, she had better make do with it. And also tell her she needs to style the junior artists. I'm not paying her to enjoy a holiday in Milan after all!' he said and got on the phone.

Shy was sitting outside the vanity van by herself when I arrived with Punjwani's message. Bela had left for her shot. A whiff of the smoke from the cigarette Shy was smoking had me craving one desperately. But I restrained myself. I had to kick this bad habit somehow.

'I have a message from Punjwani,' I said sitting down next to her on the steps of the trailer.

'If that bastard wants me to design for all the people on this set you can tell him to fuck off. He's not doing me any favours by bringing me to Milan. I have enough money to see it myself if I ever wanted to. And I get enough grief from the top actors about their clothes without needing to hear bullshit from the rest of the crew,' she said vehemently. Wow! This woman knew her mind. But now I was in a jam—I felt that Punjwani had tasked me with getting Shy to do her job. 'Also that man makes people do two people's jobs when we're outdoors. What does he think of himself? Next he'll tell me to hold the clap and dance as an extra because someone is sick. Bloody hell!'

And suddenly I realized that Punjwani was making me work as a translator for Bela as well as a location manager who would find new locations, secure permissions and move the crew in time for the shoots. That was extra work that I had just agreed to without truly comprehending how much more effort it would require.

'Come on, we're needed at the shoot,' Shy said as she got up. We both walked towards the location.

Milan is known for its high fashion and Da Vinci's *Last Supper*. But what people don't know about this place is that it is teeming with culture and history and has far more character than the other cities of Rome. I was glad we were shooting here. The brief trip that I had taken had been with Ray. It had been very cold then. We had snuggled together under the blankets in our motel and had taken a two-seater bike to tour the countryside one afternoon. But mostly we were so into each other that we hardly noticed the city. I felt so close to Ray in that moment when I paused and looked around. He had stopped and kissed me passionately at every corner, the kind of kiss that Shy had spoken about when people were together, a kiss that was unabashedly deep and profound with not a care of who was watching and what people thought. The memory of that kiss trembled through my body just then and I needed to take a break from the shoot and get away where I could reflect. I knew just the place that could give me clarity of thought.

'Shy,' I said suddenly, 'I'll be right back. There's something I have to do.' I started going in the opposite direction. I grabbed the bicycle that I had hired since I knew it was the fastest mode of transportation in Milan. Every day men and women dressed in their Armanis and Guccis would get on their bikes and ride home after their meetings. This blend of the absurd and the practical was part of the charm of Milan. I rushed to the Refectory at Santa Maria where I needed to see the one thing that made me begin to love art. Leonardo da Vinci's *Last Supper*. I had seen a painting of it when I was seven years old, transfixed by the depth that it could portray even though it was painted on a wall. I knew then that I had to study art and somehow be a part of the world that could have inhabited this man. I wanted to carry his legacy on through discourse and emulation. I parked my bicycle outside, paid my entrance fee and walked into the great hall.

Unbidden, the dialogues that Bela was supposed to say in the church burst from my lips, 'I didn't mean to fall in love, Father. I've strayed from what you taught me, what you wanted me to be. Give me a sign, Father. Tell me, should I do what is expected of me? Or should I go with my heart?'

I looked around to see if anyone had heard me but I was alone in this room. The guard came by and told me that my fifteen minutes were up. That was all that a tourist got to observe the work. I begged for some more time and since there weren't too many people around, he left me alone in that cool chamber. As I gazed at the deteriorated fresco, I could feel the genius of the painter stirring up emotions in me again. I felt relieved. I took a deep breath and exhaled. I knew I was doing this interpretation work to earn money right now. But I was determined to return to the world of art where my true calling lay. When I got back to the set an hour after the first shot had been taken and the second shot was being prepared, I was surprised to find that there was a calm in the air. Shyamolie was standing in a corner and laughing as Punjwani cracked a joke.

Bela was sitting behind the monitor studying the shot she had just given (in thirteen takes). And the crew were having tea and looking surprisingly far cleaner than they did in Mumbai.

Just then Rajvir emerged from behind one of the rooms. He was tall, fair and had light eyes—absolutely gorgeous. I had never seen him in person before. Rajvir was the quintessential Bollywood hero; young and fit, his dark wavy hair and manly aura made the women swoon and even made some men go weak in their knees. He sauntered over to the monitor and watched the shot that Bela had done and commended her on her performance. Bela smiled at him and they exchanged a few words. I watched all this from my vantage point in the back, afraid to go any closer lest someone heard my heart beating like mad. I had no idea why I was reacting like this to Rajvir. I thought to myself, 'Kaveri, you're way too old for this guy. And he's a *hero*. Stop dreaming!' But I was completely besotted. I was one of those women who fell in love in an instant and deliberated later. Even though time and experience had warned me of such situations, I was careless with my heart. I made sure it plunged deep into an infatuation before my mind could take over with logic. And here I could sense it happening again.

Bela's voice shattered my reverie, and I looked up to see her frantically waving at me. I walked towards them very slowly, hoping that by the time I reached them, I would sound like a composed, distant woman unaffected by his gorgeousness. Fat chance! Bela introduced me to Rajvir and he immediately got up from his chair and shook my hand. I blushed so hard that I would never need my Lakme blush again.

'She speaks seven languages. She's very well read. You won't get along with her at all Raj. She'll make you look like an idiot!' Bela said teasingly and laughed.

He smiled and said, 'That's true. I only speak Hindi and English and grew up in a film family. And I've hardly read anything lately other than film scripts. And even those are usually narrated to me. I hardly read.'

'Well I'm sure it's because you have no time and your profession demands it,' I said, trying to make him sound smarter than Bela made him out to be.

'No,' he admitted, 'that's not it. I don't like reading all that much. I'm a music guy though. I love listening to music and have the latest tracks on my iPod.' He took out the tiny gadget that was tucked away in his pocket and put the earphones in my ears. 'Listen to this. It's mind blowing.' He came closer to me and all coherent thought evaporated as I was enveloped in a haze of Hugo Boss that mingled deeply with the scent of his fresh clothes. And although all I could focus on was the sound of his breathing, I nodded and said, 'Mind blowing!'

He smiled at me in agreement, and at that moment, I couldn't have cared less if he was the dumbest man on the planet or Albert Einstein, I was totally besotted with Rajvir Kapur. His smile lit up his eyes and his manners seemed genuine and heartfelt. Or so I thought. Sometimes some infatuations are like mirages. The closer we think we are to the person, the farther you really are from the truth.

Sometime later they began to shoot the next scene between Bela and Rajvir. I got ready for this since Bela had said she would need help with the pronunciation of the dialogues. They were lengthy and needed emotion as well. After a point, it became torturous to watch Bela struggle while Rajvir gave one perfect take after another.

'Bela, please say, *Mujhe maaf kar do* and stop. I'll take the rest in another angle,' the director shouted. 'And Raj, just break down and begin your dialogue so she can interrupt you with— Bela listen to this—*Tum mujhse kya chahte ho*? Got it? Great. Roll sound. Roll camera.' One of the assistant directors rushed forward with a clap and said, 'Shot two. Take four!'

Bela managed to deliver her first dialogue flawlessly, but fumbled with the words of the second one. Then she took a deep breath and Rajvir calmed her down by putting a hand on her shoulder. He turned to the director and said, 'Let's take five.' Bela went towards her trailer, and Rajvir followed her inside. I wanted to go with her but she just waved me aside. Unfortunately, Punjwani caught hold of me just then and reprimanded me for not having Bela ready and wasting his time. He said if she didn't get her act together soon he would have to fire me. Fear rose in my chest, threatening to overpower me. But just then Bela and Rajvir emerged and gave a perfect take. Perhaps they had been rehearsing inside.

The rest of the scene went off well and we even got to shoot part of the song at Sforza Castle. Things went much better there since Bela was an excellent dancer. What she lacked in dialogue delivery, she made up in her dance. And since most Bollywood actresses were expected to seduce their audiences through their gyrations rather than their perfect accents and acting, Bela had become a hit amongst all the choreographers. Bela's superior dancing skills were outshone only by Rajvir's intricate footwork and the fantastic way he moved. I was just in awe of him. By the end of the day, Shy and I were dancing to the familiar Bollywood number that we knew would be a hit.

This outdoor shoot was looking like a lot of fun after all.

28

A Day in the Life of a Heroine

The next day at dawn Bela woke up to go for dance rehearsals for the remainder of the song that she had to shoot. And since Punjwani had rather rudely reminded me that he had paid for my ticket and then insisted that I go with her for everything, I went for the rehearsals as well with bleary eyes and a croissant in my hand.

For the next five hours, I drank gallons of coffee in order to stay awake, but I was fighting a losing battle. And every time I fell asleep, I was jolted back into awareness by the choreographer's voice barking instructions to Bela as she tried to match the steps to the complicated routine. And every now and then, the choreographer would shout in an attempt to be heard over the blaring music, 'Five, six, seven, eight and move!'

I had to admire Bela for her dedication. She might not have mastered her accent, but she was extremely hard working. I wondered how the dirty talk had gone with her boyfriend and more importantly, who he was. But I dared not impose on her personal life or she would take offence. Once the back-up dancers joined the rehearsals, Bela took a break and ordered some egg whites and fruit for breakfast. I thanked God that I didn't have to be in front of the camera and asked for pancakes, muffins and some muesli. Eating just egg whites would have made me extremely cranky! Being in the limelight was not easy I realized. You had to always look after your figure and your skin and spend a fortune on your clothes and accessories. Celebrities had their own share of problems. But I couldn't feel too sorry for her. After all, I was doing nearly as much work and being paid a fraction of what she was.

'Let's go one more time,' said the choreographer and everyone took their places once again. And they rehearsed it once more before 'packing up' for the day. Later, when I heard the song again on location during the shoot, I would be so fed up that I would take a stroll to La Scala and buy tickets for the opera! Oh how I loved the opera. But India didn't have any operas, only item numbers!

After Bela finished with the rehearsals, she had to attend a mini press meet with the local papers that had been arranged in the hotel lobby. We quickly went to her room where Shy had laid out the clothes she had chosen the previous night.

But Bela still complained, 'Shy, I don't think the purple dress is going to look nice today. I feel like going nude.'

I was shocked. Did she want to do a naked photo shoot for the press? That would certainly catch eyeballs and make her film a success.

'Fine. But the nude will make you look very washed out in the lighting in the lobby,' Shy said apparently understanding what Bela meant. 'How about we do nude pump shoes and nude make-up with a pastel dress? Soft and feminine and yet makes an impact. Like the heroines of yesteryears!'

Bela thought about it and agreed. She told me to go over the speech that she had prepared so she wouldn't look like a dunce with improper pronunciation. While she took a shower I looked over her speech and made corrections where I thought she would stumble. We rehearsed the speech while she was getting her make-up done and went over some likely questions so she would not falter. Within an hour she was ready and headed down for the press meet. She had decided she was going to be a punctual actress and that was what would set her apart from the rest. The press liked her for respecting their time rather than making them wait endlessly. And she was quite a hit. The press did indeed love her and she laughed and giggled when she didn't know how to say something and apologized for her language and blew kisses to a few photographers. She retained the right amount of mystery needed for an actress and revealed enough to give correct quotes for the papers. It was hard to tell if she actually delivered her speech since all the next day's papers were talking about was the ravishing beauty from India who was going to take the world by storm. There was something about that woman! She had an aura that made people like her even though she made life difficult for all those who knew her well.

After the press meet we headed for the shoot where she shot all day and she sipped on water and had sprouts. I was dog tired by the middle of the afternoon and I went to lie down behind the set while the lighting people set up a shot. I quickly fell asleep despite all the shouting and hammering and general noise. When I woke up an hour later, Punjwani was shouting at one of the spot boys while Bela and Rajvir stood in a corner, talking to each other.

'How long is this taking? Is this your father's money that you are spending!' Punjwani's voice rose above the noise and as if on cue people began scurrying about, pretending to be busy. Although there seemed to be a lot of activity on the set, nothing was really happening because the shot still took another forty-five minutes to set up.

Suddenly I missed Aditi. This had been her world for so long and she had loved it; she would have fit right in here, knowing exactly what to do.

Later that evening, after the shoot was over, Bela wanted to go back to her hotel and sleep but Punjwani had scheduled a photo shoot with her for a brand endorsement he had tied up with. As her agent, he would benefit immensely as soon as it went public and even though she was exhausted, she relented.

The studio was already set up. Bela got her make-up done and picked out her clothes from what they had brought and was ready in just half an hour. Even though she had been up since five in the morning, dancing, shooting and emoting, she looked fresh as a daisy in her slim cropped beige pants, a powdery pink silk blouse, a wide mother-of-pearl belt that made her small waist shrink further, and 'windswept' hair that was held back with a pair of Armani sunglasses on top of her head. For the next three hours, Bela followed the photographer's directions— smile, pout, sit, stand, lean back, lie down, extend your arm, turn your head, lift your chin—like a pro. Halfway through the shoot, a gorgeous, tall, blond man wearing a white shirt, khaki shorts, a sleeveless argyle sweater and a preppy cap on his head walked in. He had green eyes and a killer smile; he was delicious! He was a lead model in Milan and was in the photo shoot with Bela. I simply sat and ogled.

By the time Bela finished her shoot, it was almost midnight.

I went back to my hotel and took a long bubble bath, and drank a glass of white wine. For just some time I wanted to feel like the heroine of my own movie instead of just a sidekick.

29

Sandwiches and Sex

The next day was Sunday. And everyone had Sunday off, no matter which part of the world we were in. Punjwani was fuming at this; he had hoped the crew would work every day and wrap up shooting soon, saving him tons of money in the process. But he had no say in the matter. Shy pleaded exhaustion and took herself off to lie in bed the whole day. I went downstairs to the hotel coffee shop to have breakfast and then set out by foot to figure out what I wanted to do that day. As luck would have it, just as I was getting on my bicycle, I saw Rajvir walking towards me. I wondered if he was lost and waved at him.

'Hey! Are you lost?'

He shook his head. 'No, I was listening to my music and went for a walk and decided I just needed to go on. Such awesome tracks I've downloaded! Wanna hear?' he asked in all eagerness.

'No, thanks,' I smiled, 'but I'll catch you later, okay?'

He reached out and grasped my arm. 'Where are you going? I have nothing to do today. Wanna just hang out?'

My arm burned. The hero of this film had actually touched me. I was elated. But I thought it was strange that he had no one else to hang out with. Maybe he read my mind but at that moment he answered, 'You seem like a very interesting person. Besides, I have no one else to talk to about stuff that's not related to the movie and I really need a break. I overheard Punju saying you know a lot about Milan. Maybe you can show me around?'

I would have shown him all of Europe had he asked me! But for now I was glad to show him around Milan. I left my bike at the parking at the hotel and we walked around together. First I took him to my favourite place in Milan, the church of Santa Maria to see *The Last Supper*. We were allowed in for only ten minutes. I stood there and explained the concept of Da Vinci's form along with the rumour that the disciple next to Jesus was his wife. Rajvir seemed pretty impressed with my knowledge of history and art and asked me when I got out, 'Where did you read up about this stuff?'

I blushed for no reason and replied, 'I studied art history for more than a year in New York and then taught in Barcelona.'

'No! Seriously? I love New York!' he said with a twinkle in his eye. As he started to tell me about his favourite bar in New York, I realized a discussion on the architectural and cultural difference between the USA and Europe was best left alone.

Instead, I decided to do all the touristy things with him and took him to the Rectangle of Gold, the little piece of heaven, where every major designer in the world had a shop. We went in to a few shops where even the salesmen and women were dressed immaculately in designer clothes and looked down at you if you didn't spend at least five hundred euros. But with this gorgeous looking man by my side they seemed happy to let me try on whatever I wanted. They even allowed me to hold the latest Birkin, for which there was a three-year-long wait list, before it was delivered to the Italian prime minister's wife who had just come into a great deal of money from her alimony settlement.

I sighed and Rajvir asked me, 'What's wrong?'

I shook my head and said, 'I was just thinking that maybe one of the benefits of getting married is to at least get all that alimony when you divorce!' I laughed and he caught on to my joke.

I thanked the salesperson in her native language and left the store.

Rajvir followed me outside and asked, 'You know Spanish?'

I smiled at his faux pas but answered courteously, 'Yes. I also know Italian.'

'Oh my God! I am such a dunce. Of course! We're in Italy!' he said and grinned.

As we walked through the Rectangle, I suddenly thought of Siddharth who would have maxed out his credit card if I had wanted that Birkin. He had been creeping back into my thoughts pretty regularly these past few days. This break away from him was making me realize how important he was in my life. Life is nothing without people to love and people who love you. The trick is to understand that it is okay if they're not the same.

Rajvir and I were both very hungry by now having walked about all morning, so we decided to stop somewhere for lunch. Rather than blow a few hundred euros on an expensive place, I took him to the greatest sandwich bar in Milan, Bar della Crocetta. We ordered two paninis and two cappuccinos. I also ordered dessert, but he shook his head, claiming he had a shoot the next day and couldn't afford to let his six-pack look like a family pack. I laughed. I had heard the joke before but he said it with such ease that I loved it.

Next, we took a bus and went to the San Siro stadium, home of AC Milan. Rajvir loved it here. We sat in one of the benches looking out at the open green field bathed in warm afternoon sunlight. We were the only ones there. The security guards had shut the place for lunch time but we told them we were shooting a Bollywood movie and after a few photographs with them, Rajvir was allowed in without any trouble. The power of Indian cinema pervaded even touristy spots in Europe.

He took a long breath and exhaled. I looked at him and smiled, suddenly feeling shy. 'You're really pretty, Kaveri,' he said, smiling at me. I thought he was being patronizing but he continued, 'You're smart. Unlike anyone I've ever met and have this amazing intensity when you talk about stuff. It's really turning on.' I blushed. And then he leaned over and brought his face close to me, meshed his hand into my hair, looked deep into my eyes, pulled me closer and kissed me. It was delicious, and soft and gentle, with his cologne mingling into my hair, his mouth ardently pressing down on mine, and his tongue tenderly tantalizing my soul. It was warm and passionate, with our bodies locked into each other, a heat so raw that it emanated between us with both of us not wanting to let go for several seconds. As he moved his lips away from mine and took a deep breath holding my face close to his, I could feel his stubble brush against my cheek and the smell of his Armani cologne permeating every pore of my body. Incredible power mingled with desire and lust cascaded through my bones. I could feel a wave of immense desire welling up and taking me along for a ride as I caught my breath while he gently let me go. He was the most popular hero back in India. And here he was kissing me. My day was made. I felt this wondrous explosion of lust, love and infatuation tangled up because of the day that made it so perfect. When he pulled away my body was still tingling and I rubbed my hands against my arms. I was dying to tell Shy and Aditi, but knew that something like this needed to be kept quiet and between us. He looked away and seemed to be very far away. I didn't know if it was the kiss that had elicited such a reaction—had it been that bad?—but then he looked at me, smiled and said, 'Shall we go?'

I nodded.

When we got out the sun was still bright but it was already six in the evening. I asked him, 'Do you want to go back to the hotel or someplace else?'

He shrugged and said, 'Let's do something wild!'

I laughed and replied, 'Okay! I know just the place!'

And even though it was still too early to go, I took him to the hippest bar in town, the Loolapaloosa. We sat on the outdoor terrace watching the people go by. As the sun began to set, the bar became packed. Everyone seemed to be having a great time—the music was loud, the alcohol flowed freely, and the atmosphere was ebullient. Every now and then people would climb onto the bar and dance to the music and the cheers of the crowd. Before I knew it, I had been whisked away from my comfortable seat and onto the bar counter by one of the bartenders. My shyness took over till another girl joined me on the counter and soon five of us were doing a coordinated move on a new commercial hit. It was tremendous amount of fun having pink coloured shots and following it up with a bit of dark chocolate mousse. By the time we left, I was ready to pass out and Rajvir had run out of old Bollywood songs to croon to anyone willing to listen.

We decided to walk a little bit before we took a taxi, otherwise we would both pass out and neither of us would get to our hotels. We strolled through La Piazza, our laughter echoing in the night. Suddenly, I found myself all alone. I felt a moment of panic. Where had he gone? I heard footsteps then. Shadows playing in the dark. I opened my mouth to call out for him, when I saw his silhouette moving behind a pillar. I followed him, but he disappeared again. I started walking slowly backwards, keeping the columns in view. What game was this? Where was he? And then I walked into a body. I tried to scream, but he covered my mouth with his hand.

Armani. His smell is familiar. His touch, alien. Rough. Longing. His kiss so passionate that it leaves me breathless. I allow my instincts to run free in the darkness as I move in close and kiss him back, lust mingling with relief that it's him. I exult in his touch and the feel of his hard body along the length of mine. What am I getting into? But there is no room for coherent thought, just the overwhelming need to give in to the moment. Dear heaven, he feels so good. I tilt my head back and smell him. Musk. Sweat. He pushes me against a pillar and buries his lips against mine. Sensation spirals through my body, heating it to a fever pitch as I moan, longing for more. He tightens his arms around me, and his left hand moves down between our bodies, slowly unclasping the buttons of my blouse. Deft and swift, he knows his way around. He traces the contours of my cleavage with his fingers, and slides his hand inside and cups my breast. He catches the hardened bud between thumb and forefinger and rolls it gently until I groan. His other hand encircles my waist, slowly scratching his nails across my stomach. I inhale sharply. His hand trails over my trembling belly and slides further down in an intimate exploration that sends shards of exquisite sensation throughout my body. His lips moved down to the soft curve of my neck. He savours the delicate hollow as I hold back another sigh. His hand still inside my pants, he deftly uses his fingers to find places deep within me. Slow strokes. A passionate moan escapes my lips and he covers my mouth with more kisses. He doesn't let go as his vigour increases. Deep rubbing. He tears open my bra and takes my breast deep into his mouth, groaning as he slowly sucks on me. Holding me in place with his body, he removes his shirt. His body gleams in the moonlight. Muscled shoulders. Sculpted abs. Beautiful. A beauty borne out of hard work and discipline. Simply lithe and powerful. All male. Mine to possess. I run my mouth all over his body, devouring the man that a whole country desires. I love the feel of his body beneath my hands; I lightly caress him, feathering my fingers down his chest. He groans loudly as I reach for his belt and remove it in one swift move and unzip his jeans. The breath catches in my throat at the sight of his erection. I hear him hiss as my hands cup him and fondle him. He moans, and pushes against my hands. I let go and shimmy out of my shorts. He lifts me up, and I straddle him, my legs wrapped around his waist. I put my arms around his neck and lick his ears. I bite my lips, ever so slightly till they plump up, pink and swollen, urging him to taste them once more. We let ourselves linger; myriad sensations course through my body, heating it with a primitive hunger for him. His shoulders bunch under my hands as he lifts me again and positions me onto his carefully rigid penis and eases in. He watches as my body takes him in to the hilt, and begins to move. I moan loudly. He covers my mouth with his own, his tongue thrusting deep inside. Mighty movements. Shorter thrusts. Quicker now. A wild hunger raging in us. Urgent kissing. He holds me tightly as he takes his fill of me. Bolder moves. Harder. Stronger. Entwined in each other's embrace. Rhythmic movements. Warm skin, fiery veins throbbing with hot blood, the faint odour of sweat and musk and old oak. Urging me to the brink until I shattered into a thousand splinters. We feel a huge wave stirring, a grinding feeling that is running away, bursting, buzzing, it explodes and wave after wave of sensation wash over us. He leaves me there. Gone again.

I scrambled to make myself decent. Just as I got my breath, I heard footsteps again.

'Hey, there you are. Where did you get lost?' he asked nonchalantly as he came into view.

I smiled and replied, 'Somewhere in the shadows.'

30
The Morning After Dark

When I awoke the next morning I was lying in a strange bed, alone. The room was extremely large with an equally humongous bathroom. I tried to get up, but my head began to spin so I lay back down. Looking around, I noticed a tall glass of orange juice kept on the bedside table along with a note—Off to shoot. Take it easy. Catch you later.

And then the events of the last twenty-four hours came flooding back. The night had ended with Rajvir calling for the car to bring him back to his hotel. I couldn't believe he had the stamina to still get up and shoot after the amount he had drunk, but I supposed even an actor had a job to do that was way more important than sleeping in. Fortunately, I could pull the covers over my head and go back to sleep. I didn't need to be at my job till noon.

But I was restless and my stomach felt queasy, so I got out of bed. I was wearing only a shirt. Had something else happened after we came back? I gulped down the juice and walked slowly to the bathroom. The gold filigree work around the bathtub and the mirror was exquisite, as were the beautiful carvings on the ceiling. Soft towels were stacked on the outstretched arms of the statue of a boy who looked delighted to be where he was. The opulence seemed a bit much for a bathroom but then probably they had to cater to tourists who believed that they must be surrounded by art even when taking a tinkle.

I decided against a bubble bath and took a hot shower instead. When I came out I wondered if I could order room service. Since Punjwani was paying for this in any case I went ahead and ordered a lavish breakfast. But when the eggs, toast and my cappuccino came all I could have was one toast and sipped on the coffee very gingerly.

I couldn't shake off the feeling that I was a horrible person. I had slept with a man on what could not even be called a 'date', and I had cheated on my boyfriend. What kind of a person was I? Who had I become? Just another notch on Rajvir's bedpost? Even telling myself that Siddharth and I were on a break did not make things easy for my heart. I knew it was wrong. The only question now was should I tell Siddharth or leave him in the dark. I didn't know what to do.

I asked the receptionist to call a cab for me since I was running late, then I quickly got dressed and left before someone from the hotel or the film crew spotted me and spread gossip about the hero and the woman he brought back. Unfortunately, Bela was still in the hotel, and she walked into the lobby just as I was heading out towards my cab. She immediately spotted me and asked, 'Kaveri! What are you doing here?'

I looked towards my cab and said after a slight pause, 'I had actually come to take you for the shoot.'

'Oh but I don't have any scenes till the evening when we are shooting in a church. They're lighting up for it now. Has there been a change in the schedule? Are we shooting there in the daytime?' she asked, concerned. Bela was a professional, and while her command over the language was shaky, she knew everything about her schedule, locations and costumes. She had to if she was going to become the number one actress in Bollywood.

I quickly tried to come up with a logical explanation for my presence. Oh why wasn't my brain processing fast enough! 'Oh, I must have got it wrong. I'm so sorry,' I said lamely.

'You must be thinking about the other shoot I need to do. The still shots for the perfume campaign at one o' clock. I have an interview with *Vogue* before that. They want to put me on the cover next month and since we won't be back before they go in for print, they've sent the editor here.' No one could keep up with her, constantly flitting from shootings to script readings and appearances as she was. I wondered if she had any close friends in Mumbai. I had never seen her share anything personal with Carl or even Shy, who had been her stylist for so long.

'Now that you're here, would you mind staying for the interview? I find myself feeling a little nervous,' she asked, smiling.

I smiled back. I really just wanted to get back to my hotel and sleep, but I couldn't say no. I told the cab to go back and went with her to the coffee shop where the editor of *Vogue* was waiting for Bela. They air kissed and started speaking. The interview went off very well; I didn't have to step in even once to help Bela. It was clear she had been working hard on her accent, and her English was now perfect.

The reporter left after the interview. Then Bela turned to me and said, 'You know the advice you gave me the other day came to very good use.'

I looked at her with a quizzical expression. She explained further, 'The dirty talk. I tried it a few nights ago and it was received well.'

Received well. By whom? But I dared not ask; I didn't know how she would respond to such a personal question. So I smiled and said, 'I'm glad I could help.'

Then she surprised me by asking, 'Are you seeing anybody?'

I didn't know what to say. Last night I had seen someone intimately and a few weeks ago I had been seeing someone very emotionally. But just then I had no idea who I was seeing and if I would ever again. So I shook my head and said, 'Not really. It's complicated.'

Bela lit up what must have been the longest cigarette in the world and took a deep drag and answered, 'All relationships are complicated. That's why it's fun. It's fun to be a girl and ruin someone's life, no?' she asked in jest and laughed her small giggly laugh that made men swoon for her.

I didn't know if it was the leftover alcohol in my blood or her laugh that made her seem like someone I could confide in. Later, I would look back at this moment and think that if I had only shut up and waited for Shyamolie to come back from the shoot, I would still have a job or a life, but at that moment I had thought Bela would understand exactly what I was going through.

'I kind of . . . umm . . . slept with . . . Rajvir . . .' I said hesitantly. 'And now I don't know how to tell my boyfriend in Mumbai.'

Bela stopped and stared at me. The thin smoke emanating from the filter of her cigarette snaked up between us in a menacing dance as if to hypnotize me before it evaporated into the shadows of the columns in the coffee shop. It seemed as if time had stood still. I didn't know what to say and I couldn't gauge her reaction. She stubbed out her unfinished cigarette, got up abruptly and walked out.

I ran after her. 'Bela, what happened?'

She whirled when I caught up with her in the lobby and glared at me. In her six-inch Prada heels, even her five-six frame towered over my five-five. 'What do you mean you slept with Rajvir?'

I knew that something was wrong. I shook my head and said, 'I . . . I'm not sure. I was drunk and I woke up in his room this morning.'

'What? Then why did you say you slept with him?' she shrieked.

I knew that it would be better for me to keep quiet right now but I wanted to clear my name and appease her. So I hastily said, 'It's not like that. I took him on a tour of Milan yesterday. I had too much to drink so he brought me back to his hotel to sleep it off.'

'He was taking me to Torcello . . .' she muttered to herself. 'Bastard.'

'Bela, nothing happened,' I tried to add but she didn't want to hear anymore.

She rushed off to her room and I slumped down on a large sofa in the lobby with my head in my hands. I knew then that I had made the biggest mistake of my life. Things only got worse in the evening. I went to the shoot to find Shyamolie but she wasn't there. When I went in search of Rajvir, I saw Bela and him arguing in her make-up van. I quietly climbed into the driver's seat to hear better, and curled into a ball so no one could see me.

'How could you Rajvir?' Bela was shouting.

'Baby, I swear I didn't have sex with her. She's making it up. I was with her for only an hour,' Rajvir replied. Liar! I could go in there right now and show them the hickey he gave me on my breast.

'Then what the hell is she saying? Why did you even spend time with her? Was our sex not good enough? Didn't I talk dirty enough for you?' she hollered.

'Honey, you're an amazing woman and I would never do anything to hurt you. You've got to trust me. I knew you were busy at the spa last night, so I went out to get a drink. I was going to come back immediately after and worship your body all night, like you know I do. But I saw her at the bar and she was totally sloshed. She was saying something about how she missed her boyfriend and then she passed out. I didn't know where the crew stayed so I brought her back here so she could sleep it off. I had to sleep on the couch and you know how that affects my back. It's been hurting since the morning and you haven't asked about me even once. C'mon babe, look at yourself, you're a goddess . . . she's just an old woman. Why would I be with her when I can be with you? Come here now and rub my back like you know how,' Rajvir said. I heard someone shuffling inside, and then he moaned. 'There's my girl. Now gimme some of that dirty talk that you're so good at. You know how I like it. Come here. Let me show you what I'm good at,' he murmured.

I had heard enough. I crawled out of the van and went straight back to my hotel room. Shyamolie was sitting there coordinating all the costumes for all the artists. One look at me and she asked with concern, 'What happened? You look like death!'

And before I could open my mouth I burst into tears that lasted several hours. The misery had just begun.

31

Back to Square One

I didn't go back on set that day. I didn't know how to face Rajvir or Bela or the entire crew. My eyes were burning and my head was spinning. I didn't know what to do. Shy tried to get me to eat something but there was a churning in my stomach that couldn't even take in the sight of any food. I felt nauseous and heartbroken.

How could Rajvir do something so horrible? I knew we would never have a relationship but the decent thing to do was at least own up to it. Taking responsibility for something builds integrity. But so few realize the value of it. I hadn't come on to him. He had wanted to spend the day with me. And then after those drinks, he was the one who initiated our sex. Sure I could have stopped him but it happened all so fast that I didn't even have a moment to think about it. But even if I let all that go, he left me juice! All I could think about was that when I woke up he had left a glass of juice with a note on it. Now if a man didn't care, he wouldn't do that. But he did. He left me juice!

I knew I had truly lost the plot when I tried telling Shy this and she gave me the one eyebrow lift look. Which meant that I had lost the plot. Bad relationships bring out the true test of character. How you respond makes you who you are. I wasn't responding well at all!

Shyamolie tried to make me feel better by telling me all about what had happened with her the day before. While she had been lazing around in the room yesterday, one of the lead dancers had called her room up and asked if she wanted to go out for a bit. Since she had nothing to do, she had decided to go with him.

'The best moments in life are always unplanned and unexpected,' she babbled. Both of them had been eyeing each other for a while but they hadn't spoken to each other for fear of rejection.

'I seriously believe the world would be a better place if we stopped judging men by their accomplishments and women by their looks. Let equality reign!' Shy said.

He had got tickets to a Milan fashion show from an uncle of his who was working with an international designer and taken her there. At first she had thought he was gay. But then she realized he was as connected to his masculine side as he was allied with his feminine side. This was the type of man Shy needed. She didn't care about a macho man who was tall, handsome or rich. She had never dreamt of finding the perfect man, only the *perfect love*. After the fashion show, they had had dinner at a lovely Italian bistro where they sat and talked for hours about their dreams and hers. Shy had always lived life as though she were playing a hand of poker—she never revealed her cards until she was sure of winning. So she had always held back till now. With this man she could feel herself giving away her ace.

'Oh K,' she said, a dreamy look in her eyes, 'I think I'm in love.'

I looked at her dryly. What did she know about love? She was going to go through the spin cycle of love and come out all wrung like me.

'Trust me,' I said. 'It's overrated. And it's never going to make you happy. The irony is that just when you think he's your knight in shining armour, he turns out to be a retard in tin foil.'

'Oh, come on. You're just saying that now. But once you get married, you'll let go of all this cynicism,' Shy replied making me realize sometimes an ignorance to alternatives might be the most blissful state to be in.

'Marriage is like that light at the end of the tunnel before you realize it's an oncoming train,' I said wryly. It was what I had learnt from Aditi.

Shy came over and hugged me, 'Depression is such a waste of time. I know you're going through this bad time, but forget it, K. Rajvir is a loser. When we get back to Mumbai, you'll go back to Sid and have a rocking life. Now let's go to our shoot. We have work to do!'

But I wasn't in the mood. I told her to go ahead, I would go later.

Half an hour after Shyamolie left, I got a visitor. It was RT. Punjwani's assistant.

'Shyamolie told me you weren't feeling well. I came to check on you,' he said as he sat down on the only chair in the room that was not covered with clothes.

'That's so sweet of you. Thank you,' I replied while trying to remove some of Shy's things from the couch to make room for myself. 'Can I get you something? Should I ask for some tea?'

RT nodded. 'Tea will be nice, though I need to be rushing back soon. Mr Scunjay won't like it if I'm gone for too long. Listen, Kaveri, the reason why I'm here is because Mr Punjwani had a chat with Bela earlier today.'

My heart sank. Instead of letting him continue I distracted him with small talk, 'Do you want chamomile or Earl Grey? Here try some cookies. They're absolutely delicious. And they're free. Did you know that you can order up to three plates of cookies here and won't be charged for them? Isn't that amazing? And fruits! You can order as many as you want. That's perfect if you are on a diet, but with all that yummy Italian food I doubt anyone would want to continue with a diet. Oh look, the tea is here. Would you like some sugar? One cube? Milk?' And as I handed RT his tea I realized that I had run out of things to say. I sat down on the sofa with my cup, and waited.

For the next several minutes, RT slurped his tea and when he was done, he placed the cup on the table and cleared his throat. 'Can I go on?' he asked.

I nodded, even though I didn't really need to hear him say it. I knew what was going to happen.

'Kaveri,' RT said softly, 'you have to go home. Bela doesn't need you anymore. And Mr Punjwani doesn't want to keep any more people here than necessary. I'm sorry.'

I nodded and smiled weakly, 'It's okay. I was missing home anyway.'

RT told me that he had booked me that same evening back to Mumbai and that I could come on the set and say goodbye to everyone. I told him I would think about it. Then he left.

I knew it was because of Rajvir that Bela wanted me to leave. And frankly I didn't want to stay. I would never be able to face both of them again. I felt miserable. One small mistake on my part and I was back to square one. I thought I had evolved as a person and become wiser and more mature. But all I had done was lose my job and alienate the people who I had grown close to.

I finished packing my suitcase and sat down. I didn't know if I should go on the set to say goodbye to everyone. But before I could think further I decided I must. So I dragged myself on the set where Bela and Rajvir were shooting a scene.

'Roll sound, roll camera,' the director instructed as they took their places.

'Take five,' the clap boy shouted and the scene began.

Bela was leaning against a bridge wearing a short, fitted white skirt, a dark blue chiffon blouse and knee length boots. She ran her hand through her hair and looked into Rajvir's eyes. The single diamond bracelet that glinted in the light seemed out of place for the middle-class girl she was portraying. Another costume battle Shy had lost. I could imagine Shyamolie trying to talk Bela out of it. I would miss the moments that made a film a film. I now realized why Aditi missed being on a set. I would miss it too. It was a privilege for ordinary folks to be so close to the glamour and the madness.

'I don't know what to say to you. You betrayed me. How can I ever forgive that?' Bela said.

Rajvir looked into her eyes and replied, 'I didn't. I promise you. I love you, Maya. I've always loved you. How can there ever be another? You consume me. My thoughts, my life, my heart. You're a part of me. Like I'm a part of you. But Maya, I don't have a lot to offer you. Just a one-bedroom house where I live with my mother. And she's very important to me. I love you, but I can't afford you.'

'Maya' turned, put her hands on either side of his face and said in perfect Hindi, 'Living in that one room might be difficult, Raj. But living without you is impossible.'

Oh what a load of crap, I thought. I'll bet she wouldn't live a day without her Louis Vuitton if it happened in real life. She hardly looked like the 'girl next door' she was supposed to be portraying. She looked every inch the horrid woman who was getting me thrown off this set.

'Raj' adjusted his coat, took out a ring and asked, 'Maya Mehrotra, will you make me the happiest man on earth and be my wife?'

'Cut!' the director shouted and then gave instructions for the same scene to be shot from another angle. While the camera and light technicians scurried around to prepare the shot, Bela and Rajvir stepped down to get their make-up refreshed. Rajvir saw me but quickly looked away. That movement sent a fresh wave of hurt right through my body. Bela saw me and walked towards me.

'Hi Bela,' I said nervously, 'I'm leaving in a few hours so I wanted to say bye.'

She nodded. 'Have a safe trip back.'

Caught between rage and frustration, I wanted to tell her what a bitch she was and that I hoped the film was a flop. But just then Punjwani came over and said, 'Bachcha! I heard you're going back because your mother is unwell. How sad. But we shall meet you in Mumbai. You take care. Give my regards to your mother. All the best.' He shook my hand and walked away, without having given me the chance to say anything in response. Apparently Punju didn't want anyone to know that he had fired me as that would lead to too many questions and he hated questions and confrontations.

I walked around the set, saying bye to all the crew members I had become friendly with. Tears stung my eyes; I felt as if I was leaving a family behind. Heartbroken, I headed back to the taxi that was dropping me to the airport; Shy was walking with me.

I started speaking first. 'It was my fault. He did what he had to do.'

'He's a spineless asshole. And after this I'm definitely quitting and starting my own label,' she said spewing venom at Punjwani and Rajvir. 'And how dare that bitch who didn't know her ds from her ts fire you! Slut! How many men does she need?'

'Forget it, Shy,' I said. I honestly didn't care anymore. I had done my job and I had done it well—Bela had turned from a Russian hustler to a Bollywood diva. But I was going to miss Shyamolie. As long as I was working with Bela I had had a reason to hang out with Shy. But now that our paths would be different I wondered if we would see each other that often.

She had been thinking the same thing for she said, 'When I come back, I want us to work together on this label thing okay?'

I smiled. I didn't know how that would ever work out, but I thought it was sweet of her to offer me something to hold on to.

'You look after yourself,' she said when we reached my cab, her throat choked with tears as she hugged me tightly.

I nodded. 'You, too. And hold on to that boy. Great love is hard to find. Don't screw it up by overthinking it. And don't let these people get to you. It's just this industry.'

She sniffed and said, 'Wah! You're telling me? Then I know you're ready to move on!'

And I was. I was done with the film industry. I had seen enough of it to understand that people weren't real. They gave up little bits of themselves to the characters they portrayed on the sets, in their films, living half lives, incomplete. Sometimes the hope lies in something ending and being done with. There is a tremendous peace in a conclusion and closure.

As for me, my journey was yet to begin. And I had to face my demons before I could take the first step.

32
The Ugly Truth

It might take us years to understand that what we really wanted was wrong all along. But that revelation finally leads us on our right journey. Back in Mumbai I had a huge choice to make—should I tell Siddharth about my dalliance or not? But as I thought about it more and more, I realized it was an easy choice to make. Honesty was important in all relationships, even if it meant losing the person you loved the most. So I called him and asked him to meet me at my place.

I slaved in the kitchen, preparing his favourite dishes, even though I barely knew how to cook. I desperately wanted to please him, and when you are afraid of losing someone, you hold on just a little bit tighter. I was going to try my damnedest best to hold on to him. He came promptly at eight o'clock. As soon as I shut the door after him, he pulled me into his arms and hugged me. And then he started kissing me. And I kissed him back. It was clear from his ardour that he wanted to take this into the bedroom, but I didn't want to make another mistake. I wanted him to know the truth before we slept together again; I wanted to make a fresh start.

'Let's have a drink first,' I said, moving away from him to open a bottle of wine I had chilling in the fridge. Rather than tell him that I had been fired, I began by asking him about what he had been up to. Men always like talking about themselves and when you give them a bit of encouragement and appreciation, they can gloat for hours. After an hour of drinking and talking, I suggested we have dinner and told him that I had cooked the entire meal myself instead of ordering in.

'Yum, look at that,' he said admiring my hard work while I laid the table with bright red crockery and shining silver cutlery.

'So this is whole-wheat pasta in arrabiata sauce with all your favourite veggies. Sautéed paneer, some garlic bread with low-fat butter and mushroom risotto with red wine,' I said, uncovering the dishes and showing him.

He gave me a long kiss and said tenderly, 'I love you for taking the effort. I know you must be so jet lagged. We could have easily eaten out, yet you did all this. Thank you.'

I smiled and said, 'Let's eat.' I poured him some more wine. I told him that Shy had found a man she thought she was in love with. He laughed at my suggestion that the first loves were testing waters for the rest of the loves to come. Somehow I couldn't bring myself to tell him about Rajvir. He was being so nice. The temptation to let it go was overwhelming. Obviously Rajvir would never say anything to him and Shy was the only other person who knew, and she wouldn't breathe a word about it to a soul. I could probably keep it quiet forever.

But that was not me. I had grown up. While I could have thought of doing something like that when I was younger, with Arjun, but now that I was wiser, I was certainly not going to keep any secrets from Siddharth.

'Sid,' I started after we had finished eating and were sitting at the table with the second bottle of wine, 'I have something to tell you.'

And I told him. I told him how drunk I was, how terribly lonely I was, how immensely attracted I was, and how sorry I was. I told him that it hadn't meant anything to me. That I was feeling horrible, low and completely worthless. Siddharth just stared at me in complete disbelief. When I reached out to hold his hand, he got up from the table and went to stand by the window. He stared outside for a very long time. And all the while I watched him, terrified. No one can ever truly describe fear. Or love. I loved him so much and now I was afraid I was going to lose my love.

'Siddharth, what I did was reprehensible. I am an awful person. There is no excuse for my behaviour. I . . . I'm so sorry for hurting you.' I was crying openly, uncontrollably. 'This is the most wonderful relationship I've ever had and I went and screwed it up. Please, please find it in your heart to forgive me. I can't be without you. I learnt that the hard way. I want us to be together, Siddharth.'

'That's not your choice anymore,' he said coldly, cutting into my melancholy. 'I gave you everything. Everything! And you couldn't even be faithful to me? What's wrong with you?'

I shook my head and sobbed quietly. He was right. I was doing to him exactly what Ray had done to me. I was perpetuating the cycle of pain. I was no better than his ex-wife; she, too, had been unfaithful to him. I was breaking him as a man. I felt like killing myself. I must have said that out loud because he turned to face me, furious, 'Oh no! Don't you dare turn this guilt trip on me. You take responsibility for your actions.'

He was right. I had to be stronger. When you ask for forgiveness without any excuses or baggage, you surrender yourself. Only then you really set your soul free. I needed to do that.

I stood up and said, 'I'm sorry, Siddharth. I am truly sorry. And I love you. I really do.'

'Stop saying that!' he shouted and just like that he walked out of the door, slamming it behind him.

I crumpled against the wall and wept for another hour. You can't suppress pain no matter how hard you try. The only way to get over it is to accept it, embrace it and then release the pain. Only then, you can be completely free.

I didn't want to call anyone. I didn't want to tell Aditi. I didn't even want to call Sid to ask him where he was and what he was doing; I didn't have the right anymore.

I realized that sometimes the purpose of our lives is not what we want from it, but what others need from us. We are the reservoirs of love *they* live on. And I had failed yet again in a relationship.

33

I Do Begins with You

Siddharth messaged me the next day saying that it was *over*. He didn't want to see me or speak to me ever again. I was so heartbroken I didn't know what to do. But I decided I wasn't going to sit at home and cry. I had done enough of that in my life. I was going to get dressed and go out and find a job. Even if I was dying inside.

So I went to the art galleries and gave my résumé to the managers there and told them I was willing to work all hours for whatever pay and start immediately. A few offered me a job right away and said they would email me the details of the position. I felt encouraged. I decided to visit the gallery apartment that Siddharth had taken me to the day I met him.

Mamta greeted me like an old friend. She didn't have an exhibition on at that moment, but there were a few paintings still in the gallery that took my breath away. She noticed me standing in front of a large canvas of a woman standing with her back to the viewer. There were yellow sparks in the distance and it seemed as if the woman was looking at a light that had just gone by. I felt I could connect to it. Mamta came and stood next to me. She said, 'I've got some amazing chocolate chip mini muffins that will melt in your mouth. Why don't we go to the back room and have an espresso with them?' I nodded, wiping away a tear quickly.

When she had made the espresso and heated the muffins, she sat down on the sofa and said, 'So tell me what's wrong?'

And even though I hardly knew this woman, I felt a strong connection to her and found myself opening up to her. I told her that I had been unfaithful to Siddharth and he had broken up with me. I also told her I had no job, no love and apparently no life.

'Darling, don't focus on things going wrong in your life. Focus on how to make things right. The world is full of ways and means to waste time. It is the focused few who succeed in life. I've always felt that love should be secondary to a career. Of course, it's important, but it's not the only thing. You've made it the first and only thing in your life. All you want to do is find a man who loves you, with whom you can be forever. And your career has taken a back seat till you find that person.' And I realized she was right. Although I had enjoyed teaching at the university, I had stayed on in Barcelona for two years because of Ray, not my job. And back in Mumbai I had been content to work as an interpreter for Bela rather than chase my dreams of starting my own gallery because I had Siddharth. She continued, 'Be gentle with your own soul. Let go of the pain that comes with guilt and sadness. Others live their lives their way. You have to live your own. Holding on to negativity will only wear you down. Stop hoping, expecting, wishing and wanting from someone. Be true to yourself for a change.'

I admitted as much to Mamta. 'What the hell am I doing wrong?' I asked.

She took a sip of her espresso and mulled on that for a moment before replying, 'If you want autonomy and independence you have to earn it. Define who you are and what you want to do with the rest of your life. So many of us talk about the things we hope to do, but so few of us actually do the things we want to. So far you've done things because you wanted to earn money, or make someone happy. If you truly wanted to pursue something then you would stick to it, be what may. Your job is not to make everyone happy. Your job is to do the best you can today with the goals you've set for yourself. You need to define those goals. Circumstances play an important role in success. Intention is not the only thing that matters. Doesn't mean we give up. Only means we need to be patient.'

'Okay, that's about my career. But what about my love life?' I asked, impatient to know all the answers.

Mamta smiled as she spoke, 'Transitions are by necessity full of sadness, especially if the past is made up of some happy memories. Be kind and true to yourself first and foremost. When you have a strong connection to your internal power, the quality of your life is very different from when you let the outside world decide for you. You tell me. Were you in love with any of the men?'

I thought about it. Hadn't I really loved them? Hadn't I given everything to them? Some of them had let me down. Some I had failed.

'You need to define what your goals are with relationships as well. One minute you want to be married, next you want a live-in boyfriend, then you want to have kids, but you don't want to be settled, you still want fun. That's all a bit confusing for the universe,' she said helping herself to another muffin.

'I thought I loved Siddharth.'

Mamta shook her head, 'For a great relationship one has to be accepting of who that person is in totality. Not what you think the other person is or can be for you. Pattern thinking gives instantaneous reaction. If the same thing is happening again, take a moment to not react. Think how you can change it! A happily-ever-after doesn't begin with "I do", it starts with you. Every woman deserves to be pampered, cherished and worshiped. And every man deserves to be loved completely. It is okay to belong to the former group, as long as you don't lie about it to yourself.'

'I didn't lie,' I said defiantly. 'I'm not a cheater. I've never cheated.'

'Well then that relationship wasn't the correct one for you anyway,' Mamta said, getting up to grab the remote to change the AC temperature in the room.

I thought about it for a moment and said, 'Why do you say that?'

'Some of us go through many relationships in our lives to find the correct one. Sometimes we cheat on those we think we love hoping to find the right one. That doesn't really make us cheaters. If you cheated because you were unhappy and felt it was not right then you're not a cheater. But if you did so even though you believed that Siddharth was the man of your dreams then you did it for excitement. Then you are a cheater,' she explained.

I was shocked. Was I a cheater? Did I really do it for fun and the thrill of having slept with Rajvir? Or was it a heady infatuation that got me to deceive the man of my dreams? I didn't have the answers then. They would come to me much later on a crisp chilly evening when Siddharth would help me find them. But for now she had given me something to think about.

'Understanding what people need and giving exactly that is the key to success. Trying to give what you think is correct is just a waste of time. Life is too short!' she said waving her hands around. 'Laugh when you can, apologize when you should, and let go of what you can't change. Love deeply and forgive quickly. Make that your motto and you'll do great. When life becomes clearer, minute issues won't matter,' Mamta smiled. 'And remember, things change you for the better. You might have loved art once upon a time. But now it's just your hobby. Don't make it your job. You're not that person anymore. The reason we suffer is that we think our identity and worth as human beings is inextricably tied to our careers or relationships. It's not.'

I was shocked. Here was someone telling me that art was no longer my life. Was she right? I took a moment to think about what she had said.

'You were attracted to Siddharth because he defined art to you. He was art. The sombre, beautiful, regal, mature, deep, reflective piece that you found most attractive. You hung him on your wall of life to admire and show off. But after some time, you moved away into your bedroom where there was a pop culture poster of a film. You might still want to prove to yourself that you deserve that art and you are that drawing room. But you're not. You've changed. Identity is strongest with your personal belief and faith in yourself. Listen, sweetheart, there is no such thing as unconditional support or everlasting love. Don't expect it from men. There is only unwavering belief in yourself. Regret is the outcome of unwise choices you make today. So choose wisely from here on.'

'If the Universe is trying to tell me something, I seriously wish it would be a little clearer!' I said getting up. I had stayed much longer than I had planned. It was now time for me to become stronger and make my own decisions.

'Only when you give your actions serious consideration will you be able to face the serious consequences without fear,' she said giving me a tight hug.

I thanked her for a lovely time. I had never felt so much at peace after a break-up as I had today. Maybe she was right. Maybe I was more pop than avant-garde. Maybe my career was not in an art gallery. Maybe it was to do something else. Going back to square one only helps you make a new blueprint. Experience can never set you back. It only takes you forward. I was going to use all my experience and understanding of this world to remake myself.

34
Career Karma

I decided to give men and relationships a wide berth from now on. I wouldn't even ogle at a man lest I give him the wrong idea. I was going to figure out how to get my career back on track. I knew I wanted to do something with the film industry but I didn't know what.

I was not good at styling so I couldn't step into the gap that would be created when Shyamolie started her own label. I just didn't have it in me to throw things together and create a new look. I had been wearing the same look for years, and if I couldn't experiment on new things myself, I could hardly do it on a daily basis for celebrities. Styling and doing costumes was a gift. And the gift of aesthetics I just didn't have.

So what else remained? I sat at my window and thought about what the other elements of filmmaking were. I knew in my heart I wanted to be in films. I had to mingle the two worlds of my past—art and film. I just didn't know how. I could not go into any technical aspects like sound, editing, cinematography or lighting. I had to do something that was creative and still arty. I wished Shy was around to help me. Perhaps it was time I spoke to Aditi; she had been in the film industry for some time and could probably help me. I had not called her since I came back from Milan. I didn't want to tell her that Siddharth had broken up with me. I knew she would be on my side but a part of me felt that maybe she had put a hex on the relationship. Siddharth and I had been doing really well till she came into the picture. I know it was a silly thought but somehow it was taking up all my logical judgement. Sometimes the people who matter most to you are the ones who can really pull you down. And there are some bridges you need to burn to make new paths on your journey of life. I decided not to call her and try to figure things out for myself.

I desperately wanted to share my experience with Siddharth and I knew he would help me. But it would have been completely wrong. Detachment is easier said than done. But when done helps live life easier. So I did what came naturally to me: I went on to Twitter and asked what would best suit a girl like me with no connections and no technical finesse. Immediately I got back a few answers. An assistant director. A producer. A music director. A costume stylist. A set designer.

I thought about on my way to the new cafe I had found. It was a small Italian place behind a school in Andheri. It had red chairs with chequered tablecloths and wooden round tables. Posters of famous operas adorned the walls and I felt this was the closest I was going to get to being in Italy for a while. But what I loved most about it was that it reminded me of nothing. Which was exactly what I needed. A fresh start with a new place to call my own.

'Can I get you something?' asked the waiter who came to take my order. He was neither cute, nor my type.

'Yes. A cappuccino with a shot of vanilla and no interruptions for the next two hours until I'm ready to order lunch,' I said pleadingly.

He smiled and said, 'Of course, ma'am.'

Now to get back to figuring out my career. I sat with a diary opened. I've always believed in writing stuff down; seeing the pros and cons on paper makes it easier to arrive at a decision.

So I started off with the first suggestion: assistant director. I thought about it but realized that that was not for me. I had seen those boys and girls run around on the film set, catering to the whims and fancies of the director and the actors. I was too old to start that now. Besides, I doubted if the assistants were even paid.

I wasn't musically inclined, so anything to do with music was a bust. I was artistically inclined. Maybe a set designer's job. But how would I be hired as a set designer? I would have to assist someone first. And was I really good at doing up interiors at the drop of a hat? I hadn't even done a course for it. No one would take me.

'Here are some cookies ma'am. They're being promoted today in our cafe and our customers get a free plate for trial.' The waiter kept the plate of cookies and left me alone again.

I looked at the cookies and wondered if I should have them. Empty calories that I did not need. I had put on weight since I had come back from Barcelona. But I decided I needed one to get my blood sugar up and my thoughts flowing easier. Excuses of every overweight woman.

I was still pondering over my options when I saw a group of women enter the cafe. I recognized one of them instantly—Deepa Malhotra, the producer of the reality show I had been on. The woman who had helped me get over a heartbreak once upon a time. The waiter seated them at a table behind me and left after taking their order. I wondered if I should go up to her and say hello. I hadn't met her since I'd been eliminated from the reality show, The Perfect Bahu. Those had been fun weeks.

I plucked up my courage and went up to her, 'Hello Ms Malhotra,' I said a little shyly.

She looked up and smiled, but didn't recognize me. Maybe it was my hair. I definitely needed a haircut. 'I'm Kaveri. From the show you helped me with, The Perfect Bahu, a few years ago,' I said hoping she would remember and I wouldn't make a bigger fool of myself.

'Ah yes!' she said and stood up to give me a hug. 'You were quite splendid on the show. But you never came to collect your cheque after you were eliminated. Where did you disappear?'

I smiled more confidently and replied, 'I went on to do different things after that. I got exactly what I had needed from the show; the money just seemed superfluous after that.'

'Nonsense,' she said waving her hand around. 'You deserve that money. You must come and collect it. I'll give you my card. I'm no longer just a producer. I've become CEO of my group.'

This was so unlike Punjwani who would have probably torn up the cheque and saved himself the money. I replied with a beaming smile, 'Oh congratulations! That's such fabulous news.'

'Thank you,' she said and added as an afterthought, 'what are you doing nowadays?'

We moved slightly away from her group while the waiter served them their drinks and starters. I didn't want to impose on her, so I tried to keep it brief, 'Well, I went abroad to study art and then taught for a few years. I came back earlier this year and worked with a film crew for a few months. I'm actually looking for a job now.' I kept the details to myself. On our last meeting I had poured out my heart and she had probably come away with the impression that I was a babe in the woods. Now, some three years later, I had better appear wiser and more mature.

'Well your hot air balloon was quite the show for us. We didn't air it, though,' she said when my eyes popped. 'But I realized then that you have enough spunk to do many successful things. Forget art-shart. You're more suited for the limelight! Come and see me on Friday. I could use you somewhere!'

I thanked her profusely and we went back to our separate tables. I looked down at my plate of cookies and my diary. I didn't need either of them now.

I had an opportunity.

35

A Whole New Ballgame

Deepa had indeed moved up in life. She was now managing an entire company that had its fingers in many pies. From managing Bollywood talent to buying intellectual property, from producing films to publishing a magazine that wrote about them. I could sense the excitement in the atmosphere as soon as I entered the office. Instead of the small place that she had earlier, these offices took up three floors of a building in Andheri. The ground floor consisted of the lobby and two large rooms on either side meant for conferences. The staff sat on the first floor, and had access to a kitchen and pantry. The second floor was where the CEO and COO—Deepa and her partner—had their offices. The whole office was done up tastefully in beige with chairs and sofas in bright colours. There were large windows on every floor, and the whole office was flooded with natural light. Surprisingly, many windows were open, and unlike the false ceilings and artificial lights and AC vents that were found in most offices, this office had air conditioners in corners that could be switched off. It seemed like a very homey atmosphere. I could see myself fitting in, but my heart told me not to get too excited. Deepa might not even offer me a job here. She might actually tell me to do something completely different.

'So tell me,' she said, leaning back in her large red chair, 'what do you want to do?'

Deepa had put on weight over the last few years. Her hair had become longer and was streaked in dull copper tones. She wore several diamond rings and one couldn't tell if she was married or not. From wearing business suits, she now wore a very expensive sari. It made her look older and more formidable. If she had been like this a few years ago I would probably not have poured my heart out about Arjun and might not have found myself in the reality show.

She nodded at the office boy who brought in two mugs of steaming coffee and some cookies and left.

I thought about what she had asked. I didn't want to start with what I didn't want to do. But I didn't know what I wanted to do. I had just been thinking about it incessantly for the last couple of days, but hadn't reached any conclusions. While I was hesitating she spoke, 'Sometimes your first instincts are right. Tell me, what's your first instinct.'

'Films,' I said with confidence. 'It's taken me a while to come to this decision. I thought I would always be good with art and since I loved it so much I spent so much time learning about it and teaching and being around it. But lately I have realized that my interest in art was more of a hobby. It stopped exciting me. When I was on the sets of a film or doing costumes with an actor, I felt a little bit of glamour rub on me. I was addicted. I think I need more.'

Deepa nodded and said, 'Yes we all get sucked into the glamour. But we do not realize that glamour is hard work. All the things we see have far more blood and sweat going into them than a corporate job. There are late nights, endless changes, star tantrums, numerous adjustments . . . it goes on. The final product, the film, only takes shape after many months of hard work. There's no immediate gratification. And it takes a toll on your body. If you don't have the stamina, it will wear you out.'

I thought about that for a second. I was not young anymore. I couldn't run around till the wee hours and then be back on set early the next morning. I needed something that was not quite so hectic, and perhaps something that could be done indoors. I didn't mind the hard work.

Deepa thought about it for a while.

'I think you have a lot of spunk. You would do well in front of the camera or in a PR job,' she said looking me up and down and trying to gauge what would suit me best. 'You could even do writing work for us. You can be a reporter with the *GlamStar*, our film magazine. It doesn't pay as well as the other jobs but you would have a regular salary, and be able to interview stars, attend premiers and parties and write reviews of films and such things. Or you could be a reporter for our channel? Sort of like the paparazzi, catching the stars in action. Cutting edge film journalism. Either one would suit you. What do you think?'

I agreed eagerly. 'Fine, do a screen test in room 212 with Bharat and then meet HR in cabin 218. I'll call her right now to let her know you'll be coming. You can fix everything else with her. Best of luck!' she said, shaking my hand. 'And Kaveri,' she added as I was walking out, 'if you screw up, I will release the footage of the hot-air balloon!' My face went crimson. She smiled and said, 'Just joking!' and waved me on my way. I had far more at stake now than I did earlier.

A film reporter. Cutting edge journalism. That sounded exciting. I would meet celebrities without have to run after them. This seemed like a dream job. But when I went to the HR rep's room I understood that it wasn't as wonderful as I had imagined it would be.

'That's it?' I asked when she told me how much I would be paid. And the HR woman nodded. I would barely be able to afford anything else with my current lifestyle if I took up the job. I would just about pay my rent and have food to eat. Instead of taking the job right away I told her I would take a few days to think about it. I didn't want to make a hasty decision.

As I walked back home, I wondered about karma and coincidences. It was a coincidence that Deepa had come into my life right when I needed a job and offered me one. But was it my bad karma that it was a low paying one? If she had offered me this job a few years ago I might have taken it if I had been certain about wanting to be in films. I'd been younger then, more carefree. Now I had more demands, and comforts I didn't want to compromise on. It was not that I shirked hard work. It was just that I was afraid of the less in my life. There's a difference between working hard and working intelligently. One will lead to knowledge and the other to money.

I wanted to know how I could acquire both.

It was time that I spoke to the one man whom I still loved very deeply.

36

Parents Are Nature's Way of Showing You a Mirror

'Where are you?' my father barked as soon as I called him.

I could understand that my parents were upset with me. I had been unreachable in Milan and once I had come back I was too busy sorting out my personal and professional life to call them. It was incredibly selfish of me and I felt horrible about it, but in my defence my conversations with them didn't exactly leave me eager for more. They would keep reminding me that as a single child I had the sole responsibility to look after them. Dear Lord. I often asked why they just hadn't had another kid and spared me all the emotional blackmail. Their answer was that I had been quite a handful as it is, and they hadn't wanted to risk having another like me. Well that was reassuring.

'I'm in Bombay, Dad,' I said while twirling my hair and looking out of the window in my apartment. My apartment. The one that I had taken a whole year to set up exactly as I wanted with each corner displaying something that reflected a memory for me. Oh God, I thought, I would have to leave my apartment if I didn't have any money.

'Well, why haven't you come to see us? We should never have let you leave Bangalore. Ever since you've gone, you've turned into a completely different person. We never hear from you; it's like we don't exist for you anymore!' he said, being difficult. But I had heard this argument before. I was tempted to point out that I had not left them in Bangalore. I had left them in Moscow when he was still working in the Indian Foreign Service. I had got sick of the travel and wanted to settle down in Mumbai. After being forced to travel with him for all those years, my mother had emotionally blackmailed him into making Bangalore their base because that's where my mom's side of the family lived. She wanted to live a peaceful retired life with her sisters around. And he relented. This blackmail thing ran very well in the family.

'Dad, you can hardly tell a twenty-two-year old what to do. You didn't exactly *let* me leave. And obviously I've changed. It's called evolution, growth, coming of age, whatever you think fits, but the fact is people change. You're not the same man you were at thirty-five and I sure hope I won't be the same person at forty-five!' Dear God, please let me get through this phone call without getting into a full-blown argument.

'Okay, okay. You have your silly reasons for not calling us. Fine. We have no one else.' And with that oft-used jibe he passed the phone to my mom. Seriously having a conversation with them about things we didn't agree on—which was everything—was like trying to get through to a brick wall.

'I've shortlisted five different men,' she said without any preamble. 'When are you coming here to meet them?'

'What happened to my cool parents from four years ago who didn't care if I was married or not and wanted me to concentrate on my career and become famous?' I asked, chagrined.

'They want grandkids and their only hope doesn't show signs of becoming famous any time soon anyway!' she said with equal élan.

'Fine, I'll come,' I said, relenting. 'But I have only a few days before I have to return and start a new job. I won't be coming and going for a long time after that,' I said thinking out loud.

I still hadn't decided if I wanted to take Deepa's offer, but I was hoping that talking it out with my dad when he was being less sentimental might help. Besides, the crew was returning tonight and I didn't want to meet Shyamolie just yet. I knew she would talk about her love life and with my life in shambles, I didn't want to hear any of it. I quickly checked for flights online and said, 'Pick me up at nine tonight from the airport. I'll book my ticket now,' I said and hung up on my mom who was squealing gleefully about what a sweet child I was.

Maybe Mom was right. I wasn't getting any younger or any closer to fame and wealth. Maybe I needed to get married and have babies instead. But the idea of marriage was still very distant. I could not keep jumping into relationships. I needed to focus on better things. Like Mamta had said, I needed to make my job my focal point and then the love would fit in. But the reality was that there seemed to be a huge gap between my dreams and my bank account. And the only thing that looked promising right now was a wedding.

37

Who Knew Love Could Be Arranged

My parents were waiting for me at the airport. Even after years of living apart and all their emotional blackmail, I knew they were the only two people in the world who would love me no matter what. We piled into the car—a red Volkswagen Jetta that they had bought after having a Maruti Suzuki for the last fifteen years. We chatted nineteen to the dozen.

'And it has . . .' my dad droned on about the features of the new car, the mileage and the value for money while my mom told me about the boys she had picked out for me. It was surreal, but my family was like that. That is the beauty of the Indian family system—it is a completely organic, wonderful unit that you can't find abroad. No matter how far you flew from the coop, you were always welcomed back to this cocoon.

When we finally got home, Mom served me some sambhar and rice with avial and I stuffed myself with her cooking till I could eat no more. Dad retired to bed, seemingly pleased that his emotional blackmail had worked and I was finally home. Mom gave me some green tea and made herself a cup and we sat on the veranda to have a chat.

'So tell me,' she said as she was sipping her tea, 'no meaningful men in your life or have you just broken up with one?'

I laughed and asked, 'Why do you ask that, Mom?'

'I know you. You wouldn't give in to me so readily and agree to meet boys if you weren't suffering from heartbreak.'

'There's no point in worrying about the past, Mom. We have enough to worry about today! Now, let's see those boys!' I said with enthusiasm.

She went inside and came back a few minutes later with a bunch of photographs. She said as she was handing them to me, 'You know I admire you for your courage. It's not easy living on your own. I could never do it. And I assumed that since I couldn't, it would be difficult for you as well. That's why mothers want to see their daughters "settled". But I guess we'd all be happier people if we had some space and silence in our lives. Sometimes a marriage doesn't give you that. Even if it gives you everything else.'

'You know you can come and stay with me for a while if you want to get away from Dad,' I said.

She laughed. 'Yes, but he will follow me there the very next day. You know he can't live without me!'

I laughed too. She was right. My father was quite a pain most of the time but he was a hopeless romantic and he adored my mother. I looked at the photos of the men my mom had picked out. She had been short listing prospective sons-in-law and interviewing family members for a long time. Most of the pictures were done professionally. They were actually very good looking men and I wondered why they hadn't been snapped up yet. One was a divorce. One was in the army. One was an engineer in Bangalore. One was in the media. And one was a lawyer. I looked closely at the picture of the lawyer. It was the most unconventional of the lot. It showed a guy sitting and laughing. The photograph was a little blurry so his features weren't clear, but he did seem like someone who was completely at ease with himself.

I picked it up and showed it to my mother, 'Who's this?'

'That's Ayaan,' she said, frowning a little. 'I don't know if he's here. He doesn't live in Bangalore. He was born here, though. His parents are divorced. I got this from his aunt who plays cards with us. I had mentioned to my group that I am worried about you. They were all appalled when I told them you're turning thirty-five and are still single. If you keep this up, all your eggs will dry up and we will never get a grandchild!'

Yes, that was what my mother, and apparently her bridge-playing friends, were most worried about: a grandchild. But the man in the picture looked interesting and I was willing to give this arranged match deal a try. After all, I hadn't succeeded in finding anyone suitable for myself for so long. Although, I still thought it was a funny concept. All your life you're told not to talk to strangers and then suddenly you're asked to sleep with one.

The thing was that for so long I felt I didn't need anyone. I was complete in my life. I was happy, successful in my own way and content on being able to spend my money on myself and roam the earth whenever I chose to. I didn't know why but recently I had a niggling doubt if I really wanted to do it for the rest of my life on my own. I had given myself enough spiel about how a woman didn't need a man but I knew that if I avoided being with a man for just two more years, I could go an entire lifetime without ever getting married. There was something about being in your mid-thirties that really makes you feel the need to get married and have kids. Once the phase is over, there isn't a dying need anymore. Many women in their late thirties and early forties are content in having many guy friends who they can call whenever they want. They don't have the energy to pick up after a guy in their own beautiful home. And by then they've made their homes their haven and are so settled in their careers that they would rather curl up with a glass of wine on a Friday evening or go out with friends than wait for their man to make a plan. Obviously, I was taking all my inference from seeing Aditi.

I didn't want to get to that stage. While I could have thought about doing that if I had a sibling, I knew it would disappoint my parents to no end if I simply chose to be single for the rest of my life.

'We'll find out and let's go meet him,' I said with a big yawn. 'I'm going to bed. Goodnight, Mom.' I gave her a kiss on her head and walked into my room.

Interesting times lay ahead. I was looking forward to them.

38

Great Expectations

It turned out that Ayaan lived in London. Nevertheless, my mom called his aunt and told her that I was willing to talk to him, and got his number. I was feeling a little sceptical about 'meeting' this boy over the phone. How exactly was this going to work? I had decided to call him after lunch, when it would be mid-morning in London.

Meanwhile I went on with my day. Mom had made me a fantastic breakfast of dosas, idlis, chutney and upma and filter coffee. I was in heaven. I ate to my heart's content and then sat in the veranda with my dad while he read the papers. Or devoured *The Hindu* which he felt was the only paper that gave any real news. I was dying to read the *Bombay Times* to get my daily fix of filmdom. So I told them I was going to go for a walk and find an Internet cafe.

'But we have wi-fi,' my dad said.

I was stunned. 'Since when?' I asked incredulously. Last time I had checked, they were still using a computer that was so ancient it had an MS DOS system! But now they showed me their new computer equipped with a flat-screen monitor and a modem that had wi-fied the house. I was most impressed. My parents were moving up in life.

'We decided to spend all the money we had been saving for your wedding. We figured you wanted to be a spinster, so we spent that kitty on ourselves,' my dad said proudly.

'Gee, Dad,' I said wryly, 'thanks for the vote of confidence!'

He laughed and said, 'But we were waiting for you to come and download the programmes we need. Our computer guy hasn't been able to come since he set this up and we don't know how to access our games and social media sites.'

Trust my parents to call a 'computer guy' to fix their problems. While my father was in the IFS, some government person or another had done everything for them. All my mother ever had to do was call his secretary and say that there was a leak in the bathroom and a plumber would be sent over; a carpenter was sent when they needed any wood work done in the house. It had been a fairly simple life for them. A personal assistant had taken care of all their bills; all Dad had to do was give him the cheques and he sorted out the rest. And though it had been years since he had retired, he wanted to still rely on an entourage of helpers.

'I'll show you, Dad, so that you will never have to call anyone again,' I said booting up their computer.

The entire morning was spent downloading software for them and scanning old pictures that my dad wanted uploaded on Picassa, and we laughed at the memories. Around lunchtime, my mother reminded me to call London, and then went away with the maid to fix lunch. I was in no hurry to make the call. After I had finished downloading everything, I told my father about the job Deepa had offered me. I explained all the pros and cons to him.

'So you're telling me that my intellectual daughter who won a gold medal in physics in school, knows seven different languages, has travelled the world, read thousands of books, wants to write for a film magazine?' he asked a little disappointed.

I desperately wanted him to see it my way. Our education system made it impossible to do anything frivolous with our lives. Sometimes, all we ever want in our lives is a bit of fun and loads of glamour, but our parents always urge us to take the direction that they had envisioned for us, without letting us make our own mistakes. And those who haven't made too many mistakes in life haven't taken that many risks either. I wanted to take that risk now, to turn from my path of art and culture and into films and entertainment.

'Wouldn't it be better if you thought about it a little more?' he asked.

'Well, I don't have too much time. It was an opportunity that came out of nowhere and since I'm not working right now and I need to pay the rent I thought I would take it up and see where it leads me. I could also choose to be in front of the camera, but I'm not sure if I'm fit enough for that. I might need to lose some weight before they hire me,' I said, hoping his solution wouldn't be 'come back home' like it had been in the past whenever I said I was going broke. But it wasn't. He probably realized that I would not come back and live with them even if I was broke and there was no use reminding me about it.

'Well, if that's something you want to do then we'll support you, I guess,' he said although he didn't sound too convinced. 'It's probably not the work itself,' he tried to explain, 'but the fact that it's so menial and the money is not great. If either one made sense then I would whole heartedly support you. Besides, you're thirty-five years old and unsure of your finances—is this the best time to be changing careers? I would encourage you to accept a position with one of the art galleries. The pay might be the same as this film line, but at least it will be with something you know and love. And it could lead you in the art direction that you had always envisioned.'

'Lunch is ready!' my mother hollered and he said, 'Think about it!' before he got up to go to the table for lunch.

I felt a little disappointed. I had hoped that he would understand but his advice had left me even more confused than ever. Sometimes, even though you know what is going to happen, you can't stop them from happening. All you can do is change how you respond to them. Instead of being angry and upset that he didn't understand me yet again, I decided to see it from his point of view and give it some thought. I began to understand that we cannot change someone. We're not God. We can only live by our standards. And nobody else needs to.

After lunch my mom left the cordless in my room saying, 'I've unlocked the international code for you.' My parents thought that by locking the phone the servants wouldn't make national calls to their villages every time my parents went out for dinner. It hardly mattered to the servants who had cellphones and asked for extra money to fill their prepaid cards. It might have been cheaper if my parents let them call from their landline instead of giving them money for the mobiles, but who could argue with them?

So I dialled Ayaan's number.

'Hello?' said the voice on the other line.

I stood up abruptly and began to pace. I didn't know what to say. How would I introduce myself? 'Hi, I'm the girl your aunt in Bangalore wants to fix you up with, who doesn't live in Bangalore, but am calling from there since her mother insisted.' No, that did not sound right.

'Hello?' asked the voice again, a little perplexed with the silence.

I cleared my throat and said the smartest thing on the planet, 'Hello.'

'Yes?' he answered back.

Well, this conversation was clearly not going anywhere so I hung up.

I stared at the phone for the next five minutes, feeling like a fool. What if I had blown my only chance at marriage? I couldn't believe I just thought that! I took a deep breath and decided what to say before I dialled him again.

'Hi, this is Kaveri from India. Um . . . Bangalore actually. Your aunt Lalita gave me your number.'

'Oh, hi, Kaveri. Let me just call you back on this number, okay?' he said in a friendly voice.

I said okay and hung up. And waited. Twenty minutes later I was still waiting. He hated my voice. I've blown my chance at marriage. Damn! I really needed to get a grip. I hadn't exchanged two sentences with the man and I had already taken him to a mandap!

The phone rang.

'Hey! Sorry, I was in a meeting,' Ayaan said.

'No, that's okay, you carry on then,' I said. I hadn't taken into account that it was a weekday and the middle of the morning for him. Of course, he would be at work. He wasn't going through an Existential crisis like I was; stuffing my face away in my mother's house while I decided which career path I should choose.

'I'm done. So tell me about yourself,' he said formally.

'Didn't you get my bio-data from your aunt? I thought my mom had circulated it in every square in the state,' I replied.

He laughed. It was a wonderful laugh that made him sound very appealing. 'Well, yes, kind of. But only a little while ago. My aunt called and said you would be calling and said you were a really nice girl so I should be polite.' And then he laughed some more. I felt deeply embarrassed. Why, I didn't know. I just did.

So I decided to tell him a little about myself. 'Ummm . . . I'm thirty-five. I'm an Aries. Which means I'm full of hot air. I live in Mumbai, but I'm in between jobs right now, so I decided to visit my parents for a bit. Um . . . what else . . . I love art and films . . . and . . . oh . . . I know seven languages. I guess that's it.' I sounded like a complete idiot. Come on Kaveri, a little voice said, you're far more than that. I know that, I told the voice, but right now, I can't think what! 'Tell me about yourself. Why did you give that blurry picture of yourself?' I asked him back.

Ayaan laughed and replied, 'That was taken a year ago. I

didn't have any other prints. I do have some pictures up on Facebook. You can "friend" me there and check out my profile. I'm a lawyer. But you already know that. I'm a civil lawyer so no murky sex crimes for me. I do more of the boring litigation that Grisham won't write about. I live in London, though I travel to Mumbai quite often since my father is there. My mum lives here with me. She travels to Bangalore to visit my aunt quite often, claiming that she's fed up of me. She's been trying to get me married for a while but I've never had time. I have been in three meaningful relationships, but for some reason or another they didn't work out. I'm turning thirty-six end November. I'm a Sagittarian if you're into that whole sun sign business. That's it for me, I suppose.'

And then he kept quiet. And I was quiet.

'I'm not really into sun signs . . . I don't know why I said that,' I said softly. I didn't want to sound like a teenage girl, but the truth was that I didn't know what an arranged marriage phone conversation should sound like. Weren't sun signs the things that people generally spoke about?

I could feel him smiling the other end. After clearing his throat he asked, 'Tell me, what did you mean by you're in between jobs? Because here we say we're taking a sabbatical.'

I told him how I was conflicted about whether I should become a gallerist or take up the low-paying job as a reporter for a film magazine.

'My father feels I should do the art thing because he doesn't want his daughter to get into something that would compromise her ethics in the long run,' I said, hoping I didn't sound too much like a child unable to make her own decisions. Although I tended to fight against it, my parents had influenced my life greatly, and would continue to do so. I figured Ayaan might as well know that about me early on.

'Your ethics and integrity must always be far more important than monetary gain. Only then do you get respect and dignity,' he said with confidence. I began to like this man. He made sense.

'So you're saying I should chuck the mag and do the art gallery?' I asked, sauntering into the kitchen to make myself a cup of coffee.

'Don't make your life your job and don't make your job your life. You're a sum of more than that. It hardly matters if you're paid less with a magazine if that's what you want to do. Always good to make room for less in your life. It's the abundance that gives us stress.'

'I guess that's true. But I like the abundance!' I said candidly. And he laughed again.

'I'm sure we're all used to some comforts in our lives that we don't want to give up. That's why I don't know if I want to come back to India and work. I'm pretty happy with my life here because it gives me the luxuries I need. I know a lot of people who tell me that if I spend that kind of money in rupees, I could have a lavish lifestyle in Mumbai as well, but I have never felt the need to give up on the basics that I enjoy here. So I totally get where you're coming from. I'm sure at our age we don't want to start from scratch. And yet I know how important it is to chase your dreams. They're the only things that truly matter. Sometimes people yearn for things because society tells us those are things worth having. Achievement need not come from ambition. Just from self,' he said wisely.

I took a sip of my coffee and nodded. This man was in my head already. He knew exactly what I was feeling and thinking. I wondered—had most of my relationships started with a phone conversation? Would this begin like that or worse, would it end like that?

'Maybe I've crossed a line,' Ayaan said into the silence. 'I'm sorry if I have.'

I tried to tell him that he hadn't and I had spaced out thinking about what he had just said, but he had to hang up then. He said he would call me again later that night once he finished with work and we could talk more. I told him I was looking forward to it.

I sat in my room looking out of the window at the lawn where the hibiscus blossomed in patches and began to think about my conversation with Ayaan. He seemed extremely perceptive about my situation. How had he picked up on the one thing that was irking me? And what he said actually made sense. I could do with a little less in my life; I could take risks. What a smart Bengali he was. Ayaan Roy. I immediately remembered he had a Facebook profile and opened my laptop. But there were hundreds of Ayaan Roys. I had no idea whom to befriend. I decided to just wait for his call in the evening and ask him to find me instead. Suddenly my heart was racing. I was actually looking forward to talking to a man. It was like a blind date. I hardly knew what he looked like, but I wanted to present to him the best of me. I began to see what made the process of an arranged marriage interesting. It was the anticipation of something new, a pursuit of the unknown, the possibility of being chosen. It was like school where for sports day teams were made and people were picked. You always wanted to be called first and hoped you would never be last. Love marriages didn't have that; you knew whom you wanted to marry because you had known him or her long enough to arrive at that decision. With an arranged marriage, there was just one chance to be judged. And while that may have been sexist on the one hand, it was quid pro quo. Both parties had just one chance to be chosen or rejected. And both parties would show their best and know what they could have if they chose each other. It was also a gamble since neither knew what the worst could be. And in a way that made it exciting.

39

Conflicting Crossroads

When my parents woke up from their afternoon nap, my mother demanded to know how the conversation had gone. I tried to be as vague as possible and not give any hints that it had actually gone remarkably well. I told her I had told him that I was out of a job and she immediately hung her head and mumbled something in Kannada about what a bane to her existence I was. The shrew! I also told her that he had been in three 'meaningful' relationships that hadn't worked out.

'You mean he's not a virgin?' my mother asked. And I looked at her incredulously for a moment. Did she actually think that people would remain virgins till they got married? In this day and age? I better not tell them about the number of men that had been there in my life, then!

'Doesn't matter,' my mother said graciously. 'Things don't work out for a reason. Destiny had better plans for him. Like you coming into his life. Aah! I can see things working out,' she smiled as she made herself and Dad some tea and served it with some butter biscuits from the local bakery.

'Anyway, he said he'll call later tonight. He was at work and couldn't talk too long,' I said as I put on my running shoes to go for a walk. All that eating was making me feel terribly unhealthy.

'Tonight? But we have to go to a party,' she said. I looked at her enquiringly and she continued, 'We've been invited by Mr and Mrs Gupte to dinner. They have a lovely house in Green Acres. I mentioned that you would be here and they asked me to invite you. It would be nice if you came. They would love to see you; they haven't seen you since you were very little.'

'Mom,' I groaned. I hated going for old people's parties. I had been looking forward to practicing what to say to Ayaan when he finally called. I felt I had come across as someone who needed advice and I wanted to prove to him what a strong woman I really was. But my mother wouldn't hear of it. She insisted that I accompany them and said that if it got too late, Ayaan could call on my cellphone or I could call him back once I returned. I relented.

So that evening I wore a lovely cream-coloured Kanjeevaram sari with a large red-and-blue border that my mother had bought for me when the Nalli sale was on. I wore gold jhumkas and added a bindi just to be more traditional. My mother had insisted that I wear a sari since it was a formal dinner for the Gupte's fiftieth anniversary and forbade me from wearing my regular jeans or dresses. I looked at myself in the mirror; I looked like the perfect Indian girl. I added a few delicate gold bangles and my ensemble was complete. I thought I couldn't waste this 'bhartiya nari' image on just old people and decided to take a photo of myself and upload it to Twitter. I was quite thrilled about it. I immediately got a response from @SomewhereFarAway saying how stunning I looked. I was thrilled, but since Shy had once warned me about how there were stalkers, trolls and people pretending to be decent on Twitter, I kept my distance and did not respond.

At the party, after all the congratulations and thank-yous and how-lovely-you-looks and haven't-seen-you-in-so-longs had been said, I went to sit outside in the lawn. It was a beautiful night. Bangalore has great weather and these vast stretches of green lawns, trees and flowers made the city truly enchanting.

'You look absolutely gorgeous in that sari,' said a familiar voice—the last one I had expected to hear here—from behind me.

I turned around and replied. 'Thanks, Siddharth. What are you doing here?'

He came and sat down on the bench next to me. 'Ravi, Mr Gupte to you, is my father's elder brother-in-law. My father's elder sister is married to Mr Gupte,' he explained.

There was an awkward silence between us. He looked so amazing in his charcoal suit, white Armani shirt and red Satya Paul tie that I wanted to grab him and kiss him. He swirled the Chivas in his glass and took a sip. Maybe he was expecting me to say something.

I cleared my throat and said, 'I came to visit my parents.' As if I needed to explain. He nodded and kept quiet. So I asked him, 'How are you doing Siddharth?'

'It's taking time to forgive you, Kaveri,' he said softly, looking straight ahead. 'But I can't stop thinking about you. I loved you. And you betrayed me.'

'I know. I'm really sorry. I did a horrible thing. Rajvir never mattered to me.' I spoke with pauses and great hesitation to form the words correctly. 'You were my world, Siddharth. And then something just went completely wrong somewhere. I don't know if it was the Aditi thing or you calling me routine or you being distant. I didn't mean to do what I did. It happened. I don't even want to give any excuses for it. I don't . . . I'm sorry . . .' I was at a loss for words.

He finally looked at me, his expression saying volumes. I was afraid to respond. Most times it's the things that are unsaid that have greatest meaning. You just need to read the silence.

And then he finally said the words: 'Do you want to get back together?'

I was quiet. A part of me really wanted to because I knew Siddharth so well and he had really looked after me. I would never have to worry about finances if I was with him. I wouldn't have to worry about my career; he would have the right contacts to help me do what I wanted with my life. And we were amazing together in bed. We never understand how precious a relationship is until it's taken away. Much like everything else. When you're in love you want to be the one who completes the other person. Even if they are complete.

The other part of me really wanted to take that call from Ayaan and see where that was going. Maybe nothing would come of it, but I was excited to find out. I was so conflicted. A vital part of a relationship is growth and belief. That requires more than happiness of togetherness, it requires thought and work. Maybe Mamta was right. If I had belief in the relationship with Siddharth, and I knew it would grow to something more meaningful, I wouldn't have strayed.

'Does your silence mean you don't want us to be together?' he asked.

'No. Not at all. I was just thinking how we could even begin to mend our relationship. I mean, what do we do? Where do we go from here?' I asked, genuinely concerned.

'Well we could start by seeing a counsellor to figure out what went wrong and then we could work on solving the problems together.' He finished his drink in one long swallow and continued, 'We would need to be celibate for a bit. I don't want to sleep with you till we figure this out. It might take a few weeks, it might take a few months, but I'm sure we can work through it if we really love each other.'

'If?' I asked. If you're going to speak the language of love you must learn to speak the language of apology as well. I wanted some sort of an apology from him as well for calling me boring.

He nodded. 'I still love you, but I'm still hurting. You must understand this and take responsibility for it. Only then can the healing begin. And I will try my best to change to cater to your definition of love and be the man you need. But it must start from you.'

I sat there, looking at him for a while. Then I turned away. What he had said hadn't affected me quite as much as the tone in which he had said it. Siddharth's tone had been very condescending. I had apologized for my mistake. Over and over again. We had been taking time off to see if we would be able to work things out when I had left for Milan. It wasn't as if we were married. I didn't really want to see a counsellor. And I didn't want to spend months on figuring out if this would work or not, not when he was predicating it on an 'if'. People made mistakes, but when they loved each other, they forgave those mistakes and moved on. A relationship cannot exist in a status quo. It can change its nature, structure and meaning. But it can't be about what it was when it started.

If I went back to Siddharth, I would have to go through relationship counselling and then more therapy if I wanted to get married and have kids but he didn't. I could see a life filled with us sitting on the couch. And I didn't want that.

All I really wanted was to live a little and enjoy every day. And when I looked back over the year, I had loved every day. The ridiculousness of training Bela, the running around with Shy, counselling Aditi—I had enjoyed every bit of it. I soaked all those moments in. I finally understood it. Not everything you do is going to pay off. Some things will be there just so you experience life a little more. I thought I had done pretty well for myself. I had even had sex with the most popular Bollywood hunk of our times! I had lived an entire year being me and doing what I wanted. I didn't want to regret that.

Siddharth was disappointed by my answer. He couldn't understand why I was giving him up. But this was not about him. This was about me. This was about me wanting to be more than someone's girlfriend. If I was going to do something radically different with my career I needed to do something equally drastic with my love life.

I needed to plunge into a blind, long distance friendship with someone and live life exactly as I wanted even if it would never lead anywhere. Friendships are like mutual funds. Not all your investments are going to give fabulous returns. Some will be duds. And I was finally willing to take the risk in this game.

40
Long Distance Love

We got home pretty late that evening so I missed Ayaan's call and he was busy the next day so he didn't call during the day. This gave me time to reflect on my decision. Sometimes you don't know if you've done the right thing until you get the opportunity to undo it. If you don't, you know it's the right decision.

I didn't want to stay at home with my parents that day, so I took off by myself, saying I was going shopping. It was the one thing my mom and I never did together. She liked to browse through every section in a store, pick up random things to try on and ultimately decide she didn't like anything. I was the exact opposite. I entered a store only if I liked something on display on the mannequins. Once inside I quickly scanned the merchandise on the racks, bought something if I really liked it and walked out in five minutes tops.

Instead of trying to clear my head sitting in a coffee shop like I generally did, I decided I would hit the stores in central Bangalore for some great bargains. And as I went through clothes stores, shoe stores and book stores on M.G. Road, I found my mood improving. I was single again. I had been in one relationship or another for the last three years. The only time I had felt single was in New York when men were just a distraction when I was bored. I made up my mind that if I was ever going to be in a relationship it had to be fun and honest. We both had to be truthful and sincere with each other. But I was feeling relieved to be single. I felt relieved *not wanting* a relationship. And not wanting a man. I didn't know where anything would lead with Ayaan. But I didn't care. If he chose not to call me back, I knew it would not upset me. I would be happy knowing I was a single, independent woman in control of my life rather than a woman whining to get married.

After walking for hours and shopping, I entered a bookstore. I browsed through the shelves, picked up several titles and then found a corner and sat down.

'Can I help you, madam?' Came a voice in front of me. It was the store owner, a portly old man with thinning hair wearing a red checked shirt much too tight for him.

'No, thanks. Would you mind if I sit here and read for a bit?' I asked.

'Not at all,' he said with a smile and left.

I sat there for a long time not opening any of the books I had just collected. I often read the first chapters to see if I'm hooked enough to buy a book. Murakami's *Norwegian Wood*, Toni Morrison's *Jazz*, and a book of poems by Maya Angelou lay beside me along with a few of the latest magazines. I looked around and found that right there, right then, I was most at peace. I was the creator of my own destiny. I was unique. And I could let no one else rule my judgement or cloud my vision. I began to believe in myself again. I knew I had made the right decision. We are mistaken to believe our consciousness awakened at our birth. It is born only when we become aware of something larger than ourselves. That realization happened to me at a small bookshop in the middle of a sunny afternoon while I felt completely alone.

Everyone loses their way. Growth is not always a fantastic climb to the top. Sometimes it's a plateau to reflect. This year had been that for me. And even though I had incredible sex, made new friends and hopped onto another career track, it had given me opportunities to take new and bold steps. It had shown me that I wasn't the same person anymore. I needed to get out of my comfort zone, live out of the box, or even throw away the box and live life anew. I finally felt free of the chokehold of angst and negativity.

As I turned to pick up one of the books next to me, I noticed a girl sitting nearby. She looked to be in her late teens. In a light cotton shirt with faded jeans, she seemed more confident than I was at her age. She had a tattoo at the nape of her neck—a sort of an ancient design with some encryption around it. She looked up at me and smiled. I smiled back. I said, not wanting to look like a weirdo, 'I noticed your tattoo. It's cool.'

'So's yours,' she said.

I looked down at my left hand, at the beautiful version of love and enlightenment that I had got for myself a few years ago. How was it that I hadn't noticed it for so long? Had it just become a part of my skin that I had started taking it for granted? I had got it as a reminder that I loved myself most in the world.

'Thanks,' I said and smiled. 'What do they mean . . . the words around your tattoo?'

She tilted her head and rubbed her neck with her right hand, 'It means beautiful.' And smiled and turned back to her book.

It really was beautiful. In the middle of an unknown bookstore, sitting next to an unknown woman, I finally figured out that life was too beautiful to throw away on anyone or anything.

I opened my book, and began reading.

41

@SomewhereFarAway

Later that night Ayaan called me and I told him to call me on my mobile instead of the landline. This way I didn't have to worry about sitting within the permitted range of a cordless and have my mother listen in from the door! I opted to go for a walk instead.

'What have you been up to?' I asked in a friendly and casual tone. I wondered if he had time to go through our last conversation and realize what he wanted from us, if there even was an 'us'.

'Nothing much. Same old cases and same old nutcases. Clients from hell and bosses from purgatory. The wonderful thing is that the weather here is absolutely gorgeous. You must come and visit me,' he said this so casually that I stopped walking and wondered if I had heard correctly.

'Um . . .' I started eloquently, 'isn't it too soon for us to be meeting?'

I could imagine him shrug at the other end before replying, 'What difference does it make? Can't friends meet?'

I had to spell it out then. '*Friends* can, Ayaan. But we've met through a *match* that our elders made for us. If I was to fly out to meet you, they would think that we've decided to get married!' And then I stopped myself. Damn. Why had I said the M word? Why did I have to think about it every time he was on line?

But he was nonchalant and responded with, 'Hmmm . . . I see what you mean. But the great thing about being in London is that no one cares. And the fantastic thing about being a man in Indian society is that no one asks you as many questions as they do to the women.' And then he roared with laughter. And I giggled as well even though the joke was on me and how everyone would only be asking me questions about us. 'So what have you decided about your job offer?' he asked, changing track to a more comfortable topic.

I took a turn at the end of the street where the streetlight was broken and walked back home, 'I've decided to take it,' I said confidently.

'That's wonderful!' he said without any hesitation. My parents would have disapproved, Siddharth would have offered me a better job, Aditi would have hounded me with questions, and Shy would have said that at least it would help me lose weight!

'Yes,' I said, 'I think I need to try to do new things in my life. I can't always be worried about money. I need to chase my dreams. I've had moments where I've almost figured out what I need to do with my life and then I've let relationships distract me. I don't want to do that anymore. So I've decided to be off relationships for a year and concentrate only on my career.'

'Well, that doesn't sound too promising for me,' Ayaan said, sounding disappointed.

Damn. Me and my big mouth! He had probably been wondering where this—we—could have gone and I had made the decision for us without consulting him. Maybe I should have waited to make that decision when I had no options left. But I felt more in control of my life walking away from the table when there was an offer on it than walking away when I had no other choice.

I had to say something that compensated my arrogance. 'I'm

sorry, Ayaan, I didn't mean it like that. I meant that I was not pinning all my hopes on us. I don't want there to be any pressure because we were set up. It just seems wrong to expect you to fall in love with me. It doesn't *need* to happen. We can be friends. And we can visit each other and see where things take us,' I said turning my earlier stance.

He was quiet for a bit and I thought that maybe I had ruined even the possibility of friendship with him. But then he responded, 'I guess that's okay. That does kind of put the pressure off. So let me get this straight. I don't need to call you regularly and you won't get upset about it?'

'Nope.'

'I don't need to send you flowers, gifts and such things for one month anniversaries and other Hallmark card days?'

'Not at all,' I laughed and added, 'and you wouldn't have to even if we were together. For God's sake we are in our thirties. We need to take *passion* forward, not stupidity.'

'Okay, no teddy bears for you! You won't start planning an extravagant wedding and tell me that I can't have my rowdy friends there since they drink a lot, will you?'

I started laughing and almost choked but still said, 'No!' I knew that some long distance relationships are more solid than those with couples seeing each other every day. Maybe Ayaan and I could have a long distance friendship that could develop into something more. Or not. It didn't matter.

'Hey, this sounds like it could work. So what are the rules? Are we allowed to date other people?'

'Absolutely,' I said. But added, 'But I don't necessarily need to know about them unless you want to pour your heart out about how she dumped you.'

He laughed and agreed. And then just when I thought I had liberated myself from the cycle of unending relationships he said something that made my hair stand on end.

'So, you looked damn hot in your red and white sari.'

I had reached the gate of my house and was about to go in,

but I stood absolutely still for a moment. Had I mentioned anything about the Gupte dinner party and what I had worn? Nope. I was absolutely certain that I hadn't told him. Then how did he know? Did he have a spy? Was he a distant cousin of Siddharth's? If that was the case, I would be mortified and swear celibacy for the rest of my life.

But that was not the case. It was something that came as a complete surprise and cleared so many of my doubts.

'I follow you on Twitter,' he explained calmly, as if he could feel my blood freeze a million miles away. But I needed to know all the details immediately.

'Since when? What's your handle? But why didn't you say anything earlier? How much do you know? Jesus, I sound like a fool,' I burst out.

'I've been following you for a few months. But you don't have a photo of yourself. I already had a photo of you because my aunt sent me one that your mom gave her. When I saw your sari photo, I put two and two together. I didn't know I was following *you*!'

I had reached my kitchen and was terribly thirsty. 'Well what's your handle? Is it Ayaan Roy?' I asked while pouring myself a glass of water.

'No. I didn't want my clients or anyone in the legal fraternity to follow me on a social network.' He paused and then said, 'I go by SomewhereFarAway.'

I was going to need something stronger than water. I went to my dad's bar in the drawing room and took out a bottle of Hennessy Cognac and poured myself a drink. If he had been following me for so many months it meant that he knew everything about me—what I thought about Bela, my days in Milan, Shy and my trysts with Siddharth. He was still a stranger, but suddenly I had become an open book to him. I cursed Shy for introducing me to Twitter; the damn thing was so addictive that you poured out your entire heart in it only to realize you have exposed yourself to the world! I felt vulnerable all of a sudden.

'Kaveri, listen,' he said when I didn't respond. 'I don't check my feed regularly . . .'

'Don't lie,' I interrupted more aggressively than I had intended. 'You have responded to most of my tweets. My thoughts, my ideas, my life . . . it seems you know it all!' I said with hot tears forming in my eyes.

'Kaveri, you have to understand that I didn't know that KaveriLoveGuru and you were the same person until yesterday. I have been following you and replying because I find you so interesting as a person. I found myself drawn to KaveriLoveGuru. The realization that you are her blew me away. For the first time in my life, I have started believing in destiny. How else can I explain the fact that the woman I've wanted to be with for so long was the one my aunt had set me up with? I didn't have to reveal myself to you just now but I don't want any secrets between us, I want us to be honest with each other right from the start.'

I wanted to feel better but I was even more confused than ever. Was he making all this up? I walked into my bedroom and sat down on my bed.

'Why don't you go to bed now? It must be quite late there. We'll chat again tomorrow. Give me a missed call whenever you're ready and I'll call you right back. Just think about it. We'll be whatever you want to define us as. Okay?'

I agreed. I needed to get some rest now and I needed time to think about things. Most people lack 'depth of field'. It's what makes you see beyond words and find meaning in silences. I had finally found a man who understood the silences in my speech, the depth in my tweets and the cry for help with my career and yet had never even met me. And I had said I didn't want a relationship with him. I only wanted friendship.

Had I just made the biggest mistake of my life?

42

Back to Reality

The next few days passed by so quickly that I didn't even have a moment to think. When I got back, Shy immediately called me saying she had some urgent news and wanted to meet me. I also had so many things to tell her.

The moment we laid eyes on each other the next day we burst into speech. If chatting had been a sport at the Olympics, we'd have won the gold.

Shyamolie told me that Bela and Rajvir had been quite an item in Milan. The PR team was now going to promote the movie with this piece of information. But Rajvir had no intention of staying with Bela. In fact, he had hit on Shy during one of his costume trials. She got back at him by tampering with the inseam of his pants so that they ripped in the middle of shooting a song. The entire production unit was laughing; someone had even managed to take a picture with their cellphone camera. After that, Rajvir had flown in his own designer who brought many clothes for him but none fit since the designer hadn't checked Rajvir's measurements!

'Attention to detail is the key to being indispensable, my dear! That designer brought all clothes that would have looked good on Amitabh Bachchan but made Rajvir appear older than he actually is. The thumb rule to style is, don't dress according to your age, dress according to how you feel. You'll never feel old again!' Shy said with a flourish. She was so fantastic at her job that I wondered if she should really give it up to start her own label. But I dared not ask her that. I had learnt that if people wanted advice, they would ask for it. And if they really wanted advice, then they would ask you to agree with them. 'Anyway, all this drama meant the shoot had to be extended for four days which infuriated Punjwani and he drove everyone up the wall! RT quit half way and left. Punjwani almost had a heart attack and broke down. It was as if his wife had left him.'

'Oh wait, you mean they weren't married?' I asked in jest and we burst into laughter again. Apparently, a big foreign studio had given Punjwani and his team money to make this movie. Punjwani had thought that he would spend half on the movie and half on his personal villa and car that he was planning to buy. He had never invested any money of his own. Somehow, I was not surprised.

'So you haven't told me anything about why you went to see your parents? What happened?' Shy asked.

I told Shy that Siddharth broke up with me and then when he wanted to get back together, I had refused.

'Well that's the strangest love story I've ever heard!' she said as she sipped on her green tea while we sat in the Kala Ghoda Café at Fort. It was a beautiful place that was close to the art galleries I loved visiting when I was lonely. I often came to this café to sit and think at times of conflict. I remembered being here with Siddharth once. But somehow, memories of the people had ceased to exist and the place lived on with me. I had become more mature like that. Once, places, music, conversations, films, and things that we had talked about during the relationship would leave a hollow feeling in the pit of my stomach every time anyone referred to them or I would visit, see or hear them at any juncture. But not anymore. I had decided that if certain things were important to me, they would continue to be important even if my significant other at the time became insignificant. Why should I give up on what made me happy so I could forget the person who couldn't make me happy?

'Don't eat that. You're just going to get fat!' Shy wailed as I ordered a chocolate muffin and another cappuccino.

'Honey,' I said with maturity, 'it's about time we realize we're not going to get any thinner or younger. At least let's try to become wiser and calmer.' And I dug into my chocolate muffin while Shy watched enviously. 'Beautiful people are not those who have the perfect body or the fantastic clothes. They are the ones who make you feel beautiful, too. And I think I do that for people. And I really see people like that, too. If everyone everywhere is always on a diet, what's going to happen to all the chefs who toil away to make all this yummy food?' I laughed. I loved eating. I didn't know if I was ever going to be thin enough to fit into a pair designer jeans again, but for now I was happy with the way I looked, and that made me feel absolutely terrific.

'I got a job offer to do some film reporting for this woman I know. I think I'm going to take the job. This film bug has bitten me and I want to do something in it again.'

'I thought we were going to do business together?' she asked looking crushed and pouting with her barely there lips. Seriously, she needed to put on some weight. She was losing fat from all the wrong places!

'I didn't know what we should do and if that's what you really wanted,' I said honestly.

She went on to tell me her plan. She was going to continue working in films since she had a big enough clientele that she couldn't just give up. But she needed more management with the stars. She had spoken to her father who knew an agency that managed stars and he had said I could have a job there. So I would be managing two or three stars' portfolios who worked with Shy as well. So in a way I could help her but manage my own thing.

'Shy this is perfect!' I said as I got up to kiss her.

'And don't worry, an agency won't jilt you of payment. They'll pay you a pretty decent bit to keep you looking good while you're hanging out with the stars!' she added.

This was exactly what I needed! I decided to turn down the other offer and went to meet Deepa in person the next day. I explained to her why I couldn't do the job but thanked her profusely for having offered me something when I needed it most. She was most nonchalant and said that if I chose to throw my life away chasing after actors who wouldn't care for me, then that was my problem. I thanked her for her understanding and left. Neither a Deepa nor a Punjwani would affect me again. I realized that such people exist in this world to give themselves an ego boost. They were only using you as a stepping stone to do that. And while you might feel grateful to them for doing something for you, you had probably given them enough as well to walk out of that relationship with your head held high. Yes, your relationship with an employer is far more delicate than the one you have with your partner, because that's the one that can make or destroy your confidence. I chose to build from it.

I left Shy that day without telling her about Ayaan. That was too complicated for me to explain. Her love story had ended in Milan itself. Once she came back she had realized that she was far too ambitious for a dancer and she needed more from her life. I could see glimpses of my old self in her, but I refrained from giving her unsolicited advice. She needed to make her own mistakes before she became wise in relationships. Everyone has to fall in love before they rise in it. And I knew that since we would be in close proximity, I would always be there to help her.

43
Old Friendships and New Ties

Aditi called me when her divorce was finalized. She was once again a free woman and she needed to see me.

We met at our favourite place, a shopping mall. The quintessential shopaholic, she shopped when she was depressed. She shopped when she wanted to celebrate. She shopped when she was bored. She said it was better than sitting and eating in a coffee shop like I did. At least her way, she was on her feet and burning calories instead of consuming them. So we went to the biggest mall in Mumbai and darted in and out of stores, talking across shelves and changing rooms, not caring who heard our conversation.

Aditi told me that she had got enough alimony from her husband to keep her fashion business going. Her lawyer was smart and wonderful and played to the gallery and her husband had relented. He had felt guilty that he had ignored her but admitted to her that he had been seeing someone else. She had seized on the opportunity and told him that if he wanted a quick divorce to be able to marry the other girl, he needed to shell out a pretty packet immediately. And he had. She had been the one having the affair with the brother-in-law and yet she was the one who had emerged the winner from this marriage!

She was going to keep her store in a smaller place but prominent locality so that she could get enough customers and she was going to expand into the jewellery side as well. I wondered how I had got stuck between two fashion businesswomen but I guess you attract like-minded people into your life and sometimes unknowingly you transform them too.

'Isn't that dubious?' I asked.

Aditi tried on a dress and came out to show me. She said, 'If you want something in life, you need to know how to ask for it correctly. If you haven't got it, you need to change your method. The universe doesn't always know what you want. If God looks the other way, it just means we finally need to start working harder.'

I was amazed. When had she blossomed into this mature woman? My jaw dropped. Aditi smiled at my reaction and said immediately, 'My boobs look great in this don't they?'

I laughed. They did. The little boobs that Aditi did have, she knew how to enhance so they would seem just perfect. I asked her about her brother-in-law and what she was planning to do about him. She shrugged. 'He hasn't spoken to me. I was careful when I was having the affair. I didn't have anything in writing. I never sent any suggestive SMSes or emails. It could all be seen as harmless flirting. At one point he called to say that I should drop the alimony because I had been unfaithful as well. But I thought about that. I had given four years of my life to my marriage and Rajat had been cheating on me for most of that time. So why should I give up on something that is truly mine? Besides, Rajat will make his riches again, but it will take me much more time to establish my character and business in this cut-throat society. So I said no and told him that if he tried to defame me, it would leave his mother feeling deeply betrayed by his actions since I was already on my way out. He kept shut after that. I don't think he loves me anymore!' And with this she collapsed into peals of laughter. And I joined her. I may not have agreed with everything Aditi did, but she believed in herself so much that she had an attractive confident quality that made it extremely difficult to argue with her. For whatever she was, I was proud of Aditi. She had given me my space when I had wanted it and let me realize on my own that she truly loved me. My True Love had to extend beyond my own core. It had to include my friends as well. For without Shy and Aditi, I would not be me.

I still kept Ayaan all to myself though. I never spoke about him to either of them. But I did confide in my mother. I began to call her and tell her about my day and the celebrities I had met. She tried occasionally to run my life for me and tell me what to do, but I would tell her every now and then, 'Mom, you telling me to do something doesn't mean I'm going to actually listen. It's only going to mean I won't want to call you the next day.' Slowly she stopped trying to advise me and began to just listen and ask questions. She stopped judging me for running around with stars and not doing something 'intellectual' with my life. She stopped nagging me to take my relationship with Ayaan forward.

'Guess what Ayaan said today,' I asked her when I was on my way to meet Shahid Kapoor to show him a new collection that Shy had designed for him.

'What?'

'He said that all this time we've been friends with benefits, but he hasn't seen any benefits yet!' I said with a laugh.

Mom giggled, 'Well, maybe you should make a trip to London to see if you can give him some benefits!'

'Is this my mother encouraging me to have sex? Even though I'm not married? Oooh! This is a red-letter day! I think I might just like this new mom!' I teased.

It felt great to know that she supported me. It was a different feeling than having friends support you or a man encourage you. Having a parent believe in you was a different kind of a high. I slowly understood what people had been saying about family. You can do everything on your own and enjoy your life, but when you have family to share that happiness with, it gives a far deeper satisfaction than it does with anything else.

44

I Did It My Way

Pretty soon Shyamolie and I decided to start a company together. Shy would still work as a stylist for Bollywood celebs, but she would only go for initial meetings with me and after that I would interact with them on sets and shoots and other things they wanted styling for. She would send the appropriate clothes and accessories from which they could choose. This way I could deal with them since I had a better temperament and greater convincing power than the two of us and she would still be able to design clothes. Aditi joined our company too; we figured she could manage the store since she was great with customers and didn't want to run around too much on sets. And she could bring in her clients for all the accessories that she designed and made and look after our finances since she was a wizard with numbers. I thought it was completely fantastic working with my two best friends.

There were days when we fought like mad and refused to talk to each other but soon enough we desperately wanted to discuss something new happening with the label or the store or a client and we were back to chatting with each other. I liked how we were such different personalities and yet got along so well with each other. A fantastic conversation can do far more for you than even a facial can. That's why we looked as good as we felt. There are many routes to the final destination of your dreams. Taking the easy one wastes the most time. Push yourself to do better. That's why I was finally in a happy place with my career. Because I chose to take risks with my life.

Although I loved my new career, I had not been able to let go of my fascination with art. I still visited Mamta often. We had become close friends over time, and I frequently turned to her for advice. She had the most beautiful exhibitions and I even met some of the painters who came for it. Every now and then when the stress of an exhibition got to her, she would tell me to just take over the gallery so she could sit at home or do something else with her life. But I could see that she had an intense passion for art and it would be difficult for her to give up the gallery. I always made sure that Siddharth was not there at the time. I didn't want to bump into him at any point. She told me that he was doing extremely well in his business. She never mentioned his personal life and I never asked.

Before we knew it, it was the middle of November and Ayaan's birthday was in a week. Ayaan and I had been chatting everyday for the last six months. He would call me in the middle of the day to catch up with me and at night we would web chat. From being 'just friends' we had gone to being friends who lusted after each other. He made me laugh so hard that I would forget my worries for the time being. And he listened to me agonize about issues with my business partners, the tantrums my clients threw and the things I wanted to do. I felt he was helping me evolve more than just being in love. It was a different feeling all together. And instead of doing it in a judgemental manner, it would be more of a push to better myself.

One day when I was telling him about a party that we needed to attend but I just didn't want to go, he demanded, 'Then why are you going?'

'Because I have to! I have to network and build our brand. If people don't know of us, how will we get work?' I lamented.

'By being exclusive. The more friends you make, the more difficult it will be to ask them to do something for you. Then you'll be asking for a favour. You're better than that. You've got to be so fucking brilliant at what you do that people will come to you. And Shy and Aditi already have their clients. Concentrate on work and reaching people through word of mouth. I mean, for God's sake that's a country of more than a billion people. If everyone told everyone about you, you'd be in so much demand. Don't lower yourself by networking! Use the time and energy in marketing!' he said in his Brit accent that I absolutely adored. And then he added, 'You're a star in my head. You don't need to stoop to anyone's level. You need to mix with the right people who are stars too. Up your game! Sometimes, doing nothing is the best action you can take.'

'See that's why I love you. Because you wrap all your advice in such wonderful compliments. I could get used to having you around for the rest of my life.' Damn it! I had done it again. Had I no control over my tongue? 'As a friend . . . you know what I mean,' I added quickly.

'Sigh,' he said with a sheepish grin, 'we're never going to stop being *friends*, are we?'

And I laughed and said, 'No! We'll never stop being friends. So what plans for your birthday?'

He rubbed his chin and replied, 'Nothing much. Too old now. The same old people will probably want me to take them out drinking so we'll do that. That'll last till the morning and we'll go have some pancakes and coffee and then I'll head to work! Unless . . .'

'Unless?'

'Maybe you could do something more exciting for me for my birthday,' he said with a naughty smile.

'Such as . . .?' I asked warily.

And he replied, 'You could do a strip tease for me on web cam.'

I was a little taken aback. What if it got recorded and put on the Internet? It was a bad idea. But I could see he wanted a little more than our regular conversations now. I answered, 'I'll think about it. Pictures and videos on the Internet are not really a good idea.'

He laughed and we got off web chat that night. I always went to bed happy after I had spoken to him but that night I became apprehensive. Would our long distance relationship last if we didn't take it a step further?

45

Sometimes It's Not the Hours in Our Life that Matter, It's the Life in Our Hours

For the next few days I was very distracted at work, but I refused to tell Shy and Aditi what was going on since I didn't want them to make fun of me. I didn't know what to do. I also had to buy a present for Ayaan that said I really liked him, but I didn't know what he already had. Finally after two days of watching me surf the Internet for gifts for men and hearing me complain that my relationship was doomed, Aditi and Shy sat me down in our office room at the back of store. They placed a plate of mini chocolate-chip cookies and a cup of cappuccino in front of me and asked what was wrong.

I looked at the plate of cookies and realized they must be really worried because they never allowed me to eat junk food in front of them. I had told them some time back that there was a new love interest in my life but I hadn't given them any details other than his name and where he lived.

I sighed, 'Ayaan's birthday is on Saturday and he wants me to do a strip tease for him on the webcam. First I don't know how to do a strip tease. He'll probably laugh at me and then I'll lose my nerve and our relationship will be over. And second, I don't think it's safe. What if it is recorded by a hacker and posted online? If my parents see it, I will have to shoot myself. So now I'm trying to figure out a fantastic present to make up for disappointing him but I can't seem to find anything as fantastic as getting him horny! See what I mean?' I asked in exasperation.

They looked at each other solemnly, and burst out laughing. I was most upset. 'I need some sympathy here people!' I said but they continued to hold their stomachs and laugh hysterically. Aditi even had tears rolling down her eyes with the amount she was laughing.

'Forget it!' I said with annoyance, 'I'm never talking to you people again.' And I took a few cookies in my hand and stuffed them in my mouth. That immediately got them to shut up. They sat down properly on the two chairs next to me.

'Don't worry. No one on the Internet is going to see you strip for him,' Shy said.

'No one will even want to,' Aditi guffawed at her own joke till Shy gave her a stern, mischievous look.

'I'm sure you'll find "how-to" videos on performing a strip tease on the Internet. You can practice in front of a mirror a couple of times,' Shy continued.

'And remember it doesn't matter if he laughs. It's supposed to be fun. And enjoy yourself. Don't think you're a serious pole dancer or anything. Feel sexy first. He'll feel it too,' Aditi piped in.

I wasn't convinced. Just because Aditi had had some fifty men in her life and had done it all and Shy was a super confident woman, didn't mean I could exude that confidence at all. I shook my head and said, 'You people are useless. I shall go back to surfing the net for a present. I'm not doing that strip tease.'

They both shrugged and replied, 'Suit yourself. You can get him a stripper there. And pay for it online. Maybe he'll get lucky then!'

I was horrified. I didn't want him to get lucky with anyone

else. I had the awful feeling that I may have inadvertently fallen in love with him. It seemed silly to say that I had fallen for an arranged match but that was the truth. It didn't matter that he was so far away and we had never even held hands, or even kissed; I needed him in my life. I couldn't send him a stripper! It would send all the wrong signals. It would mean I didn't care if he was with another woman and that our relationship was just friendly and there would be no benefits. I decided to send him a really expensive watch. That would show that I was ready for a commitment since I had spent enough on him. I hoped.

But Thursday evening, the day before his birthday he seemed a little distracted, and finally said, 'Listen, I won't be able to come online tomorrow. I'm going out with my friends. And they're all a rowdy bunch so we'll probably finish at some five or six in the morning and then I'll sleep for the entire day. Don't get all worked up if I don't pick up your call okay?'

'Sure, no problem,' I said with a fake smile.

'Okay, great. I have to go back to work now. So I'll talk to you later. Bye!'

The Skype window closed even before I had a chance to say goodbye.

I switched off my laptop. And then I cried. I had really hoped I would be the one going out with him and I would be the first person he spoke to on his birthday. But I guess that would not be the case. I would be the last person since he would wake up late and then call me. By then the entire world would have wished him. I had no idea why I was feeling so betrayed and broken but I was. I decided to stay in my pajamas and have a pity party and watch films all weekend long at home.

And that's what I did all day on Friday. At midnight I looked at my phone and wondered if I should send Ayaan a message. Did he care enough to call me and hear my voice? Should I call him? I thought for a few minutes and dialled his number. It took forever to connect. And it went straight to voicemail. He had probably switched it off so he wouldn't be bothered by calls while he was out having fun. I didn't leave a message. I didn't want to seem needy. I went to bed and lay there for a really long time hoping that he would call. Eventually I feel asleep.

The next morning I woke up and checked my phone. There were no missed calls from him. I felt a deep sense of disappointment. He hadn't even wanted to hear my voice on his birthday. And now he was probably asleep. I would have to wait for the whole day to hear his voice again. This long distance thing was seriously tough. While I made my coffee I wondered if he was with another woman. Had some girl kissed him at midnight? Had he become tired of our friends-with-no-benefits arrangement and decided to be with another woman? My mind began to wander.

I took out the trash and picked up the newspaper. I spent an hour reading it but if someone had asked me what the headline was I wouldn't have been able to answer. Tired of staring at my phone and willing it to ring, I went to the bathroom and took a shower. The phone rang just as I turned off the water. Oh the irony! I ran towards it and almost fell but answered it just in time.

'Hello,' I said breathlessly while clutching on to my towel.

'Sexy morning voice, huh? Is it for my birthday?' Ayaan asked from the other end.

I tried to sound casual even though my heart was racing at the sound of his voice. 'Yeah, especially for you. From doing my morning yoga, you know. Nude.'

'Oh yeah?' he said all excited. 'We've been Skype-ing at all the wrong times. We should do it now!'

'Shut up!' I said smiling and added softly, 'Happy birthday, Ayaan. I really wish you a fab year ahead.'

'Thank you,' he said formally. And then there was a pause. I was tempted to ask him about his night with his friends, but didn't lest he mention a girl and break my heart. 'So,' he began, 'I didn't really want to go out drinking with the guys yesterday so I did something that you may not like.'

There it was. I knew it. He had brought another woman home. I held my breath.

'Well,' he said, exasperated, 'aren't you going to ask what?'

I sighed and told him the truth. 'I'm afraid to. I don't want to know if you were with another woman.'

Then he laughed and said, 'No! I wanted to spend it with my woman. You. Come open the door. I'm outside your house.'

'What?' I screeched as I went running through the house to look through the peephole. I couldn't believe my eyes—there he stood, talking on the phone with me. I took a few steps back and said into the phone, 'Can you give me two minutes?'

'Umm . . . sure,' he replied, sounding puzzled.

I quickly went to my room and raided my closet for my best underwear. I couldn't let him see me nude. Not yet! I wore my new silk red flowered bra and matching panties and threw on a soft, white chiffon dress that I had bought soon after coming back from Barcelona but never worn. I dabbed some perfume, lined my eyes with kajal and wore a hint of lip gloss. I could not look drab the first time we saw each other in person. I had to make a good impression. I couldn't believe he had come all the way to see me. My heart was racing so hard that I had to take deep breaths and tell it to calm down.

I walked slowly to the door and opened it. I would be meeting my arranged match for the very first time.

46
Happy Endings

Ayaan was even more handsome in person than he was on web cam or in his photos. He was tall, with legs that went for miles, broad shoulders, a lean body, lustrous olive skin and sparkling eyes. He had gorgeous curly brown hair and a smile that sent electric shocks through my spine. He was immaculately groomed even though he had been on a flight for twelve hours. He was sitting on his suitcase and toying with his phone when I opened the door.

'I thought you were doing nude yoga?' he said, standing up.

'Ayaan,' I whispered, barely able to control my excitement.

He grabbed hold of me, picked me up and kissed me so passionately that my heart spun out of control. I was captivated immediately. He freed one hand and yanked his suitcase into the house before kicking the door shut. All the while nibbling my neck, sucking on my ear and finding my mouth to kiss me again.

'Oh my god,' I whispered when I could catch my breath.

I felt like I was drowning. Liquid fire ran through my body as I succumbed to his touch.

'I want you,' he mumbled.

I felt the warmth of his palm as it slid under my dress to cup my breast. His mouth rested on the hollow of my neck, nibbling sweetly, tantalizing, caressing till I let out an inaudible moan. With fingers as light as a butterfly's touch, I unbuttoned his shirt, slowly running my fingers down his chest, across his taut stomach, teasing the outline of his navel before trailing a slow path to sink my fingers into his taut behind. He inhaled sharply. We sank to the floor, still wrapped in each other's arms, our clothes a thing of the past. I pushed him onto his back and straddled him. I leaned over him, slowly teasing and tempting him with my lips, the tip of the tongue . . . the gentle nip of my teeth. I cupped his balls, gave them a gentle squeeze and traced the length of his erection with the tip of my finger. His stomach contracted in a rapid reflex and he flipped me over and pinned me to the floor with his body.

I could see him properly now. I drank him in with my eyes. His strapping arms, an immaculate bone structure, the Shiva tattoo on his shoulder. A strong, masculine, musky smell that sent ripples through my body. I silently let out a sigh as he gazed deep into my eyes. I could feel every inch of his powerful male body throbbing with desire.

He played with my breasts, taking his time to gently caress one hardened nipple before moving on to its twin. He flicked his tongue over them, teasing so tenderly that it sent shivers down my spine. He kissed me again, passionately; his passion fuelled by our time apart. The air between us pulsed with immense desire, desire that an ocean had separated for all these months. I felt as if the current of heat that was coursing between us had swirled around the room to leave its impression on everything it touched.

I drew him close to my body and whispered, 'Don't you want to go into the bedroom?' while flicking my tongue in his ear.

He shook his head. I smiled, knowing he could not wait any longer. He was thick and ready. He clutched my hair and pulled it back softly, biting my neck, sending my body spiralling into a free fall of unimaginable lust. I moaned loudly. He covered his mouth with mine, kissing me urgently. I felt my wetness building up. I trembled as he moved down, his tongue finding the crevasses of my body and possessing them until I cried out. All I felt was a primitive hunger for him . . . only him. He held me firmly as he used his mouth, his tongue and his fingers in an erotic tasting that has me writhing in ecstasy as he took his fill.

He loomed over; his eyes darkened with passion and raised my legs ever so slightly. I questioned him with my eyes. He lowered himself and slowly pushed inside me, penetrating deep into my wetness. I wrapped my arms around his shoulders and hooked my legs around his waist as we caught a rhythm . . . long, lingering strokes that drove me wild, becoming harder, faster, bolder, more frenzied until, together, we shattered into a million pieces. His mouth took possession of my own in a kiss that was incredibly sensitive. I felt a wave of heat crashing against my body. Magic. Innumerable sensations defying satisfactory explanation.

I didn't open my eyes for a long time. I had never felt this way. A timeless ripple of love, desire, lust, heat and an erotic need. We lay there catching our breath, not knowing what else to do, or where to go from there. It had all been so sudden, wonderful, rabid, raucous that we weren't even sure we should make any conversation. A mere twenty minutes ago we had been on either side of the front door, and here we were lying next to each other. Naked. He tucked my head into the curve of his neck as if it was the most natural thing to do in our position. My hair was in disarray and my make-up definitely smudged. But I didn't care. For in that moment I felt like the most beautiful woman in the world!

'You want some water?' I asked as I slowly got up and tried to see where my clothes had gone in this mad rush. I felt a little embarrassed to have surrendered to him so quickly. It went against everything I believed about waiting and letting the man long for you. I grabbed my dress from the floor and headed to the kitchen without waiting for his reply. I just stood there for a while giving him time to get dressed. When I got back, the living room was empty. Ayaan emerged from the bathroom in his jeans, still buttoning his shirt. God he looked so good.

'Those benefits were certainly worth the wait!' he chuckled.

I smiled shyly in response, unsure of what to say. Then a thought hit me, he must be hungry after all this travel. 'Do you want to go out and get something to eat or do you want me to make something for you? I'm sure you must be famished,' I said feeling very concerned.

'Let's go out and get some nice breakfast. Isn't the Marriot close from here?' he asked as he rummaged through his bag for something. I took a quick peek at the mirror to make sure my kajal wasn't smeared and my hair was in place again. 'You know what I was thinking?' he continued conversationally. 'I was thinking we should get married.'

My heart stopped at his words. When I turned around to face him, he had a small box in his hand which he opened to reveal a beautiful platinum band with a single two carat, immaculately cut solitaire. A proposal. Finally!

He said very softly looking into my eyes, 'Kaveri, my love, will you marry me?'

Love when it's real, permeates your very core. It instructs your body to yield. It demands your mind to be ecstatic. It becomes a strength of power so deep that you want the world to stop and let you soak in that moment completely. It makes you so happy that you know it can never be anyone else. That person becomes the pivot on which you want your whole life to rotate and there is a harmonious, congruent fitting of souls that you've never felt before.

'Yes, Ayaan Roy, I will marry you.'

I was finally ready for this new chapter in my life. Marriage and kids. With the man of my dreams.

Acknowledgements

A trilogy is never easy. A writer thinks that they have one story and it ends when the book is done. But the success of *Losing My Virginity and Other Dumb Ideas* made people want to know more about what happened to Kaveri. And hence I had the opportunity to write another book.

Honestly just to hear people say that makes me feel so humble and proud. A success. Of my story. I am truly grateful to God for letting that happen.

So first and foremost I need to thank each and every person who bought my debut novel. Your small act helped me accomplish a lifelong dream and I shall love you forever for it.

I hope you loved where Kaveri went with that book. Do write to me on Twitter or on my blog about it. I have tried to reply to everyone to the best of my ability.

I also want to thank my best friend Bharati who gives me tremendous support and love. She remains the beacon of light in my life. Can't live without you babe.

Thank you to Vaishali who believed in me every step of the way. Love you.

Thank you to Bala who always tells me to act from a place of confidence and not fear. You inspire me. Love.

Thanks to Mom, Dad, Ani, Meera for giving me support and peace and to Ayush and Aneesh—the two pieces of my heart.

Thanks Parikshit for being there. For fulfilling every whim of mine with a smile on your face. Love you forever.

Thanks Sunaman. A lifetime will never be enough for me to thank you for what you give me. But I will try every day. Muah!

Thanks to my mom-in-law Veena who adores me and chats with me every day. I'm the luckiest woman to have a MIL like you.

Thanks to my women friends who have such tremendous strength and power to live life on their own terms and who are awe-inspiring for me—Reshma, Shivaani, Anuraadha, Chandreyi, Vidhu, Neha, Ridhi, Sikha, Annie, Sulbha, Barkha and Olivia. You are all amazing in so many ways and so important in my life.

I am but a sum of what I write. I hope I can give back as much as I have received. And then some more.

Till next time . . . Kiss!